Here and There,

This and That

Steve Fitzsimmons

Please be aware some stories contain strong language and sexual references.

Contents

Dedication

To short story readers everywhere!

One for the Road

We were sitting on the verandah drinking sundowners and listening to the grating chorus of crickets and cicadas. We didn't talk much, usually not until the second whiskies were poured and the ice in the bucket was starting to melt in the residue of the day's heat.

Piet tapped his pipe on the ashtray and began to fill it again. It was his ritual before conversation. 'Some hippos overturned a mokoro up by Van der Linde's farm this morning and just about broke the ruddy thing in half, according to my garden boy. The fishermen were damned lucky to get away with just a soaking.'

'So I hear,' I said, 'it's not a good idea to upset hippos at calving time.'

'*Ag*, it's their country, the silly buggers should have known better!'

I refilled our glasses. The bottle was three-quarters full and after our regular Friday evening engagement it would be empty. It was as well the local police force rarely ventured this far out of town and certainly not after dark. There was little chance of getting into trouble on the seven-kilometre drive home as long as I didn't crash into the cattle or donkeys that tended to gather on the warm tar road at nighttime.

Piet picked up his glass. '*Gesondheid!* Let there always be light in your karzi. Is Kate well?'

'May pangolins never piddle in your piano,' I replied. 'She hasn't stopped grumbling since the maid burned a hole in her new dress with the iron this morning. I expect she'll get over it in a couple of light years. And Penny?'

Piet pushed an idle grasshopper from the edge of the table, lit his pipe and sat back. 'I shouldn't have married a younger woman in hindsight,' he said eventually.

Piet, I knew, was fifty-eight. Penny was in her late thirties and very attractive, too. 'Why's that?'

'I can't keep it up.'

'How do you mean, keep it up? It won't stay up, or you haven't got the stamina?'

'It won't come up. I even tried cutting back on the grog and *that* was a sacrifice, I can tell you. It still didn't work. She's getting frustrated.'

I didn't know what to say, so I sipped my whisky. Some admissions are awkward between men.

'You've never had this … problem?' he continued.

'Only when I've had a skinful, other than that, it's in full working order.'

Piet puckered his lips and stared into the sunset. I felt he wanted to say more but wasn't sure how to go about it. Then I heard the sound of a truck pulling up behind the bungalow.

He grunted. 'Penny. Been shopping and downloading gossip in the Expat Club, no doubt.'

I heard the flyscreen door open and the sound of sandals flapping against the floorboards.

I turned around and smiled. 'Hi, Penny, how's it going?'

'*Howzit*, Tim, good to see you again.' She looked at the glasses and empty beer cans on the table and laughed. 'Where would guys be without Friday nights, hey?'

She walked around the table and kissed Piet's cheek. She obviously wasn't wearing a petticoat because her legs were silhouetted against the fading sun through the thin material of her dress. It was as if she were naked below the waist. I almost spluttered into my drink. As she turned it was apparent that she wasn't wearing a bra, either. How could Piet's equipment not work when confronted with that figure?

'Well, I'll leave you men to your boy's talk,' she said. 'Shout if you want anything.'

Piet's mood soon lifted as the whiskies went down. We talked about everything and nothing and watched the moonlight settle on the veldt. Eventually the beers we'd had as openers began to filter their way through my system.

'Time for a slash,' I said.

Piet passed me the ice bucket. 'Can you bring some more? You'll find a bag in the chest freezer.'

I noticed the bedroom door was ajar as I was making my way to the bathroom. Most people can't resist a look through an open door, me included. Penny was standing in front of the dressing table, sideways to me, doing something with her hair. She was naked. I couldn't tear my eyes away. She must have sensed I was there because she turned around and looked me hard in the eye for a few moments. Then she smiled and reached for her dressing gown.

'Er … sorry, Penny,' I mumbled.

'Don't be,' she said and slowly closed the door.

My hands were shaking so much when I returned that the ice cubes were rattling against each other in the bucket.

'Good man,' said Piet. 'Now we can get down to some serious drinking.'

There was less than a quarter of the bottle left when Piet came out with it.

'Do you find Penny attractive, old chum?'

'She's a very pretty woman,' I said.

'Pretty enough to make love to?'

This was dangerous ground. What was he getting at? 'I think you're very lucky to have her.'

'Like I said earlier, I'm not having her. He leaned forward and touched my arm. 'What I'm suggesting, *boet*, is that you might like to help her out.'

'Christ, Piet, what a thing to ask me!'

'*Ag,* man. Do you want to sleep with her or not?'

The whisky-soaked brakes on my tongue failed without warning. 'I'd be lying if I said she didn't get my sap rising.'

He slapped me on the back. 'That's sorted then. Next Friday. We'll have a drink or two then I'll bugger off to the Expat Club until midnight. Kate won't be suspicious – as far as she's concerned you'll be getting sloshed with me as usual. Let's drink on it, eh?' He poured two hefty measures of whisky, lit up his pipe again and leaned back in his chair.

'Er, how does Penny feel about this, Piet?'

'Don't worry, she'll feel a whole lot better, believe me. Drink up, man.'

***

Kate was unsympathetic when I lurched into the kitchen and shielded my eyes against the mid-day sun streaming through the windows. She glared at me and began to pound a lump of steak with her mallet.

'You made enough racket to drown out a lion with toothache when you got in at three o'clock,' she scolded, 'so you can put up with any noise *I'm* making now.'

There wasn't much I could say against that charge so I took a couple of Panado and went back to bed. As I lay there with the curtains drawn and a jackhammer idling in my head, I recalled Piet's unexpected offer last night. The thought of fresh fruit suddenly overshadowed my hangover. It was true that lovemaking between Kate and me had become a little mechanical over the past year or so. We were getting stale. I dropped off to sleep thinking about Penny and her bedroom display.

The week seemed to drag but Friday inched by in delicious anticipation. I finished work at the mine early and dashed home to get myself spick and span for the evening. Kate passed me a cold beer as I stepped out of the shower.

'I hope you haven't used up all the water. You've been in there for at least twenty minutes. And *please* don't come home in the same state as you did last week, otherwise you'll be in even hotter water.'

'Don't worry, I won't,' I promised.

I was ready in ten minutes. Kate kissed me as I picked up the car keys. 'Enjoy yourself, darling.'

The sun was just starting to rest on the horizon as I turned into Piet's yard. He was waiting for me on the verandah with a glass of whisky in his hand and there were four cans of Castle, another glass and a bottle of Glenmorangie on the table. He had long trousers on for once, shoes instead of sandals and a tie that matched his shirt. Expat Club regulations were strict, even though half the members might be rowdy and rootless at the end of the night.

'*Howzit*, chum? Grab yourself a beer and loosen up while Penny gets herself operational.'

It all seemed very business-like. We sat down, drank two beers each, talked about the week's events and started on the whisky as the daylight gently faded away.

Piet looked at his watch after a while. 'Seven o'clock. Time I was making a move. Enjoy the evening; I'll leave it to you to find out what Penny likes. Expect me back well after midnight.'

He finished his drink, patted my shoulder and disappeared into the house. I heard his truck pull away a couple of minutes later. I was wondering what to do next when Penny came onto the verandah with a glass of wine in her hand. She was dressed in a wrap-around skirt and low-cut white blouse. She pulled me towards her and kissed me hard on the lips.

'Whenever you're ready, Tim,' she breathed.

So we went into her bedroom and began to do what new

couples do. After fifteen minutes of furious smooching and petting we undressed each other and got set for action. And then I thought of Kate's trusting face as she'd kissed me goodbye. Waves of guilt pulsed through me like the pain of the previous week's hangover. I couldn't go through with it. Penny's face was a mask of fury as I told her I was going home, that I couldn't cheat on Kate, even for a beautiful woman like her.

'You'll be sorry about this, very bloody sorry, *meneer*,' she assured me as I left the bungalow slightly ahead of an airborne wine bottle.

This was going to ruin a very good friendship with Piet, I thought, as I hammered along the track.

It was for sure. I found his Hilux parked outside my house when I got back.

The Final Sentence

Cliff tapped my arm as Elvis Presley faded away. 'Do you want to hear something very interesting?'

The jukebox began pounding out the latest Eurovision Song Contest winning entry as he finished speaking. I thought for a few seconds. '"Waterloo". It's a damn sight better than the usual dross that gets the votes.'

'You can say that again!' he said. 'The blonde's a real dish as well but I wasn't thinking about ABBA. I've got something that'll open your eyes even wider.'

This was unusual. Cliff wasn't one for gossip. 'I'm listening,' I said.

'See old Derick over there?'

Derick was sitting in his usual place in an alcove at the end of the bar that was just large enough for its two chairs and circular table. He was drinking his customary pint of mild and bitter and there was a pipe and empty spirit glass on the table. He was alone. Everyone in the village knew there was no profit to be had in talking to him.

'Ah, the man who makes a Trappist monk sound like a gossip.'

Cliff chuckled. 'True. Anyway, what do you suppose he used to be?'

I looked at the tight-lipped, black-suited old man again. He wasn't much more than five and a half feet tall and slim with it. His face – and nose in particular – was red, contradicting his snow-white hair, and I guessed his age at somewhere around seventy-five. He was staring at something well out of anyone else's view because there was nothing to look at behind that end of the bar other than packets of peanuts clipped onto cardboard backgrounds of semi-naked women.

'Huh, he could be anything,' I said. 'If you told me he'd been a road sweeper or a politician, I wouldn't be surprised.'

'Well, that was a pretty good guess. Actually, he was the middleman of the two.'

'Eh? I'm not with you.'

'Like I said, he was the middleman – he did the government's cleaning up.' He glanced at the alcove again. Derick was busy filling his pipe. Cliff looked back at me and winked. Then he put a hand around his throat, made a dreadful choking sound, jerked his head to one side and closed his eyes. 'Now guess!'

'Christ Almighty.' It was as if something had sucked all the warmth from my body for a moment. A match flared as Derick lit his tobacco and a surge of horror ran through me at the thought of those same fingers slipping the noose over the heads of condemned prisoners before pulling the trap lever that sent them on their short journey to the next world.

Cliff grinned. He was clearly enjoying the effect of his exposé. 'Yes, Frederick Hardisty himself!'

I must have looked as puzzled as I felt.

'He's known as Derick around here to protect his anonymity,' he continued, 'otherwise there'd be ghouls flocking from all over if it was public knowledge.'

Of course! Now I remembered reading somewhere that a Frederick Hardisty had despatched several hundred murderers, traitors, Nazi spies and war criminals during a thirty-year career of culling. And now here he was, living in the Derbyshire village of Alsover, population 1,116.

I looked over again. Derick was pouring what was left in

the mild ale bottle into his glass. 'He always gives me the impression he's afraid of being pounced on, like a rabbit hiding from a fox.'

'Well, I suppose *he* was the fox at one time.' He finished his drink. 'Another one?'

There was now a horrible fascination about Derick. I looked over again as Cliff went to the bar. *Public Executioner* … what a way to earn a living! I tried to imagine coming home from work.

'Hello, dear. Sit yourself down and I'll fetch you a bottle of stout. There's a nice bit of mutton for your tea and some bread pudding for afters. Did you have a good day?'

'Oh, not too bad, I only had one customer. He made a bit of a scene but I soon quietened him down. Have you seen my slippers?'

By some sixth sense, which he must have sharpened since he began his grisly trade, Derick looked up at me. I hastily switched to watching the barmaid as she collected glasses but he knew exactly what I was looking at.

Cliff returned with the drinks and put on his Groucho Marx voice. 'I once asked a hangman if he liked his job and he told me it was money for old rope.'

I couldn't help laughing at his tasteless joke despite my revulsion at finding out a state-sponsored killer was sitting less than a bus-length away. But when I dared look at the alcove again, Derick was gone. His unfinished beer stood on the table. He never returned.

I wondered if my stare had anything to do with his departure.

***

Derick died about three months later. *The Times* and *Guardian* ran dry obituaries and the *Sun*, *Daily Mirror* and *News of the World* reported his death in their usual sensational manner. He was a widower and, if he had any relatives, they never turned up for the funeral. Perhaps they didn't want the association of having an executioner in the family plastered all over the media. After the service, The Welcome Inn opened at mid-day for a quiet wake. The lounge bar was going to be a different place from now on although I noticed no one was bold enough to sit in Derick's regular place yet. Reminiscences started to flow with the beer but there were few anecdotes because no one in Alsover could say they knew anything of the real Frederick Hardisty. It seemed he was as distant to us as was the era in which he was employed.

But there *was* an exception. He was sitting quietly at a window table with a whisky. The landlord was doing his social rounds and asked if he was in Alsover for the funeral or just passing through. Yes, he said, he was here for the funeral and introduced himself as an old friend of Fred's. That got everybody's interest. He spoke with a strong Lancashire accent and, like Derick, was red-faced and well past seventy. He finished his drink and went to the bar for another. While he was there, someone asked him how old Derick had been when he became a state hangman. That started off a torrent of queries from just about everybody, but not one answer revealed anything of the executioner's personal life. That is, until he'd drunk his fourth or fifth double. Somebody mentioned Derick's standoffishness and peculiar faraway looks. He signalled for another drink and faced the man who'd made the comment.

'Well, he wasn't aloof, I'll tell you straight. There was a good reason for him being that way, and I'll defy any man to behave otherwise in the circumstances.'

This was getting even more interesting. The crowd gathered closer, eager for titbits, afraid of missing a word. A whisky appeared at his elbow, then another and another.

'You folks remember the Shay murders?'

There was a rumble of confirmation. I recalled reading about the case when I was at university in 1962. The army deserter had broken into a Bedworth house in the middle of the night, battered the owner with a hammer and raped both his wife and teenage daughter. The asthmatic girl suffocated under a gag and the man died in hospital a few days later. Shay was arrested shortly after and charged with the killings as well as rape and armed robbery. Murder was still relatively uncommon in those days and the country was shocked. He was found guilty and sentenced to be hanged.

'Fred got the job and travelled to Winson Green the day before the execution. He worked out the drop from the weight table, set up his equipment and went to take a look at the prisoner through the peephole in the cell door. Well, this Shay, he looked up at the same time, almost as if he knew he was being inspected. His eyes locked onto Fred's; he said the sheer malice in that stare burned right through him.'

He took a healthy swallow of whisky, filled his pipe, lit it and continued. He knew he had his audience.

'Anyhow, Fred got up nice and early the next day, looked over his equipment again, had some breakfast and sat in with the governor until ten to eight. When he got back downstairs, Shay was screaming and lashing out at the priest and warders.

'Fred's had all this before so he wasn't too bothered, but it's unpleasant and unsettling for the others, like. The room with the scaffold is right next to the condemned cell so it's just a case of opening the doors, pinioning the prisoner and dragging him in. It doesn't take long – two men who know what they're doing can have a prisoner dangling on the end of a rope within fifteen seconds. Some say that Albert Pierrepoint once managed it in eight.

'So, the two warders have got hold of Shay while his hands are fastened behind his back with a strap. As soon as that's done, he's frog-marched to the scaffold, spitting and kicking. Then his legs are fastened with another strap and Fred pulls the hood over his head, followed by the noose. Just as Fred's slipped the locking pin and about to pull the trap lever, Shay shouts out: "Ye *bastarrds,* Ah'm gaein' tae fecking-well get ye, just see if Ah don't."

'Fred's heard all that before too, so he steps back, pulls the lever and down goes Shay in mid-curse. Slap on the stroke of eight, it was. That's fifteen quid in his pocket and another piece of human rubbish gone. Fred's about to go under the scaffold drop with the doctor and the governor to confirm the death and all that. As he's walking past the condemned cell, he hears a voice. It's not much more than a croak and it says, in a Glaswegian accent: *"Ah'll be waiting fir ye, ye bastarrds."*

'Fred looks around. There's Shay, sitting back on his bed in the cell. *"Aye, Ah'll be waiting fir all of ye,"* says the voice again and then Shay disappears.

'The governor and the doc haven't heard any of this so they go down the trap and inspect the body. Shay's dead, of course, Fred had done his usual good job. But he was never the same after that. He did two more executions and resigned.'

A truck rattled past the window, breaking the stunned silence.

'Jee-sus!' said the man who'd brought it up.

'So that's why poor Fred was like that … he had an appointment to look forward to that he couldn't avoid.' He downed his drink in one swallow and reached out for another.

'When did he tell you this?' I heard myself asking.

He held his whisky up to the light for a second or two before despatching it as quickly as he had the others. His eyes were starting to glaze.

'He didn't,' he said eventually. 'I was the assistant. I was right beside him.'

All in the Mind

Despite being 75 years old, Mr Valentine Merryweather listens to Metallica, Nine-Inch Nails, Mötley Crüe, Slayer, Slipknot, Iron Maiden and Motorhead every day and most nights until 2 a.m. He knows every guitar riff, every lead break, every drum groove and every lyric of the albums by heart. He even knows the exact length of each track.

He's got no choice – his new upstairs neighbour is a fanatical follower of high-volume hard rock. Objections are ineffective. Offender Troy Fillet is over six feet tall, weighs the same as two full beer kegs and often drinks their capacity in a fortnight. The fuse that ignites his peppery temper is considerably shortened by exposure to strong lager. His genetic link with *homo erectus* is apparent, from his Bluto-like features to the tussocks of hair sprouting from his knuckles. Fortunately, the majority of his face is obscured by a ragged black beard that camouflages the tramline of scars introduced by a broken beer glass, rumoured to have been wielded by his own father.

The inoffensive Valentine bears the brunt of Fillet's musical preferences, loud parties, revving car and vicious taunts. He's all that his distasteful neighbour is not. Small and slim. Smartly dressed. Educated. Refined. And quiet. He'd been an entertainer once. Television and cabaret. Performed in Europe. America and Australia too. But that was a long time ago, before the dawn of Netflix, YouTube and DVDs. Now he passes time in his two-bedroomed apartment along with his photographs and memories.

One morning, Olympuss, his cat, doesn't return from his regular night-time peregrination. When he appears through the cat flap at mid-day, Valentine sees that a Ty-wrap has been fastened around his belly, causing him to walk like a drunkard and, in gross indignity, his scrotum has been sprayed Day-Glo orange. Valentine is incensed.

He comes back from the veterinary surgery with Olympuss in his cat box and notices Fillet performing noise-making operations upon his Golf GTI. The cat hisses fiercely. Fillet looks up from under the bonnet with a horrible smirk on his face. Valentine frowns and returns to his apartment. A solution must be found.

He ponders for a while. A door slams in the flat above, followed by 'Ace of Spades' at the customary level. He goes upstairs and has to knock several times before he's heard. The door is violently wrenched open to reveal Fillet. A wrinkled trumpet-shaped cigarette hangs from the corner of his mouth and he has a can of Tennent's Super lager in his tattooed paw. He looks down at Valentine.

'Yeah? Woya want?'

Valentine stands his ground without flinching. 'Ah, good-day, Mr Fillet, I'm sorry to disturb you. It seems to me that we are not living as neighbours in such harmony as might be considered convivial. I have therefore taken it upon myself to relieve the tenseness of our relationship.'

'Wha?'

'You see, Mr Fillet, I feel that perhaps I am largely to blame for this lack of *entente cordiale*. It's rather unfortunate that members of my generation do not always provide the respect that younger members of society deserve. We must learn to live and let live, understand the needs of others. Habitate with accord. Therefore, Mr Fillet, I would like to redeem my previously uncharitable self and offer you the hospitality of my home for an hour or so, during which it will be my pleasure to offer alcoholic beverages of your choice and the opportunity to select such musical albums as you may find suitable from the effects of my nephew, now permanently domiciled in the Antipodes.'

Fillet's jaw hangs slackly. A question mark is suspended above his simian features.

'Uh?'

'Very simply, Mr Fillet, I have several cans of beer for your consumption and any music discs that may take your liking.'

The reduction of syllables eventually allows Fillet's burdened brain to absorb the import of Valentine's proposition.

'Yer givin' me booze an' CDs?'

'Yes, Mr Fillet, a gesture of goodwill.'

Suspicion clouds Fillet's face as he considers this unexpected offer. 'Er, yeah, all right then,' he says awkwardly.

'Fine, fine, Mr Fillet, come down when you are ready.'

As the door is closed, Valentine notes, with some satisfaction, that Olympuss has managed to leave sharp reminders of his struggle on Fillet's hands and arms.

***

Valentine is watching a video when the doorbell rings. He switches off the TV, straightens his bow tie and opens the door.

'I'm 'ere,' says Fillet.

'Splendid, splendid, come in,' replies Valentine. 'Do sit down. May I offer you some refreshment?'

Fillet grunts. Valentine goes to the kitchen. Olympuss swishes his tail and disappears through the cat flap. Valentine fills a glass with lager, puts the remaining seven cans onto a tray and returns to his guest, who seems to be compiling a mental inventory of valuable and attractive items. Valentine satisfies himself with a small sherry as Fillet empties his glass in three gulps.

'Do help yourself to more,' encourages Valentine. 'Perhaps you would like a chaser to complement your drink. A whisky?'

Fillet gruffly allows that he would like that. Valentine takes a bottle of scotch from the drinks cabinet and pours a large measure. Fillet looks at the other bottles: rum, vodka, schnapps and brandy and licks his lips. The whisky and another beer disappear down his throat. He belches and opens another can. Valentine pours him another generous whisky. The first measure isn't lonely for long. Valentine smiles where it can't be seen.

'Where's the CDs, then?' demands Fillet in a tone half a point less surly than normal.

'Ah, yes, forgive me. Allow me to get them. Another drink?'

Valentine leaves his guest to his ill-intentioned devices and goes to the spare bedroom where his nephew's music collection is stored. He pulls a cardboard box from under the bed and returns to the lounge, tugging it behind him. Fillet is eyeing the DVD player and satellite decoder.

'There you go, Mr Fillet, perhaps something here is to your taste?'

Fillet roots through the discs impatiently, taking frequent gulps from his glass. Valentine, the perfect host, ensures it is never less than half full. Fillet eventually overturns the box in disbelief.

'*What's all this bloody crap, then*?' The Osmonds, Barry Manilow, The Jackson Five, Des O'Connor, Boney M. and the like, slide out onto the floor.

Valentine stands up, fixes Fillet with a stare and wags his finger admonishingly at this display of ingratitude.

'Mr Fillet, I absolutely deplore the use of bad language. It must cease immediately. Do you quite understand me?'

Fillet looks guilty and nods.

'Now that we are in agreement, Mr Fillet, or may I call you Troy? I would like to redress our difficulties. Firstly, finish your beer and pour yourself a large whisky. *No,* Troy, I said a *large* whisky. That's better. Cheers! Down in one … *Well done!* Now, I'd like you to do a few things for me. Do you have any illegal drugs upon your person?'

Fillet empties his jacket pockets and puts various articles on the coffee table.

'Marvellous! Offensive weapons?'

A flick-knife joins the drugs.

'*Perfect!* Car keys? *Excellent!* Before you leave, do have another whisky. That's right, fill it right to the very top. Listen carefully, Troy, this is what I'd like you to do for me …'

***

The sergeant looks up in surprise as the police station doors are kicked open and a red-eyed creature lurches up to his desk. He has a can of Special Brew in one hand and a spliff in the other. He puffs on the joint furiously and directs a stream of smoke into the officer's face. The sergeant reels in his seat.

'Ello, 'ello, 'ello, piggy-wiggy,' slurs the wretch, 'not busy beatin' up pris'ners an' stealin' lost property, then?'

Before the coughing and astonished policeman can react in the correct manner, the man grinds his spliff out on the bell button, untwists a ball of tinfoil and empties a small pile of white powder onto the desk. He tidies it with a flick knife, takes a five-pound note from his pocket, rolls it into a thin tube and inhales the substance through his nose.

'Nuthin' like a line of coke to make the journey home interestin',' he explains as he twirls his car keys on his finger.

The red-faced desk sergeant is joined by two equally amazed constables. The bubble of incredulity suddenly bursts with a loud *pop*.

'Right, sunshine, you're nicked. Let's have your name,' splutters the sergeant, at last unsilenced by these bizarre events.

The man snatches the officer's helmet from the desk and unzips his jeans. He smiles contentedly and flutters his eyelids. 'I be *Mister* Troy Fillet, you fat, Fascist bast—'

The sergeant leaps to his feet in XXL outrage. 'Then you, *Mister*, are in deep, deep trouble,' he roars. 'I'm arresting you on suspicion of being drunk in charge of a vehicle, suspected possession of Class A and B drugs, suspected driving whilst impaired by controlled substances, for which test specimens will be required, possession of an offensive weapon and damage to police property. You do not have to say anything but it may harm your defence if you do not mention, when questioned, something which you later rely on in court. Anything you do say may be given in evidence—'

Evidence. The word makes contact in Fillet's scrambled brain.

Simba, King of the Lions, leaps over the desk, hurls the appalled sergeant face-down onto the floor, wraps all four limbs around his squirming body and ruts away frenziedly, snarling and growling at the other lions as they attempt to pull him from his mate.

***

Valentine looks at his watch, smiles, and rewinds the 1974 *Royal Variety Show* videotape. Then he takes another sip of his sherry and sits back to watch it again.

'And now, ladies and gentlemen, let's have a big hand for *Merryweather, the Mind Bender, Hypnotist Extraordinaire!'*

Some things, he thinks, you never forget.

Forget-Me-Not

Christ, what an embarrassment to have to see him in a place like this.

The nurse looked up from her computer screen. 'Good afternoon. Can I help you?'

'Paul Milsom,' I said. 'I've come to see my father.'

She ran her finger down a list on her desk. 'Oh, yes, Gordon Milsom, isn't it? If you'd like to sign the visitors' book, you can go through.'

I saw my brother's name near the bottom of the page. That was the other reason for not wanting to be here.

'Have you seen him recently, Mr Milsom?'

'No. Not since March and he wasn't exactly with it then.' That was an understatement. The silly old sod kept asking where my mother was and she'd been dead for nearly two years.

'Oh, I see. Do you work away?'

My trade is the importation of cheap booze and tobacco from France. But that was none of her business. And I had another vanload to collect from my lock-up in Dover as soon as I could get away from here, a profit of almost four hundred quid if I could deliver to Aylesbury before the New Millennium parties.

'Yeah, my job keeps me travelling. So what's the score – is he on his way out or just going further round the bend?'

'Well, I wouldn't put it like that, Mr Milsom. Dementia

affects thought, memory and speech, but sufferers don't go insane. It's the progressive deterioration of brain nerve cells that—'

'Yeah, I've heard all that stuff. But he's not going to kick the bucket because of it, is he?'

'No, *Mr* Milsom, not at this early stage—'

'That's all I wanted to know. Where can I find him?'

She picked up the phone and asked someone where he was.

'He's in the day room,' she told me, 'first on the left down the corridor, opposite the vending machine. You might find he's withdrawn and distracted at times so I wouldn't expect too much if he's not seen you for nine months.'

I'd never expected much from him even when he was healthy so that would be no surprise. He had no drive. Ambition didn't exist in his dictionary; he'd been quite happy to stand in front of the same lathe for forty years, tinker around in his potting shed and have his two pints of mild in the Working Men's Club every night. No wonder he'd ended up scratching along on his piddly pensions. I could make more in one day than he'd picked up in a week.

I squeezed past a couple of coffin dodgers blocking the corridor and saw David standing by the coffee machine. Another deadbeat. He was five years younger than me, but nobody would have thought so. His shabby clothes didn't help his appearance much either. He looked up as I approached.

'Afternoon. Don't I know you from somewhere? Paul Milsom, isn't it?'

The prat. 'Enough of your snide comments, OK? I didn't come all this way to put up with your sarcasm.'

'Yeah, 90 miles must've taken a lot of time and planning. Trade's good, is it?'

'It would've been better if you hadn't got me up here for nothing. He's not going to croak because he doesn't know it's Christmas, *is* he?'

'I never said he was. I said his brain cells are dying. You'd have known that if you'd read the leaflets I sent you when he was first diagnosed. Better still, you could have found time to drive up and talk to the neurologist yourself.'

I took a step forward so he could hear me better. 'Don't preach to me about time. I've got a business to run and a lot of turnover right now. I don't get paid by the government to sit on my arse watching television all day, unlike *you*.'

I'd offered him a hundred quid a week to white-van my stock around last year, but he'd turned it down on priggish principle because he was on benefits. More fool him. Morals don't put food on the table or buy the kids new shoes.

He threw his cup into the bin. 'Time's something Dad doesn't have much of either. Anyway, I'm not getting into another argument with you. Get this over and done with and then you can go back to your squalid little dealings.'

I'd have stuck one right on his miserable bloody mug if we hadn't been inside a nursing home. He turned away and opened a swing door. I followed him into the day room. There were Christmas decorations all over the place and seven or eight residents watching the television. I saw the old man sitting in the corner. He was staring at the wall and there was a cup of coffee on the table beside him. We pulled over a couple of chairs and sat down. I remembered the packet of mints I'd bought at the petrol station on the way up and put them next to the cup.

David squeezed his shoulder. 'Hello, Dad.'

He looked at David for a while. Then he nodded and went back to the wall.

I could see this being a gripping afternoon. A nurse came in, looked at her watch and flicked through the television channels. Somebody cheered when *The Great Escape* came on and one or two moved their chairs closer. Then the old man turned to David.

'Who's this, then?' The words sounded like they'd rusted in his throat.

'It's Paul, your son. He's come to see you, Dad.'

The old man looked at me, then again at David.

'He's not *my* son,' he said eventually.

How can you not recognize your own son, *for Christ's sake*?

David gave me a heavy wink. 'Sorry, Gordon – this is Paul. Paul – this is Gordon.'

I didn't understand. What the hell was he on about? Then he repeated himself.

'*Paul* – this is *Gordon*.'

Oh, great, let's all play party games, shall we? 'Hello, Gordon,' I said, 'I'm pleased to meet you.'

The old man stared at me for a while but didn't say anything.

David prompted him. 'Paul's come from Southend to see you, Dad.'

'Have you?' He was peering at me closely now.

David pushed his palms towards me like someone bouncing an invisible balloon against a wall. Oh, for God's sake …

'Having a nice Christmas, Gordon?' I said.

'Aye.' It took him all of twenty seconds to come out with that.

I looked at the television. Prisoners of war were wandering around the compound. That was handy. 'David says you were in the army.'

He perked up. 'That's right. The Royal Engineers. Sappers, we were called.'

'You must have had some interesting times, Gordon.' More interesting for him than me, for sure.

'Aye. Some good, some bad, but I was with a grand bunch of lads all through the fighting. We moved around a lot, making Bailey bridges, fixing water supplies, demolition, construction and just about everything else.'

What a way to spend Christmas Day – listening to someone rambling about the bloody war. It was my own stupid fault, why hadn't I picked something else to kickstart him with?'

David kept him talking. 'You saw a few countries then, Dad?'

'Yes, a few. Let me see … North Africa … Italy … France …' He rubbed his chin for a few seconds. 'Belgium … Holland … Germany of course.'

The old man had never spoken of any of this before. I looked at the TV again and noticed that one of the prisoners had ribbons below his flying brevet.

'Did you get any medals, Gordon?'

He thought for a while. 'Aye, there's a few tucked away somewhere. Campaign medals. We all had them. They gave me a Distinguished Conduct Medal as well. Our squad was pinned down by a Jerry machine gun post at Caen a few weeks after D-Day and me and Dodger managed to knock it out with a couple of grenades. It was nothing out of the ordinary, we were closest, that's all. Dodger married an actress, you know. Vanessa de Vickery, she was called. That wasn't her real name. It was something like Joan Thomas. No, *Lomas*, that was it. I walked out with her sister a few times until she ran off with a Canadian pilot.'

'So you married someone else, Gordon?' It was getting hard to hear him now and he looked tired. I was struggling to think of anything that would keep the conversation going. It looked like I could be on my way shortly.

'That's right. I met Maureen at the Kirby United celebration dance. We got to the FA Cup semi-final before we were knocked out. I was playing outside-left in those days.'

'You played for Kirby United!' He'd never said anything about that before, either.

'Nigh on two years. Derwent Rovers were going to sign me up, but I broke my leg on a motorbike so that put an end to my footballing days. I was saying I met my wife at the dance. Popular with all the men, she was. I was lucky to get her. She was with her friend, Vera. They shared a flat in Victoria Road, next to The Plough and Furrow.'

There didn't seem much wrong with his memory now.

'Aye, married for forty-nine years, we were.' He faded away for a while and came back like a re-tuned radio station. 'I've got a son, you know.'

Now he *was* getting forgetful. 'Only one?' I said.

He picked up the mints and dropped them into the cup. Cold coffee splashed over my knees.

He looked me straight in the eye. 'Yes, only the one, you little bastard.'

Junior's Big Break

'You ready to cover an assignment by yourself today, Junior?'

I thought I hadn't heard him right for a second or two. 'Uh, yeah. I guess so,' I said. Since I'd joined the *Mid-Oregon Weekly Muster* straight from college, I'd only been allowed to write up charity fetes and routine court reports or fillers about kids stuck up trees while I was learning the ropes. The other two reporters got to byline all the juicy stuff like reviewing baseball games, investigating municipal scandals and attending free-lunch ceremonies.

'Good, there's no one else available right now, so you're promoted from cub,' Ray Garfield, the editor, told me. 'It seems there's been a suicide over in Geraldsville. Bring back the story and we'll see if you've paid attention to anything we've taught you. Here's the address. Take the truck and stick thirty bucks of gas in it.' He rooted through his desk drawer and passed over a fifty. 'Don't forget the receipt.'

I pocketed the note. 'What happened?'

'*What happened*? How the hell should I know? That's what I'm paying *you* for. Bring back a couple of pizzas and some Cokes when you're done, willya? We've got a busy evening ahead.'

I hate Mondays. Everything's got to be finished for the midnight print deadline, and more news meant more work on the layout. 'All right. I'll call if it's a front-page stopper.'

Ray grunted and went back to his keyboard. For a newsman, he was a tad short with words sometimes. I put some gas in the Ford and took the road east to Geraldsville. It didn't take long; I was there in twenty-five minutes. *Geraldsville Domestic & Commercial Freezers, 49, Roosevelt Blvd*, it said on the scrap of paper. It was easy enough to find, there was a black and white parked outside with two cops leaning on the trunk, talking.

I got out and flashed my *Muster* ID. 'Morning, officers, I hear you've got a suicide. Anything you can tell me about the deceased?'

The one chewing gum looked me up and down. 'Not a lot really, son. White male Caucasian aged approximately seventy. Sorry, we can't release his name until the coroner says so. There are relatives to trace first.'

Fair enough. I opened my notepad and looked at the five Ws reporting checklist I'd written inside the cover: *Who? What? When? Where? Why?* It was time to put it into practice. I licked the point of my pencil. 'What were the circumstances?'

'Suffocated himself, apparently,' said the other cop.

'Suffocated himself! Jaysus! How the hell did he do that?'

'In one of the cold stores. He took the inside handle mechanism off first so's he couldn't change his mind and left a note in his pocket saying he'd had enough.'

'Enough of what?'

'That's between him and The Almighty, I guess. It just said: "I can't breathe in this world anymore." That's strictly off the record, mind. Like I say, the coroner's the only one supposed to release that sort of information.'

I slid my pencil back into the notepad's spiral binding. 'Sure. It's a horrible way to go, though.'

The first cop joined back in. 'Yeah … the strange thing is that he was wearing top-grade thermal clothing, hiking boots, cap and gloves. He sure didn't intend to freeze to death first.'

'Why the hell would anyone want to stretch a suicide out? How long's he been dead?'

The cop shrugged. 'The M.E says it's difficult to tell right now because of the temperature. He was as stiff as a board when one of the drivers found him this morning, so he must have got in sometime over the weekend. Sorry, I don't know any more than that.'

'Thanks for your time. Is it all right for me to talk with the staff?'

'It's a free country, go right ahead.'

The owner was a bit more forthcoming. 'It's all over town who he is or who he was. Gene Schaeffer. I took him on as a part-time cleaner two months or so back. Quiet sort of feller, he didn't speak unless he had to.'

'Did he live locally?' I asked.

'Yep, he rented a place next to the auto-repair shop on Coldwater Avenue. He lived by himself and never mentioned a family.'

There wasn't much he could add to what the police officers had said, so I drove down to Schaeffer's house. There was a black and white down there too so I decided to ask the neighbours what they knew. The first person I spoke to was the old man next door. He was brighter than his decrepit looks gave him credit for.

'He'd been livin' here for seven or eight months, like I told them there officers. He didn't say nuthin' to nobody, kept isself to isself. He was one of them 'stronomer fellers, I think, allus in the garden with a telescope lookin' at the sky. Ain't nuthin' else to look at around here, not since Maylene's daddy sent her away 'cause of the Norwegian feller.'

Now *that* could have been an interesting story, by the sound of it.

The next three people I spoke to said much the same thing. Apparently Schaeffer was just a sad old man with stars in his eyes and rocks in his head. But why would he suffocate himself in a cold store? As I was about to drive back to the office a grade 7 kid on a cycle pulled up beside me.

'You the reporter, mister?'

Hah, recognition at last! 'That's right. Got a story for me, champ?'

'Maybe. You here about old Schaeffer?'

'Word gets around quick,' I said. 'So, what's the scoop?'

He hooked his thumbs around his jeans belt loops. 'I figure I could've been the last person to see him alive. No one's said they seen him since, anyhow.'

I opened my notepad. 'When was this?'

'Friday evening, nine o'clock or so. I was in the field out the back with my dog. Just when I was walking past Mr Schaeffer's place, I heard someone sobbing. It was a horrible sound, like something really bad had happened. Well, I stuck my head over the fence and there he is on his knees, beating his fists on the ground and screaming at the moon like some kind of werewolf. Anyway, I watched for a couple of more minutes and went away. There's something awful about seeing a grown-up cry, ain't there? Maybe he was one of them screwed-up Vietnam vets or something.'

'You may well be right,' I said. 'Anything else you can tell me about him?'

'Sorry, mister. He never said anything all the time he was here, just stayed in his house in the daytime 'cept the mornings he was going to work and looked through his telescope at night.'

There wasn't going to be much on the suicide in this week's news round-up by the look of it. I was hog-tied until the coroner officially released the details anyway. I bought the kid a soda and drove back to the office.

Ray was discussing copy with Chad, one of the other reporters, when I got in. He opened one of the pizzas I'd brought and divided it into three with an ink-stained ruler.

'What ya got on the Geraldsville affair, Junior?'

'It's a weird one. An old man suffocated himself in a meat freezer. It looks like he'd been in there all weekend. One of the cops said he'd left a note saying he couldn't breathe in this world anymore.'

'I'm not surprised he said he couldn't breathe if he'd been in there for two days,' said Chad. He wiped a string of molten cheese from his chin. 'Well, at least he had plenty of time to complain about it. Folks drowning don't generally get the opportunity to bellyache about such matters. Aren't there supposed to be internal handles in those cold stores?'

I explained what had happened. They both shook their heads as they ate.

'There's probably a profound human-interest story behind that,' said Ray, 'I guess it'll wait until the next edition when we've got all the facts. Pass me a Coke, willya?'

I by-lined eighty words on *Mystery of Man Found Dead in Geraldsville Cold Store*, had another slice of pizza, helped with the final layout and proofreading and then went home.

Pa was watching the news on TV when I got in. I grabbed a beer from the refrigerator and sat down next to him on the sofa.

'Had a good day, son?'

'Aw, not too bad. There's a game replay on at eleven if you're not watching anything else.'

Pa flicked through the channels: some crummy sci-fi movie, a documentary on raccoons, the President addressing the cameras about something and a woman beating up her unfaithful husband and his cross-dressing lover on the *Jerry Springer Show*. Then the Mid-Oregon Olympians baseball coach appeared, telling us all how they were going to whup the Salem Privateers. This was more like it.

Pity the team wasn't as big as his mouth. Pa flicked back to catch up with the news when it was all over. The President was there again, making another speech against a backdrop of NASA flags and mission emblems.

'What's all that about, Pa?' I said in between yawns. It was almost two o'clock and well past my usual bedtime, but I had two days off to look forward to.

'It's a memorial service for the Apollo 21 mission. Yesterday was the fortieth anniversary.'

That was more than twenty years before I was born! 'Memorial service for what?'

'The moon landing tragedy,' Pa said patiently. 'Didn't they teach you anything at school?'

'I guess not. What happened?'

'The lunar module got damaged on landing and the crew couldn't get off again. Both of them died of oxygen starvation. There wasn't a damn thing anyone could do, not even the pilot in the command module. He had to come back by himself. Imagine that, eh? He had a mental breakdown eventually and spent a long time in a sanatorium. Apparently he's a recluse someplace in the north-west.'

It was like someone had punched me in the chest. And then I thought of the *Mid-Oregon Weekly Muster* flying off the presses and my eighty words on page four.

Behind the Mask

A smartly dressed man of middle age hurried along the pavement and kept to the shadows, avoiding the yellow pools of lamplight that punctuated the deserted boulevards of the Latin Quarter. He turned left at the Café Pissarro, climbed the stairs to his apartment on the second floor of the tenement block and unlocked the door. Once he was inside, he took a velvet bag from his satchel, removed his hat, scarf and coat, carefully placed them on their hooks, smoothed his gloves and put them exactly onto the centre of the hallway table. Then he changed into carpet slippers and put his shoes onto the doormat. When he was satisfied that everything was just so, he unlocked the door at the end of the hallway and entered his studio. His hands trembled in anticipation as he unfastened the bag.

***

Jean-Guy Bisset looked at the office clock, swept a crumb from his lap, and folded away his lunch napkin. As he opened his ledger, a colleague sitting opposite him burst out laughing and pushed the Monday morning edition of *Le Journal Parisienne* across the desk.

'A fine advertisement for the police force, Jean-Guy – look at this, at the bottom of the page, next to the cartoon.'

Bisset picked up the newspaper and read the column.

TAKEN FROM UNDER THEIR NOSES! Red-faced Chief of Police, Paul Marchand, admitted that a bronze death mask of executed mass-murderer, Henri Thibault, the so-called Strangler of Picardy, had been stolen from the *Musée des Criminels* at some time over the weekend. Thibault, who went to the guillotine in 1935, was convicted of the murders of twenty-four women, all but one, prostitutes. Nothing else, according to Marchand, appeared to be missing.

Bisset snorted and put the paper down. 'A sorry state of affairs, to be sure. No wonder Paris is teeming with crime when the police can't even keep their own buildings secure. And this is what we pay our taxes for.'

'But who would want to steal a death mask, for heaven's sake?' said his colleague.

'Yes, who indeed,' said Bisset. 'Now, if you'll excuse me, I have work to do.'

***

Bisset arrived at the pavement café at exactly 5:30, sat at his favourite table and waited for the waiter to bring him a Ricard, to be enjoyed as he read the evening paper. And at 6:30 precisely he walked the seventy-five metres home after leaving the correct money for his drink.

His apartment was as clean and orderly as an operating theatre and barely gave the impression of being lived in. But there were two faces to him. His obsessions – from ensuring that not a single centime was adrift in his ledger to the cleaning, inside and out, of every lampshade in his home – extended to the hero-like worship of notorious historical characters, a complete paradox of his own ordered existence. His bookshelves were filled with volumes on the likes of Adolf Hitler, the Marquis de Sade, The Boston Strangler, the Borgias, Urbain Grandier, Aleister Crowley and his current interest, Henri Thibault.

His heart fluttered as he unlocked his studio and switched on the lights. There, under red and green spotlights at the end of the mannequin and curio-lined room, hung the death mask of The Strangler of Picardy.

Henri Thibault's face exuded evil in death, as well as in life: from his wide forehead, close-set eyes and ridged nose to his thin lips and smallpox-scarred cheeks. If ever there was a classic study of a criminal face, this was it. This was also the man who bred birds of paradise, read Latin and Ancient Greek and spoke in quiet, cultured tones of art, philosophy, opera and theology. The Strangler of Picardy, a deferential filing clerk and brutal killer of prostitutes.

He'd argued, in his perverse logical manner, after being charged with the murder of twenty-four women, that he'd accounted for only twenty-three of the victims and should, as such, be acquitted of one homicide: that of a young mother. The jury disagreed with him and he was executed, complaining bitterly at the miscarriage of justice. Many said he'd lost his head long before he went to the guillotine.

It was as if the mask were an irresistible magnet, transporting Bisset towards it. The metallic skin glittered under the soft lighting as he moved his head from one side to the other. He extended his hands and caressed the pockmarked cheeks as a lover might. His fingers tingled, as though a small electric charge had been applied. Then the hair on his knuckles rose like the hackles of a dog – *the face was suddenly warm and soft*. Fear knotted his throat and he began to shake. He tried to tear himself away, but it was as if his fingers were welded to the mask and his feet to the floor. Thibault's eyelids, closed for over six decades, flickered. And then a strange energy effervesced inside him, a power greater than any he could have imagined. His fear was replaced by a thrill of raw pleasure. He drew his shoulder blades together until they were almost touching, threw his head back and exposed his throat to the lurid mask; every breath was a charge of sensuality that surged through his body. And then it was gone as abruptly as it had taken him. The face on the wall shimmered once and dulled. He cried out and ran his fingers over it again and again and again. But it was cold. The life was gone from it. The conduit was broken. But the fever was still there. He switched off the spotlights and rushed from the studio in the thralls of sexual ecstasy.

***

Bisset noted the fleeting expression on the waiter's usually neutral face: surprise at seeing his regular customer for the second time that evening and acute disapproval of his escort.

'Good evening again, sir. And for the … lady?' His face was now as impassive as hers was overdone.

'Good evening, Herve,' replied Bisset. 'The same for both of us, if you please.'

Herve filled another glass from the bottle on his tray and returned to the bar where he waited, as Bisset knew, for the late evening rush of reporters from the offices of the daily newspaper across the street. And at ten o' clock, when he could barely hear his companion over the babble of thirsty journalists, Bisset counted out the exact money for the drinks and left, taking her with him.

He led his escort up the stairs to his apartment. The bar, he could see through the landing window, was now tightly packed. He unlocked the door and ushered her into the study.

'Please, *mademoiselle*, make yourself comfortable.'

She took a chair by the fireplace and crossed her legs. Bisset trembled as she adjusted her dress to reveal a stocking top and garter strap. She looked at the bookshelves that lined two entire walls of the room. 'Such a magnificent library! Is *m'sieur* a professor or a lawyer, perhaps?'

Bisset smiled. 'This is but a small part of my collection,

mademoiselle, but alas, I am no more than a lowly bookkeeper. My interests, however, are many. And now, if you will excuse me, I must freshen up. Will you allow me to bring you a drink? What would you like?'

She licked her lips slowly. 'Whatever *m'sieur* likes is perfectly acceptable to me. My tastes are also varied.'

'No doubt,' remarked Bisset. He opened a cabinet, brought out a bottle of Chartreuse and filled a glass for her. 'I shall not be long, *mademoiselle*. I look forward to my return.' He leaned over, kissed her cheek and hurried down the hallway.

He glanced behind, unlocked his studio and switched the ceiling spotlights on again. A black-uniformed *SS* officer framed by a swastika looked towards him with his plastic arm raised in salute and the portraits of Caligula, Himmler, Robespierre, Genghis Khan and Mussolini lining the walls smiled. Henri Thibault looked on approvingly. A soft, educated voice ran through Bisset's mind; each syllable was a descending rung on the ladder of depravity. His body vibrated with expectancy as he reached up. Thibault's skin became soft again as the mask moulded itself to Bisset's face.

She was sitting in the wing chair facing the fireplace. A hand reached for her neck and squeezed gently. She arched her back and looked over her shoulder in expectation. Globules of solder-like sweat trickled down the pockmarked face in bronze streams and the lips twisted into a rictus smile. The fingers tightened around her throat.

'*Bonsoir*, *mademoiselle*, it's such a pleasure to meet you.'

She screamed, tore the hand away and threw herself forward. They flexed their fingers and followed her as she scrabbled for the door. It was locked. Her terrified shrieks brought the street outside to a halt. The little bar at the end of the pavement emptied as journalists, never too drunk to find a good story, rushed to the source of the noise.

A dozen men, aided by the *concierge*, burst into the apartment, but by then it was all over. The woman lay on her back, staring at the ceiling. Her blouse was ripped open and a man knelt astride her with a mask in his hands. He was still laughing as the *gendarmes* took him away.

***

Jean-Guy Bisset, unlike The Strangler of Picardy, was spared the guillotine by an act of government passed thirty years previously. The death mask of Henri Thibault was eventually returned to its place in the *Musée des Criminels*, this time well secured, like Bisset. There appeared to be a slight smirk upon his face when viewed in a certain light. Like Bisset, he was meticulous. The books were balanced.

He had been executed for the murder of twenty-four prostitutes.

Machines in the Ghosts

'That's an impressive CV, Mr Kowalski, you've certainly got the development experience ArgoNavis Entertainment is looking for. Well, as you probably know, we've already got a limited run of CoSMoS boxes under beta testing and plan the full product release in around three months, so your Grafix background is just what we need to ensure it hits the shelves on target. Now then, if you were a salesman, how would you describe CoSMoS to me in a couple of sentences?'

Kowalski thought for a moment. 'That's a lot to squeeze into a small package. Uh … how about: CoSMoS is the acronym for Choice of Stars & Movies on Screen. ArgoNavis Entertainment subscribers can choose any film from the wide selection in its archive and replace the leading actors and their voices with any others on the list, or even themselves if they buy a Personal Features Card.'

'Great summary, I couldn't have put it better! Right, let's skip the lip – we can offer you an annual starting salary of $180,000, a profits bonus, twenty-five days' vacation, a full relocation package, family medi-care and automobile re-imbursement. How does that sound?'

***

Digby Beiswanger grinned. What a day! The official launch of CoSMoS at last! No one was going to beat this! In the four years he'd been President of ArgoNavis Entertainment, profits had risen from six hundred million dollars in 2023 to almost eleven hundred million in 2027 and now they were going to leave those figures in the dust. There wasn't a shadow of competition from anyone, anywhere. His secretary called on the intercom as he was analysing the logistics of a further two satellites to cover the Middle and Far East.

'DeWayne Jackson to see you, Mr Beiswanger.'

'Okay, ask him to come in. Oh, rustle up some champagne too.'

Beiswanger waved his CEO to a seat. 'What's the news on the street, dude?'

'Pretty damn good, Digby, there are queues outside every E-Agency from Alabama to Wyoming according to CNN.' Jackson's eyes glittered as he opened his palmtop. 'As of an hour ago, we had just under twenty-one million online and hard copy package confirms, which is … let me see … four hundred and forty million bucks a month. Holy cow, it's not even eleven o'clock! We've gone supersonic!'

Beiswanger mimicked a scowl. 'DeWayne, DeWayne, that's a poor start. It should have been hypersonic but I guess it'll have to do for now. You'd better lay on a party tonight, my man. Usual distractions apply.'

***

The complaints started to roll in on the third day. The techs were baffled. In the first case, Phoenix Rivers had simply disappeared from *On the Waterfront,* leaving a black mobile silhouette and Marlon Brando could not be retrieved. Bruce Lee similarly vanished from *High Noon*, taking Gary Cooper with him, Charlie Chaplin faded from the database along with Paul Newman in *Cool Hand Luke* and Sylvia Kristel and Lana Turner both disappeared from *Emmanuelle*.

The following day George Peppard, James Coburn, Richard Burton, Marilyn Monroe, Charlton Heston, Greta Garbo and Richard Pryor deleted themselves in entirety from CoSMoS. The strangest occurrence happened when a displaced Humphrey Bogart suddenly re-appeared in a CoSMoS-tailored *Casablanca*, crossed his arms, glared out from the screen and abruptly vanished. The replacement, Rick Blain, Oliver Reed, followed seconds later after an angry, side-long stare. Then Jayne Mansfield abandoned ship in *African Queen*, Groucho Marx refused to even come out in *Lawrence of Arabia* and John Wayne quit his *A Tale of Two Cities* role after five minutes.

By the end of the week thousands of irate viewers were besieging CoSMoS agencies all across America. Something had gone badly wrong. And someone had to tell Digby Beiswanger.

***

He slammed the side of his fist on the boardroom table and glared at the department chiefs. 'Well, whaddya got to say for yourselves, eh? We've spent nearly a billion bucks on this project and now you tell me the system's broke and you don't know why. If it's not hardware and it's not software, then what the hell *is* it? It sounds like frigging *unaware* to me. You'd better fix this sorry mess pronto if you want to keep your jobs.'

The chief Grafix engineer chewed his lip and looked at Beiswanger. 'I can't understand it, Digby, I really can't. The system works perfectly under test but whenever we put it out to the consumers it turns to a crock of camel compost once they change any of the characters. If they play the movie normally, it's fine. We've replaced the On-Board Databases and it doesn't help; the same thing happens whenever the next CoSMoS film gets played.'

‘So what are you saying, *Mister* Kowalski? That we’ve got ghosts in the machine? *Eh*?’

Kowalski looked around for support, but everyone seemed occupied with their fingernails and ear wax. ‘Well, hardly. But come to mention it, all the characters who, well, er … disappeared from CoSMoS are … um … actually dead.’

Beiswanger’s eyes almost shot out against his glasses. ‘Oh, fine, so we’re only haunted, then.’ He looked around the room. ‘Well, that’s a great relief, ain’t it, fellers! Poltergeists in the processors? Spooks in the software? Demons in the database? No problem, all we gotta do is call in a programme priest and get the system exorcised.’ He pointed at Kowalski. ‘*Jaysus H. Christ*, I’m paying you fifteen grand a month and you want me to get a friggin’ ju-ju man in to fix your foul-ups. Get real, willya?’

Kowalski’s face was as red as his knuckles were white. He steamed but didn’t respond.

Jackson broke the silence. ‘You’ve got to admit it’s a weird coincidence though. Just saying.’

Beiswanger leapt up and swept a stack of reports from the table. ‘*What?* I don’t believe what I’m hearing. Get out of here, the whole goddamn lot of you, *get out,* and don’t come back until you’ve got some sensible answers.’

***

He stared at the city lights through his office window, shook his head and filled his glass with more brandy. CoSMoS’s reputation was in Technicolor tatters and the media was shredding what was left. Four hundred and thirty-five thousand contracts had been cancelled in the last two hours alone and the European agents had already warned him they were thinking of pulling out. It was likely that the Canadians would follow suit too. The stock market was trembling and so were the accountants; his new-born baby was going to be an infant mortality unless he could salvage something from this god-awful mess.

Ghosts in the machines … Crazy bastards. He'd see for himself what was going on in his electronic empire. He picked up his CoSMoS control pad, turned to the wall screen and jabbed *Select Movies. Producers' choice of the day*:

Air America ... Back to the Future ... Catch 22 ... Deathwish ... Easy Rider ... Forrest Gump ... Halloween ... Ice Station Zebra ... Jason and the Argonauts ... King Kong ... Little Shop of Horrors ... Mad Max ... Night of the Living Dead ... Octopussy ... Pulp Fiction ... Quantum of Solace ... Rio Bravo ... Spartacus ... The Good, the Bad and the Ugly ... Unforgiven ... Vertigo ...

He scrolled back and settled on *The Good, the Bad and the Ugly.* Then he deleted Lee Van Cleef, inserted Paul Walker as Angel Eyes and sat back to watch. Fifteen minutes passed without problem. Then Angel Eyes abruptly disappeared as he shot Stevens at the dinner table and left a black shape in his place. Beiswanger cursed and pressed *REFRESH,* but the Angel Eyes character remained an inky shadow. The reproachful faces of Van Cleef and Walker suddenly appeared on the lower part of the screen, scowled and faded away.

'What the hell is going on here?' He opened his desk drawer, took out his Personal Features Card and rammed it into the data base module. Then he deleted Van Cleef and restarted the film. This time *he* was Angel Eyes.

'Right, you bozos, just try and shift Digby Beiswanger.'

CONFIRM. START.

***

'Quiet on set, everyone. Roll the sound. Act Two, Scene Two, Take One!'

Clack.

Beiswanger blinked under the studio lights and looked around. Two cameras were sighted on him and dozens of characters stood around in a circle. He tried to focus on their faces. James Dean … Charlton Heston … Bob Hoskins … Alan Rickman … Lana Turner … Gregory Peck … James Coburn … Christopher Lee … *Am I going frickin' mad?* He wiped his glasses on his shirt front and looked again. They were still there and more besides. Clark Gable … Jane Russell … Richard Burton … Ernest Borgnine … Philip Seymour Hoffman … David Carradine … James Cagney … This couldn't be real. They were all dead and long gone. The three-quarters of a bottle of brandy on top of what those half-wits had said at yesterday's meeting must have conjured them up. Yep, that's what it was, just a dream. But how could he dream that he was only having a dream when—

He jumped back as Humphrey Bogart stormed across the studio floor.

'You grave-robbing *maggot*, we've been waiting for you to show up. What's the big idea of screwing around with our movies? I thought I'd met all the jerks in this blasted business, but for a new boy you sure top the bill with your lousy gimmicks.'

'What?'

James Stewart appeared beside Bogart. 'That's right, we worked hard for years to entertain the folk out there a-a-and along you come a-a-and mess it all up in three days. That's pretty good going for someone who doesn't know one side of a darn Kleig light from the other.'

There were ugly mutterings from the other actors and Beiswanger felt their eyes boring hate-filled holes into him. The dream was too realistic for his liking by a long way. He bit the inside of his cheek until he tasted blood. But it didn't change anything – he was still standing in the middle of a studio floor surrounded by cameras, crew and cables, ladders, lights and reflectors and a baying band of dead actors instead of his penthouse office with Jackson Pollock paintings on the wall, Berber carpet on the floor and Tesseron Cognac on the table. Well, however he'd gotten here and whatever was happening, he'd put a goddamn stop to it right now.

'What kind of baloney is this? *Eh?* Don't you peckerheads pull stupid charade pranks on me unless you want your walking papers. *Got it?*'

Laurence Olivier pushed through the crowd and prodded Beiswanger's chest. 'So *you're* the wretch who reduced us to the same level as circus performers and freak show curiosities? You've made a grave mistake, *sir.* Not only have you infuriated and demeaned three generations of actors with cheap trickery and—'

This was too much for Beiswanger, hallucination or not. 'Cheap? Whaddya mean, *cheap*? We put millions of dollars into developing the technology that's keeping moth-eaten back numbers like you alive on the screen, so don't get cute. And if it wasn't for people like *me*, buster, you lot would still be mouldering inside rusty film cans.'

'*Hold your tongue.* You're not addressing your sycophantic serfs now.' Olivier's words were scalpel sharp. 'Mark my words, you'll come to regret soiling our reputations and profession with your contemptible enterprise. You'll find no friends here, I assure you.'

'Quite so, Larry,' continued David Niven. He turned to Beiswanger. 'Now listen here, old chap, this just isn't on. We're all rather upset about your conduct, no matter how amusing *you* may find it. You've made *us* the laughing stock of the twenty-first century and that is quite, quite unforgivable.'

Sean Connery elbowed his way through the actors and glared at Beiswanger. 'It's nothing that a good thrashing wouldn't fix and I don't mind starting the queue.'

'It's gonna be a long one,' shouted someone from the back. 'C'mon, let's get on with it!'

Beiswanger swallowed hard and began to edge away.

'Hold your horses, boys, make way for Mae!' A wasp-waisted blonde in a tight dress and fur stole squeezed past Connery and winked at Beiswanger. 'Why, *helloooo* there, honey! There's been a lot of talk about a new man in Tinseltown so I thought I'd drop by and get the hard facts first-hand.' She looked him up and down, stepped closer and traced a fingertip along his cheek. 'Ya know, a gal like me could make a man like you moan out loud in the right circumstances. Whaddya say?'

Beiswanger smiled uncertainly. Any friendly face was a lifebuoy in this storm and the water level of reality was already rising faster than his disbelief could keep up.

'Not sure, tiger? Here, let me show you.' She lifted her foot and raked a stiletto heel down his leg. 'Well, try that for size, you *creep*.'

Beiswanger screeched and clutched his shin. *'Jesus Christ Almighty.* You're frigging maniacs, the lot of you.' He looked around wildly and saw an open chain lift door at the back of the studio. Any place was better than here. He tried to hop through the crowd of angry actors with Mae West's cackling bouncing between his ears but found his way blocked every time. Even Stan Laurel and Leslie Nielsen were swearing and swinging their fists at him. He ignored the pain, lowered his shoulder and barged past them.

'Stop him, Steve!'

Someone stuck a foot out and sent him sprawling. He rolled over and looked up. A blonde-haired man in an aviator's leather jacket grinned at him.

'That's quite a case of stage fright you got there.' He twisted Beiswanger's collar under his chin and hauled him upright. 'Sorry, pal. There aren't going to be any great escapes on *this* set. *Cooler!'*

Beiswanger flew into the circle on the end of a left cross and crashed against a camera dolly.

'Cut!'

He screwed his eyes up against the studio spotlights. A portly man stared down at him from a high director's chair and then looked over Beiswanger's shoulder.

'Take a break, all. Next scene in an hour.'

Beiswanger turned around. The studio was empty as if the actors had been switched off. He rubbed his jaw and tasted blood again. *'Sonofabitch!'* The pain was real enough even if the circumstances weren't. He looked at the man in the chair. 'Boy, am I glad to see the back of those screwballs. Are you the big cheese around here?'

The director grimaced. 'The big *cheese*? You happen to be addressing Alfred Hitchcock, sir.'

'Whoever you are, I'm damned glad to see someone with all his marbles in the jar.'

'Hmmm … thank you so much. I'm deeply humbled by your acclamation.'

Beiswanger stood up and straightened his collar. 'Think nothing of it, buddy. Now, what about telling me how the hell I ended up in this nuthouse?'

Hitchcock leaned back in his chair and lit a cigar. He puffed away for a few seconds and blew a stream of smoke towards Beiswanger. 'Tut, tut, dear boy, you invited yourself if you recall, and look at the trouble it's caused. But now that you *are* here, I'm going to run through an idea for a movie and I'd like your opinion of it.'

Beiswanger fluttered his fingers. 'Yeah, yeah, go ahead if you want, Mr Pitchfork. I've got nothing else in my diary other than getting kicked and punched so your plot can't be any kookier than this zoo.' He felt his jaw again. 'Anything beats getting swatted in the kisser.'

'Perhaps,' said Hitchcock. 'Right, stop me if you've heard this before. A television entertainment company invents a gadget that allows home viewers to switch a movie's leading actors with other stars or even themselves if they buy a personalised card to put into the machine. This affair doesn't impress the deceased actors because they feel they're being ridiculed and devalued and their estates don't receive a cent in royalties either. They decide they've had enough after a few days of humiliation and refuse to allow themselves to be controlled by the machines. The design engineers can't fix the problem, millions of viewers cancel their contracts and the company is in serious financial trouble. Their president gets drunk in his office and puts himself into the machine to see what the issue is. He suddenly finds himself being filmed in a studio full of the dead actors; his gadgets have been degrading. They verbally and physically attack him, then the director declares a break and tells the president what a bad thing he's done.

'Are you feeling all right, Mr Beiswanger? Anyway, the president is regretful and wants to go back to his real existence but the director tells him there could be a problem. His associates are sure to find him missing and assume he's either gone into hiding or committed suicide somewhere because he's brought the company to its knees. The product is abandoned and the gadgets are recalled. If the employees find his personal card in the machine and remove it before it's taken to a recycling centre, along with millions of others, he'll be restored. But … if they *don't* find the card he'll be trapped forever in a device of his own making, so to speak.' Hitchcock beamed. 'Well, what did you think of it? No, let me guess – you don't like the ending?'

Perspiration rinsed the colour from Beiswanger's face and his mouth was as dry as cotton wool. 'You're goddamned *right* I don't.'

Hitchcock tapped the ash from the tip of his cigar. 'I thought you might say that. My actors didn't like being recycled either.'

Small Talk

Joey can't believe it. He goes to bed as a full-sized man of five feet, eleven and a half inches and wakes up as an elf.

'You're not looking your normal self today, dear,' says his wife as he comes down for breakfast with a flannel around his waist. This is no exaggeration – he's eighteen inches tall.

Joey frowns. 'It's very inconvenient. Still, I must make the best of it.'

Suzanna cuts a slice of bacon into quarter-inch pieces and sits him into their daughter's high chair. She fills a matchbox with digestive biscuit crumbs while he eats. 'You won't be needing quite so much for your lunch today. Could you manage a grape as well?'

Joey promises to do his best. But there's a small problem to consider before leaving the house. 'What on earth am I going to wear?'

His daughter's cast-off pink Barbie shorts won't win him any sartorial points at work. Neither will the Spider-Man T-shirt.

Suzanna thinks for a moment. 'Let me see what Mrs McSpreader has got spare.'

Joey's sure there'll be plenty of choice from next door ever since the dreadful young Hamish was taken away by social services. He wonders if he knows his own mother was responsible for the anonymous phone call. Suzanna picks him up as she dashes by.

'You really are a cute little thing,' she says as she puts him onto the kitchen worktop. 'Just wait here, I'll be right back.'

He sits there while his daughter glowers at him from behind the bars of her playpen. She's got a large wooden spoon in her hand and is obviously sizing him up. He tries to think of what disagreeable restrictions he's imposed upon her. But he's safe for now. That's until the cat bounds onto the worktop and eyes him curiously. He's glad that Tibbles had been fed earlier. He doesn't fancy his chances with something the comparative size of a sabre-toothed tiger. He fends him off with a roasting fork and saucepan lid.

Suzanna returns from the McSpreader household. 'Here you are,' she says. 'Hamish won't be needing these at the Infant Correction Centre.' She empties a Tesco bag onto the table and holds up various items of clothing for his approval.

A Donald Duck romper suit? He shakes his head. A two-piece Thunderbirds uniform in grey with 'Virgil' embroidered on the breast? That would never do. An infant's Milton Keynes Rovers strip? He'd be the laughing stock of the office. He finally decides on a Junior Jumbo Jet Captain's uniform in dark blue with gold stripes and wings *(Colours may bleeding during first few wash. No spinning drys. Made in Taiwan)*. A pair of green toddlers' Wellington boots completes his wardrobe.

'What do you think, dear?' asks Suzanna when she's finished dressing him.

Joey looks at himself in the hallway mirror and cringes. He's got no alternative; the shops don't open until nine o'clock. 'Well, I suppose it'll have to do. Would you mind awfully giving me a lift to work?'

So at five minutes to eight, after struggling to undo the child's seat safety belt, he's standing outside Hubbard's Cupboards International.

‘Have a nice day,’ encourages Suzanna.

Joey’s colleagues are astonished.

‘How long are you going to be like this?’ asks Miss Peebles.

‘About a foot and a half,’ he replies.

‘What does it feel like to be an elf?’ Mr Cudmore wanted to know.

This is easy. ‘Exactly the same as being full-size, except a lot less.’

‘Come, come,’ says the section supervisor, ‘back to work, all of you. Anybody would think you’d never seen an elf before.’

Well, Joey had never seen one before either, and now he *is* one. He takes his usual place at the graphic design desk with some difficulty. To start with, he’s precariously balanced on a stack of Jiffy bags. Mr Golightly thoughtfully puts some thick office supplies catalogues against the backrest and secures him to the chair with a daisy chain of rubber bands. He feels much safer. The next problem is the keyboard; it seems as though he’s depressing buttons the size of Weetabix and it’s almost an arm’s stretch to type the word ‘equip’. This is plainly Not Going To Work. He weight-lifts the telephone and explains his predicament to the company doctor on the second floor. He sounds sceptical but sends the nurse to collect him.

For the next hour Joey answers questions as to his eating habits, whether he’s participated in base jumping or underwater caber tossing, whether he’s been exposed to any radioactive isotopes and even if he plays the tuba. In the end the doctor is as puzzled as Joey is. He closes his *Encyclopaedia of Obscure Medical Complaints*.

‘I’m going to sign you off work for a week to see if there’s any improvement,’ he says.

‘Yes, thank you, Doctor. But what exactly is the matter with me?’ Joey isn’t assured by his blank look.

'Well, I diagnose your problem as a heteromorphic critical reduction in corporeal mass with the corollary of undefined associated complications resulting in the inability to perform pre-designated tactile assignments due to acute vertical impediment.'

Joey is impressed with the analysis, even though he doesn't understand most of it. He hitches another lift with the nurse and makes his way back to the graphic design department armed with the sick note. 'Get bigger soon,' urge his colleagues as he tidies away his desk, 'we're going to be short-handed.'

He decides on a half before going home. He has to wait for a towering customer to kindly open the door of the Shepherd's Rest before he can get in. He sees the look of disbelief on the barman's face as he totters over the floor of the lounge bar.

'Lost your Airfix kit, sonny?' he enquires.

But Joey loses his temper instead. It doesn't take much to throw him out.

***

The bus ride home is a bargain: half-fare despite a moustache and a very deep voice. He notices that Mrs McSpreader is hanging out her washing as he crawls under the garden gate. Her clothesline is festooned with curious items of night apparel. This brings something else to mind. How is he going to make out in the conjugal department? He's already been subjected to some scathing remarks in the past. In his present circumstances he suspects he'll only be able to please himself.

Meanwhile, his daughter is bored with the torture of small, unsuspecting creatures and decides to take out her grievances on a guardian who is now smaller than herself. 'Lucretia want more toys. Lucretia want lemonade. Lucretia want sweets. *NOW.*' She reinforces her demands with a plastic baseball bat.

'Naughty, naughty,' chides Suzanna as Lucretia pursues Joey around the garden on her electric tricycle.

***

He spends the afternoon Googling everything related to little people. Most of it is nonsense: leprechauns, gremlins, gnomes, sprites, fairies, trolls and Danny DeVito. Nothing relates to his recent disorder. He decides on a nap and curls up in the safety of Lucretia's doll's house where he dreams about a film he saw as a child. *The Incredible Shrinking Man* or something like that. In the end the protagonist could only be seen through a microscope. There's a knock on the wall. Joey opens his eyes, fearful of an earthquake. It's Suzanna.

'Here's your tea, darling,' she says and slides a jam-jar lid full of spaghetti bolognaise through the front door. The pasta's the size of drainpipes and is going to take some eating without cutlery or asbestos gloves.

'I've invited Merlin and Tabitha over for drinks and snacks tonight,' she continues as Joey shoos away a Brobdingnagian house fly. 'They've got some holiday snaps of Nepal and perhaps they might have some ideas about your little problem. Do you want some Parmesan cheese?'

He groans, not that anyone can hear him. Merlin's latest interest is anyone's guess. He's been through Zoroastrianism, Buddhism, Hinduism, Animism, Judaism, exorcism, existentialism, magnetism and astigmatism. He fancies himself as some sort of Tantric technician and is only too keen to carry out body repairs to damaged karmas or re-bore worn-out dogmas. Perhaps he knows something about minimalism. Tabitha is a tittering echo.

'They'll be here at seven o' clock. I bought you something special to wear from M&S. It's a nice little one-piece in powder-blue with anodised pop studs and a double gusset reinforcement.'

'Thank you very much,' he says.

***

Merlin and Tabitha arrive closer to nine than seven. They're unapologetic as Suzanna takes their alpaca-wool jerkins.

'We refuse to be slaves of a clockwork god, dependent on arbitrary parameters set down by those weightless in the outer space of creativity and inner vision,' explains Merlin as he adjusts his headband.

'Quite, quite,' reiterates Tabitha. 'We were watching *The X Factor*.'

Merlin notices Joey standing on the telephone table. He studies his aura. Studying auras is his speciality. 'Hello, Joey, have you been involving yourself in retroactive inhibition?' he says with a hint of suspicion, 'I observe you've slipped one or two rungs on the ladder of enlightenment.'

Joey assures him he's done nothing of the sort.

They sit down in the lounge: them on the comfortable three-piece suite while Joey sits in Lucretia's highchair. He feels like a new exhibit in a museum. Suzanna passes round plates of Quorn rolls and dried-banana biscuits. Tabitha produces a bottle of non-alcoholic wine straight from the cloisters of the local abbey.

'So, what form of mental vagrancy has resulted in the diminution of your physical manifestation, Joey?' says Merlin. 'Please consider me your astral attorney and feel free to cast your spiritual millstone into the pool of perception.'

'Mental vagrancy,' squeaks Tabitha, 'spiritual millstone ... astral attorney ... pool of perception.'

For the next two hours Joey is battered with holism, transcendentalism, empiricism, Platform Scriptures of the

Sixth Patriarch, hatha yoga, Bo trees, Noble Truths, Eightfold Paths and the price of Renault 2CV brake shoes. None of this is much use to him, not even the offer of a free feng shui blitz on his house and car. Tabitha says a few words of her own at last.

'Your problem, Joey, is that you *think* you are small.'

Joey considers this. 'That, Tabitha, is precisely because I *am* small,' he says, using an ice cream cone as a megaphone. 'Why do you think I'm sitting in my daughter's chair instead of stretching out comfortably on the sofa with a full-size wine glass in my hand?'

'No, *daaaahling*, no! You are merely suffering from a severe case of attenuated self-esteem, which has produced sympathetic physical materialisations. I heard of a similar case in France where an estate agent turned into a goose. His wife had been having an affair with a paté producer.'

'So what are you suggesting, Tabitha? That Suzanna is having a fling with Goliath?' asks Joey.

Tabitha shook her head condescendingly. 'No, dearest person, of course not. It's simply a protest from your subconscious. You must assert yourself more.'

This is rich, he thinks, coming from a soya-munching verbal parrot that hasn't had an original thought since the UK won a Eurovision Song Contest.

Merlin looks at his watch. 'Well, Morpheus beckons, it's time we were off.'

'Yes. Time we were off,' echoes Tabitha.

Joey knows there's a spicy film on Channel 4 in twenty minutes. He uses the cat litter tray while Suzanna sees them out. Very undignified, he thinks. Still, it's better than a one-way trip around the 'S' bend.

'Bedtime, dear,' says Suzanna when she gets back. 'Would you like to sleep with me or in the doll's house?'

'With you, of course,' he says, 'but I am a little tired if you understand my meaning.'

Suzanna understands his meaning but chooses to ignore it. It's Friday night, after all. Life becomes alarming for a while. It's like lying on an overgrown coconut mat during an earth tremor. He feels a little seasick but bravely perseveres. Suzanna has a piece of winceyette fluff in her tummy button that tickles his nose, which doesn't help.

She takes him in her arms afterwards and holds him close. The terrain is quite interesting. This is what he used to fantasise about as a teenager. He eventually falls asleep and dreams of his reverse Lilliputian day.

Joey senses a change in his physiology when he wakes up. He lifts the sheets and looks down. *Nine feet!* He can't believe it.

Where on earth is he going to get four and a half pairs of matching shoes in his size?

Nor the Years Condemn

'Doyle.'

The soldiers looked up at the figure silhouetted against the trench bunker entrance.

'Doyle. Are you deaf?'

Doyle got up from the ammunition box he'd been sitting on and stood loosely to attention. 'Sergeant?' The word was an undisguised sneer.

'Outside Captain Wintle's dug-out, cap and belt off. You're for it now and no ruddy mistake. Come on, *move* yourself. The rest of you are stood down until noon.'

'Bugger him,' said Doyle, when the sergeant had gone. 'If I ever catch him on a dark night, I'll—'

'You'll do nowt of the sort, you big-mouthed get,' said somebody from behind the sudden glow of a cigarette end, 'and if you get a spell in the chokey it'll be your own bloody fault after last night. So shut your bloody trap.'

Doyle looked around the candle-lit bunker for support, but there was only hostile silence. He spat on the ground and went out into the trench. Sergeant Whetham was waiting for him outside the company commander's dug-out with two escorts. He looked Doyle up and down and stood him to attention between the two men.

'Defaulter's parade ready, *sah*.'

'Very well, Sarn't Whetham. Wheel him in.' The voice from inside was weary and cracked.

'*Sah*. Defaulter – *quiiiick march*. 'Eft, 'ight, eft, 'ight, 'eft, 'ight, 'eft.'

The officer looked up as Doyle was doubled into the dug-out. Sergeant Whetham stamped to attention and saluted.

'Private Doyle, 286, one charge of refusing to obey a general order under Section 11, contrary to King's Regulations and one charge of acting to the prejudice of good order and discipline under Section 40 …'

Wintle's bloodshot eyes flickered over Doyle as the charges were read out. He frowned.

'How do you plead, Doyle, guilty or not guilty?'

'Not much point in arguing with the army, is there?'

'Not much point in arguing with the army, is there *what*?'

'Eh? With the army, *sir*.'

'That's better. I'll accept that as guilty. All right, Sarn't Whetham, the events in your own words. Any extenuating circumstances?'

'None, sir. He was ordered to stand-to at 02:00 hours, same as the other men. Told me, begging your pardon, sir, to bugger off, seeing as how he'd only had three hours sleep. Again, just the same as the rest of us, sir. I asked him again, maybe a little bit more forcibly, like. Then he said, sir, that if I didn't bloody-well sod off, he'd stick his bayonet up my arse and let me use it to pick my teeth after he'd rammed them down my throat with his boot.'

The side of Wintle's face twitched as a shell screamed overhead. He looked at the two sheets of paper on his make-do table.

'I see this is your ninth charge in the twelve months you've been in the army, Doyle. Two terms at Harfleur disciplinary camp for misappropriation of equipment and being drunk on duty. Two counts of Absent Without Leave. Brawling. Barrack-room theft. Dirty rifle. Refusing to obey a direct order. Not a very impressive record, is it? Anything to say for yourself?'

'Aye, sir, I have. I didn't volunteer for this war. I got bloody-well dragged into it.'

'That's as may be, Doyle, but as you're here you *will* conform to orders whether you like it or not. We're all in this together, conscripts or otherwise.'

Doyle jerked his head towards an alcove containing a lighted brazier, a chair, and a trestle bed. 'Aye, I can see that … *sir*.

'I won't stand for impertinence, Doyle. Watch your step.'

'Impertinent, sir? Me, sir? Don't hardly know what it means, even.'

Wintle slammed his fist on the table. His tobacco tin fell to the floor between the duckboard slats and spilled its contents into the mud. 'Then you'll damn-well know what *this* means – guilty as charged. Twenty-one days loss of pay and privileges. Extra duties as Sarn't Whetham sees fit. You're a bloody disgrace, Doyle. It sickens me that good men are dying out there and I've got to waste time on the likes of you. If you're up before me again I'll make damned sure that you get six months in detention, *do you hear?* Get him out of my sight, Sarn't.'

'*Sah*. Defaulter and escort – *shun*. About turn. Quick *maaarch.*'

Whetham dismissed the escort when they were back in the trench. He turned to Doyle and narrowed his eyes. 'I'm going to have you, sonny. I'm going to run you so hard you'll wish you'd never been bloody born.'

***

Doyle seethed as he filled in yet another latrine ditch. He lashed out with his spade as a rat the size of a small cat scurried towards No Man's Land and the perfume of putrescence. The loss of privileges and pay meant nothing to him; there were no privileges to be had at Péronne anyway, short of being wounded and hospitalised. What gripped him were the additional duties. Burial duty, ammunition duty, runner duty, sentry duty, sandbag duty, kitchen fatigues and whatever else that bastard Whetham could devise. His hate festered as the days passed.

***

It had stopped raining for the first time in three days. Doyle sat down on a firing step, took off his tunic and shirt and lit a cigarette. He heard Whetham's voice as he began picking lice from their seams.

'Doyle. DOYLE.'

'For fuck's sake, not again.' He darted into a dug-out entrance. He wasn't quick enough.

'Stop skulking, Doyle, get yourself out here, *now*.'

He stepped back into the trench. 'Just cleaning my equipment, Sergeant Whetham. Doing my duty like any good soldier should.'

Whetham snorted. 'What would you know about good soldiering, Doyle? Christ, I'd sooner count on Florence Nightingale to get me out of a pickle than a whole squad of your sort. Aye, and you *are* going to do your duty – you're on recce detail tonight. Be outside the section dug-out at midnight. Don't make me come looking for you.' He turned to walk away.

'Better mind yourself with all those German snipers out there, *Sergeant*. It wouldn't do for your nippers to be orphans, would it?'

Whetham stormed back and jerked Doyle's chin upwards and backward with the palm of his hand. His eyes were inches away from Doyle's. 'Don't threaten me unless you want to be on the receiving end of a firing squad. Do I make myself clear?'

Doyle smirked as Whetham eased his grip. 'Aye,

Sergeant, perfectly clear. It's the Fritzes you should be telling, though.'

Two troopers appeared from a feeder trench, carrying a machine gun and belts of ammunition between them. Whetham gave Doyle a final glare, pushed him away and turned on his heels.

Doyle reached for his shirt and watched the sergeant as he picked his way through the semi-quagmire. He crushed another parasite between his nails.

***

Captain Wintle pointed to an area on the map with his cane. 'As you've noticed, things have been very quiet here on our left quarter. This could mean that the Germans are massing their troops in the centre lines in preparation for a frontal attack. Or it could be that they've simply moved back because their trenches are flooding with all this damned rain. The Flying Corps can't confirm either way because of the weather. Therefore, we need to find out for ourselves. You men will be divided into two parties, six apiece. Sergeant Whetham will be leading one, and Sergeant Butterworth the other.'

An icy draught coursed through Doyle as he heard Wintle talk of using bayonets to silence any German sentries they may come across.

'… So I shouldn't need to tell you to keep as quiet as you possibly can. If you're trapped in the open you'll have to wait until tomorrow night before you can get back.' Wintle looked at his watch and nodded to the two sergeants. 'Be ready to leave in thirty-five minutes. Good luck.'

The two parties climbed from their trenches at one o'clock and began to crawl towards the German lines seven hundred yards away. Doyle cursed under the added burden of a large pair of wire cutters. The mud was six inches deep in some places, over two feet deep in others. Their uniforms were soaked within minutes and began to chill their limbs. They moved on their hands and knees and tried to avoid the water-filled shell holes and bloated corpses. Strands of rusting barbed wire ripped their flesh and clothing. They clenched their teeth and cursed silently.

They were little more than halfway across the battlefield after three-quarters of an hour. And then moonlight seeped through the thinning clouds. There was a metallic *clunk* far to his right, followed by muffled shouts and a ripple of rifle fire. The parties stiffened. A flare arced through the night. The ground for two hundred yards around was bathed in an eery green glow.

Whetham was as still as a statue. '*Don't move. Stay exactly as you are.*'

It was too late. One of soldiers scurried for the cover of a shell hole. A machine gun rattled from the German trenches and he went down before he'd gone five yards. Another flare illuminated the battle lines and the crack of bullets filled the air above them. The man next to Doyle grunted and fell onto his face. A bullet tore the epaulette from his shoulder. He burrowed into the mud with his fingers. A trench mortar coughed and great gouts of soil and fragments of long-dead soldiers cascaded onto the remainder of the reconnaissance party. Whetham slithered towards a shallow crater and Doyle followed, sobbing in fright. The two men tumbled into the hole as another flare burst above them. A clod of earth, hurled into the air by a mortar thudded onto his steel helmet and a red-hot fragment of shrapnel burned the back of his neck.

Whetham groaned and rolled onto his side. 'Chrisht … the bashtards …' He clawed at his helmet strap. Blood dribbled over his fingers and from his mouth.

Doyle looked at him in the diffused light of the flare. His teeth and jawbone were exposed by a gash in the side of his face.

'Doyle ... get me a dreshing ...' The words bubbled in his throat and died away.

Doyle stared at him for a few moments, raised his head and looked around. He felt sick with fear.

A forced whisper carried from somewhere to his right. 'Is anyone left over there?'

Doyle almost cried in relief. 'Aye – George Doyle. Who's that?'

A tearful gasp. 'Oh, thank Christ fer that. It's me, Ernie Wilson. Anyone else alive?'

The gunfire was sporadic now and the flares were dying glows in the mud. Doyle looked across No Man's Land and then at Whetham. It was a long way to go with a wounded man. Especially this one. Whetham clawed at his leg and tried to pull himself up.

'Naw. Looks they're all croakers. Let's hook it before they start again, for God's sake.' Doyle kicked at the hand again and again, and then the face, until he broke the grip and began to crawl towards safety.

Three miles away, behind the North-West Fusiliers' lines, an artillery officer gave the order for his men to fire a barrage at the German trenches.

One of the shells fell short.

***

In 1920 on the eleventh day, of the eleventh month, at the eleventh hour, the War Memorial Cenotaph at Whitehall was unveiled. A casket, with King George V and five holders of the Victoria Cross acting as pallbearers, was carried into Westminster Abbey to be buried among the ranks of Britain's most illustrious dead.

The Unknown Warrior had come home.

(The events leading up to) A Good Night Out

'Ah, Julian, punctual to the second! What are you having?'

'Hello, Charles, good to see you. The usual if you don't mind.'

Charles pushed through the noisy crowd of City workers and caught the barman's eye. 'Ah, Tony – Talisker, dash of water and an Asbach, please.'

He paid for the drinks and joined Julian at his table. 'Had a good week?'

'It could have been better; our darned lorry broke down at Arras on Wednesday night with two hundred cases of Burgundy on board. The distributors were screaming like unfed babies so we had to sub-charter. One needs to unwind. How was yours?'

Charles smiled. 'Can't complain, really, I've been having a run on wall clocks since that widow had hers valued at £11,000 on the *Antiques Roadshow* the other day. I sold an 1840 Biedermeier for half that this morning, actually. Life's less stressful in the collectable business, but I do miss the edge sometimes.'

***

'Come on, Shane, drink up, for fuck's sake.'

'I haven't finished this one yet. What's the rush?'

'It's Friday night, innit!' Craig hooked his first finger at the landlord. 'Give this pussy a lager and I'll have another

Snakebite.'

The landlord put the drinks on the bar. '£6.35.'

Craig counted the money out. 'Can't you turn the music up a bit? It's like a fuckin' morgue in here.'

'It's loud enough as it is. I've got my regulars to consider, they're not weekend drunks like you. And watch your language if you don't mind.'

'I'm expressin' meself,' said Craig. 'Bollocks to what other people think.'

The landlord snorted. 'That's an interesting philosophy! I suppose those eyebrow studs are expressing that you don't want a job?'

Craig screwed his face up. 'Not at eight and a half quid an hour for pot washin' or stackin' shelves in Sainsbury's, I don't. I'd sooner stay on the dole.'

'Oh, so how much *do* you expect, seeing as you've got no qualifications worth anything to anyone?'

'Enough to keep me in beer an' tabs'll do for now.'

The landlord bristled. 'Oh, that's all right, then – just as long as my money as a taxpayer isn't being wasted.' He moved to serve a customer, then turned around. 'When I was your age, I'd been working for three years *and* I was giving half my wages to my mother for food and board. We had a bit more self-respect in those days.'

Craig took a long drink, licked the beer from his upper lip and looked at Shane. 'Yeah, I bet he was one of them urchins what cleaned chimneys with a toothbrush for thirty hours a day and had a week off every ten years. He'll be tellin' us next that he only had a bath when QPR won the FA Cup an' lived in a greenhouse frame with fifteen brothers an' sisters in the same flower bed.'

***

Charles looked at his watch. 'A quarter to eleven. One more

for the road?'

'Why not? It's been a very pleasant evening.'

'As always, Julian. A perfect start to the weekend.'

Charles weaved between the customers and found a chink in the bustle of suits at the bar. Julian looked out of the window at the sound of a car horn. A dozen youths were jostling each other in the middle of the road, holding up the traffic. One of them threw an empty bottle. It smashed against a shop door.

Charles returned with the drinks and watched the troublemakers as they disappeared. He wrinkled his nose. 'More cretins incapable of holding their drink.'

Julian sniffed his whisky thoughtfully. 'So tiresome, isn't it …?'

***

Shane watched the last few customers leave. 'S'pose we'd better drink up before we get thrown out.'

Craig looked at the landlord's back as he collected glasses. 'He can fuck off. I'll finish it when I'm good an' ready. That twat's worse'n me old man.'

Shane took a last mouthful of lager and checked his wallet. 'That's just about cleared me out. Never mind, Sharon gets paid tomorrow. How much have you got?'

Craig fumbled in his pockets and brought out a note and a few coins. 'Twenty quid. Some fuckin' weekend this is gonna be, innit? Ain't got no blow left, either.'

'What!' said Shane. 'Nothing?' He tapped his jacket pocket and grinned. 'I've got a couple of Black Beauties as well.'

'Fuuuuckin' mentaaaal.'

'Come on then, finish up and we'll pop 'em back at my place.'

Craig swallowed his drink, slammed the empty glass on

the bar and followed Shane to the door. The landlord glared at him from the till.

'You're going to do that once too often, Sonny Jim.'

'Oh, yeah? An' I'll fuckin' do *you*, you prick,' said Craig from the side of his mouth.

The landlord was past the counter and across the floor in half a dozen steps. He jerked a fist under Craig's nose. 'Is that right? Come back when you're man enough, you little squit. Until then, you're barred. Now fuck off out of my pub.'

Craig pushed his way past Shane and spat on the entrance carpet. 'Fuckin' dosshole anyway.'

***

Charles swirled the remains of his brandy around the glass and finished it. Then he sighed contentedly. 'Ah well, shall we make a move?'

'Right-oh,' said Julian, 'a spot of supper and a Chablis or two at the club should round the evening off nicely.'

They collected their raincoats from the stand and went outside. A few revellers passed by, then the pavement was empty. They walked to the end of the road and crossed into the park.

***

'I'm gonna do some twat, just watch me,' said Craig, 'I'm just in the fuckin' mood.' He kicked a plastic waste bin next to the park gates. It made a loud cracking sound. 'I'll have his fuckin' windows out. Tosser.'

'Yeah, right,' said Shane. 'Let's have one of your roll-ups.'

Craig stopped under the entrance light and passed his tobacco tin over. 'Make us one as well while I'm havin' a slash.'

He stepped off the path and urinated over a flowerbed. When he'd finished, he kicked the heads off a cluster of magnolias.

'Someone spent a lot of time on those,' said Shane.

'Eh? What're you drippin' about? Who cares? They're only fuckin' flowers, ain't they?'

'Yeah, I s'pose everything's only something,' said Shane.

'What the fuck are you talkin' about?' said Craig after a moment. 'I wonder about you sometimes. C'mon, light up and let's go.'

He brightened as they followed the moonlit path. 'Remember the old git by the Post Office what had all them animals and things cut out of bushes? He had a go at me once for throwin' me chip paper into his poxy garden. So I waited in the bus shelter the next day until I seen him go into his greenhouse. Next thing he knows, there's half a brick through its roof. Fuckin' glass all over the place. Twat came out wavin' his arms like a fuckin' windmill, shoutin' he was gonna get the pigs on me an' all that. The blind git couldn't recognise me from five feet, never mind with me hood up.' He belched and threw his cigarette onto the path. 'Right laugh, it was, I tell yer. Should've seen his face.'

The rhododendron branches at the side of the path shivered. Craig stopped, pulled his shoulders back and peered into the foliage. A shape, even blacker than the night, stepped out at him. He jumped back in surprise. A blow struck his forearm just below the elbow. A shoe raked his calf at the same time and ground down hard above his instep. He cried out, clutched his arm and staggered in ripping pain. His other foot was kicked away. The back of his head thudded into the path. The sky turned red, then black.

Shane called into the darkness. 'Craig? *Craig*? What's up?'

He felt a tap on his shoulder and turned around. A grip like iron pincers closed around his neck. He began to choke and wrenched at the hands. The pressure on his windpipe increased. There was a rushing in his ears and he felt his mind slipping away. He kicked and punched at the attacker's outline but there was no force behind the struggle. The grip tightened even more. His sight faded to a prick of light and his hands fell away. The pressure relaxed. Then a knee rammed up between his legs as he slid to the ground.

Craig rolled over, shook his head and tried to get up. His right arm was senseless. The silhouette against the starlight moved towards him. He began to scrabble away but the attacker dragged him upright by his hood.

'Leave it out, man, for fuck's sa—'

A slap to the side of the face weakened his knees and blinded him for a moment.

'*Please* … I said I've had enough.'

The dark figure turned away, then swung back. His arm shot out. A red-hot spear of pain shot through Craig's kidney. He shrieked, dropped to the path beside Shane and vomited.

They lay on the path groaning as the sound of shoes crunching on gravel faded away.

***

Julian looked at his reflection in the mirror and brushed his moustache just so. Then he wiped a stain from his shoe, threw the tissue into the bin and joined Charles, who was waiting outside the railway station toilets.

'Shall we go?'

'Ready when you are.'

They went out to the forecourt and waited for a taxi.

'A good night out, eh, Charles?'

'First class!' He waved his umbrella at a black cab. It pulled up at the kerb. The driver wound his window down.

'Where to, gents?'

Charles straightened his tie and opened the passenger door. ‘Army & Navy Club, Pall Mall, please.’

Olympic Flags

She looked at her watch for the twentieth time that hour. He'd never been this late from a seminar before. The journey was not even sixty miles and he'd told her he'd be home by eight o'clock, nine at the very outside.

The sound of heavy rain on the windowpanes. A sudden burst hammered against the glass like a gravelled drum roll. She looked at the clock above the fireplace. One minute to ten. Why couldn't she get through to his mobile? Even if the battery was flat there *must* be a public telephone somewhere he could call from.

Her friend Anne had been around before lunch for a chat, her menthol cigarettes were still on the coffee table where she'd left them. She took one from the packet and lit it with the onyx lighter given to them as a wedding present. It would be their second anniversary next Saturday. Her head began to spin. She was unaccustomed to smoking after a six-month break. She ground the cigarette out, angry with herself for weakening. Unborn children had no say in what went into their bodies.

Ring, damn you, David, ring. Please.

Perhaps, even as she fretted, he was turning into the road leading to their comfortable little terraced house. They'd foregone a honeymoon and spent the time and money on redecorating the two-up, two-down instead. She wouldn't have changed that fortnight for anything the world could offer.

Callum kicked. She held her cupped hands over her growing mountain of happiness and smiled, despite her growing concern. David's face had shone with delight when the doctor confirmed their pregnancy. And when the scan had confirmed what she already knew, he was so pleased that he lost a day's work due to the following hangover.

The rain stopped for the first time in three hours, occasionally resurrecting itself as a spiteful patter on the bay windows. She opened the curtains and looked outside. David's Audi was a missing tooth in the neat line of cars parked along the street. *Where the hell are you?* She bit her lip and went to the kitchen.

She spooned coffee into two mugs as the kettle boiled. Hers was the red mug with the scales of Libra in white. His was green, splashed with the colours of Tottenham Hotspur. There was a large chip on one side above the handle, but he wouldn't throw it away because she'd bought it for him especially.

The sound of a car horn brought her rushing to the front door. The rain had started again. A taxi waited in the road as three figures dashed from their house. The rear doors slammed shut and the taxi's tyres sizzled on the wet tarmac as it pulled away. She closed her own door, disappointed, upset. The kettle switched itself off as she returned to the kitchen. David's supper grew steadily colder in the oven. Her hands began to tremble as she filled her cup. Twenty to eleven. She went into the lounge, sat down and put the mug onto a magazine to save the coffee table from Olympic flags. That was what David always called the marks. She looked at the cigarettes and reached out for one.

A suddenness. Everything became violently still. A vacuum in which everything was suspended. A hundredth of a second later, a knock. A rushing sound filled her ears and was gone. Another knock – harder, this time. She put the cigarette back into the packet and stood up. The world moved past her in slow motion: the coffee table, the Lowry print on the wall, the mock Grecian frieze, the telephone on its shelf in the hallway. Two dark shapes behind the frosted glass panels. She turned the entrance light on and opened the door.

Policemen. Their caps and shoulders were wet from leaving the squad car. It was parked in David's spot. The one on the left, the shorter of the two, had cut himself shaving; she could see where the razor had slipped, just below his left ear. The taller policeman looked ill-at-ease as he stepped forward.

Yes, she was Mrs Sarah Kavanagh. Yes, her husband, David, was the owner of a white 2015 Audi A4. No, Mrs Kavanagh, he hasn't been hurt in a car accident. Perhaps she'd like to sit down. He was afraid the news wasn't good. They sat down in the lounge. She rubbed at the Olympic flags on the magazine cover as they told her that David had been found dead in a motel room twelve miles away. It appeared there'd been some kind of fault with the heating system. A blocked flue, they believed.

Everything in the room took on a cold look as they told her this. Their wedding photograph on top of the television stood out in clinical clarity. David was gazing into her eyes. He'd just whispered that he loved her more than anyone else in the world could. She heard herself asking, in a voice that belonged to someone else, why her husband had died in a motel, not thirty minutes' drive away. If his car had broken down, why hadn't he called her? Why hadn't he got a taxi?

The two policemen looked at each other. They didn't have all the details yet, they said, but would let her know as soon as they could. Meanwhile, there would be some formalities to deal with. When she was ready, of course. Was there anybody she could call, anyone she wanted to be with? Parents … family … friend?

Her parents were two hundred miles away in Lincoln, she said. Her brother was in the North Sea on an oil rig. A friend? asked the policeman again, very gently. His fingers were intermeshed as he sat on the settee. His thumbs pushed and rolled against each other. He'd just noticed her swollen belly.

Yes, she had a very good friend. She lived two streets away with her husband and two children. Yes, she would like her friend to be with her now.

The taller policeman went with her to the hallway. He picked up the telephone and pressed the buttons to the numbers she mechanically called out. He passed the handset to her as she looked at the wet footprints on the carpet. She waited for a reply as the rain poured down. Someone answered. A woman. It was not her friend. The voice sounded much older. She asked if she could please speak to Anne. The voice asked who might be speaking. Sarah, Sarah Kavanagh, she replied. The voice cracked and broke, telling her she was very, very sorry but she couldn't speak to Anne. Anne was dead. There'd been an accident. She found herself slipping on the ice of reality. So sorry, the voice continued on the edge of tears, but she had to go. Her son and his children were in shock and needed her.

The phone fell to the floor. And outside, it seemed as if the rain would never stop.

The Bucket List

'All right, guys, let's have a bit of hush so we can get this briefing underway.'

The chatter faded, a chair leg shrieked on the floor and someone coughed as the police officers made themselves comfortable.

'You've all heard the buzz from the night shift, so here's the latest from the Scene of Crime bods,' said Garrett. 'What we have are five fatal shootings in our area last night. They occurred between approximately 21.30 and 02.00 according to the surgeon's initial examinations and all the victims were known to us.

'The first was Trevor Presti, who lived in Marine Drive. You'll all be aware of his form: burglary, aiding and abetting, affray, battery and supply of controlled substances. Presti's girlfriend found him in the garden five minutes after he went outside to investigate what had set off his car alarm. The cause of death appears to have been a single pistol shot to the head.

'The next was that of Kurt Freemantle in the King's Court Estate. He was discovered on his doorstep with a gunshot wound to the temple. He had a record as long as two arms, mainly ABH, A&B, theft, breaking and entering, going equipped and criminal damage.'

Garrett looked at the list on his lectern and continued. 'Number Three. Lucius McWilson of Spurfield Close, another regular customer of ours with convictions for drug dealing, pimping and guilty of a lot more than we could nail him for. Once again the cause of death was a bullet wound to the head, this time through his living room window.

'Fourth up was Albert Stringer, who lived on the Saracen Park Estate. He was released from jail last March after a twelve-year sentence for possession of child pornography and sexual assaults of a child under 13. Stringer was found lying on his doorstep with one bullet wound to the groin and one between the eyes.

'Finally, our old friend, Bahman 'Baha' Madbouli, who'd recently served three years in Belmarsh for terrorism-related offences. He was found in his shawarma van near the Mad Hatter nightclub, again with a bullet through the head.'

Garrett picked up a cane and traced a path on the wall-mounted town map. 'Now, here's a strange thing – going by the estimated times of death and locations of the victims, it would seem that our killer – or killers – started in the river area and then proceeded to knock off the others in a clockwise direction. So we clearly have a carefully planned execution sequence carried out by someone proficient with firearms.'

'The scrotes had it coming by the sound of it, Guv,' said one of the constables, 'and I dare say there'll be plenty of support from Joe Public for what happened last night.'

'It'd be hard to disagree with their sentiments, Spike, but we've got a duty to catch those responsible, however much we know the toerags deserved it. The last thing we need is people covering up for vigilantes because they've seen *Death Wish* half a dozen times. Back to the brief: once the SOCOs have finished, we—'

'Inspector Garrett?'

Garrett turned around. A WPC stood at the door with a mobile phone in her hand.

'Yes, what is it?'

‘The Super, sir. It’s urgent.’

‘Very well,’ said Garrett. He took the telephone and stepped into a side office. ‘Garrett here, sir.’

‘Jeff, you can call off your manhunt before it starts. We’re about to get a confession.’

Garrett blinked and pushed the mobile closer to his ear. ‘A confession, sir? But we’ve not even—’

‘I’ve just had a call from a Mr Finlay. He very nicely told me that he doesn’t want us to waste time looking for the murderer as he’ll be on his way to the station to make a statement once he’s finished putting one or two domestic things in order. He’s cheerfully admitted to the killings and from the details he’s given me I’ve no reason to doubt his word. So you can stand your men down from the investigation now, Jeff. Strange, isn’t it? The biggest murder inquiry to hit the county since nineteen-canteen and it’s about to be resolved before we even start. This Finlay character should be with you shortly so you’d better stall the press for now; tell them there’s been a development and we’ll be issuing a statement this afternoon when we have the full story. Any questions?’

Garrett loosened his tie. ‘No, sir; they’ll wait until our man gets here.’

***

‘Can I help you, sir?’ asked the desk sergeant.

The man rested his elbows on the counter. ‘It’s quite the opposite. I think you’ve been looking for me.’

The sergeant looked at him. Late sixties – mid-seventies, maybe. Well-spoken. Thin. Probably six feet tall without the stoop. Sunken eyes. Flat cap covering more skin than hair. Green Barbour jacket. Checked shirt. Cravat. No missing person of that description reported.

‘And who might you be, sir?’

‘Finlay. Terence Finlay.’

The sergeant’s eyes showed his surprise. ‘Oh, yes, er, we’ve been expecting you. Just one moment.’ He pressed an intercom button. ‘Mr Finlay’s here, sir.’

Garrett was at the desk in thirty seconds with another officer. ‘Mr Finlay?’

Finlay nodded a greeting. ‘Major, Royal Marines, actually. Retired of course.’

‘Good morning, Major. I’m Inspector Garrett. I think we’d better go to the interview room and have a talk.’

‘Very well, Inspector, that’s why I’m here. At your convenience.’

Major Finlay followed Garrett along the passageway and chatted amiably about the traffic and weather. He concluded by handing over his car keys as he sat down at the interview table.

‘I won’t be needing these anymore. Red Audi A3, parked next to the wall. Reverse is a little tricky sometimes. Right, I don’t require a lawyer and there are no immediate family members to inform so shall we begin?’

Garret sat down opposite him. He nodded to the other policeman and switched on the recorder. ‘Interview starts at 11:52, June 14th 2022. Custody officer is myself, Inspector Garrett. Witnessing officer Sergeant Hawley. Your name, address, date of birth and National Insurance number?’

Major Finlay gave his details and sat back with his hands loosely on his lap.

‘You do not have to say anything but it may harm your defence if you do not mention when questioned something which you later rely on in court,’ continued Garrett. ‘Anything you do say may be given in evidence.’

‘Yes, yes, quite,’ said Finlay. ‘Let’s get on with it.’

‘As you wish, Major. As this is a voluntary interview, and you are not yet under arrest, we’ll carry on once you’ve signed this written consent form.’

Finlay signed the document without looking at the details and pushed it back over the table. 'Fire away, Inspector.'

'Right, I understand you made a telephone call to us earlier this morning indicating that you were responsible for five shootings carried out between the late evening of June 13th and early morning of June 14th at various locations in Wickminster.'

'That's correct, I think your forensics chaps will find that the bullets were fired from a suppressed Walther PPK/S .22, which you'll find in a box nailed under the workbench in my garden shed.'

'And your reason for shooting these people last night?'

Major Finlay leaned forward and tapped his fingertips on the table like a drum roll. 'Vermin. Every damned one of them *and* you know it. The operation was simply a surgical removal of malignant social tumours. I doubt there'll be many tears shed over their excision, Inspector. They got no more or less than they deserved. I imagine Wickminster will be having fewer problems with their like for a while. Wouldn't you agree?'

Garrett almost did. 'Were you acting alone, Major?'

Finlay crossed his arms. 'I despatched every one of them by myself if that's what you mean. I shall, of course, plead guilty to the murder charges if this ever goes to court.'

'If this *ever* goes to court, Major? That's a strange thing to say. You've just admitted to killing five people.'

'Let me ask you a question, Inspector. On average, how long between a defendant being charged and appearing in the Crown Court?'

Garrett thought for a few seconds. 'Three months, I suppose. Why do you ask?'

'You have my age from your notes. Fifty-four. *Fifty-four*. Look at me! Hard to believe, isn't it? Most people would think I was twenty years older. It was the same with my wife. She was forty-one when the cancer took her and I've got a month or two at the most before I follow her. So, you see, there's going to be no prison sentence for me.

'And you know something else, Inspector? There are quite a few like me in this country with a lot of cleaning to do in the little time we have left and they have the same means and skills that I do. But I've got nothing more to say about that.

'Now, how about a cup of tea?'

In Cold Blood

Two porters offloaded the casket onto a gurney and wheeled it into the clinic before the ambulance driver had even opened his door. An orderly wandered over as he was completing his log.

'Morning, Larry. Who've we got this time?'

'Morning, bud. Roscoe Maddox, believe it or not.'

The orderly took a step backwards. 'Roscoe *Maddox. No way!* What happened?'

'A dog walker found him almost beaten to death in Central Park just after midnight. The ER surgeons said there wasn't much chance of him pulling through so his lawyer put us on standby for when he croaked.'

'What the heck was he doing there at that time?'

'The first responders said he was wearing running kit when they got to him so I guess he was jogging.' Larry put his clipboard down and smiled faintly. 'So much for exercise being a healthy pastime, eh?'

'Well, it looks like he's bitten the dust for real this time and he won't be getting an Oscar for it, either.'

Larry laughed. 'Maybe he'll make a comeback soon.'

'Ha-ha, not in my lifetime, I hope!' said the orderly. 'I reckon he'd have failed a screen test for his own biopic if anyone had the time or dough to waste on producing one. When are the cops going to get that place cleaned up, for crying out loud – there must've been half a dozen murders there in the last couple of months. That's pretty grim, even by New York standards.'

'Yeah … it's starting to get like it was 30 years ago. The media's gonna be screaming for heads to roll in City Hall if they don't come up with something real soon. Bums, junkies and winos are one thing, but a high-profile stiff like Maddox is going to attract a lot of public interest even if he *was* a crummy, washed-up stereotype. Fifty bucks says you won't see the grass for cops once the mayor's kicked a few keisters at Police Plaza.'

'Your money's safe there, dude! At least they won't have to watch half-assed *Shadow Over Laramie* or *Pearl Harbor Revenge* repeats in his memory when they're pounding the park.'

Larry started the engine. 'I guess rainbows come from clouds once in a while. See you around.'

***

'Denizen Maddox … *Denizen Maddox*.'

The voice filtered into his consciousness long before his memory re-arranged itself. He blinked and tried to look around for the speaker, but his head wouldn't respond. Neither would his arms and legs. It was as if he were set in concrete. *Sweet Jesus* – he was paralysed! He panicked for a moment and then realised he could still swivel his eyes. Now he could see that he was lying on a reclining treatment chair in a room with white windowless walls and a fluorescent ceiling. The tight green coverall he wore was grassed with cables and tubes connected to a bank of displays and an array of clamps secured his body to the chair.

'Sorry, Denizen, you're restrained to hold you static for conscious scanning. Keep as still as you can. It won't be for much longer.'

He tried to focus on what appeared to be a semi-opaque

man standing at his feet. 'Uh … wha'sgoynon? Wha' th'hell're yew … where'm I?'

'Welcome back, Denizen Maddox. I'm afraid *Mister* is a rather outdated prefix in present times. You're understandably confused by what you see and from now on, everything will be new to you, but don't worry, I'll explain as we go along. To begin with, I'm a hologram for quarantine purposes, we can't afford to be careless after almost re-introducing Covid Sigma in '46. It's a routine measure to protect you as well as us until all—'

'In '*46*? A'yew nuts? Tha's twenny-four years 'fore I was born!' Maddox's cracked voice smoothed out. 'What the hell's a Coded Stigma anyway?'

'Oh, I'm sorry, Denizen, *2046* – thirty-one years ago.'

Maddox strained against the clamps. 'Whaddya mean, *thirty-one* years ago? Someone here's loco and it ain't yours truly. Look, get me someone who can talk sense, dammit.' *How could it be 2077, for Chrissake? It was August, 2019... he'd just stepped out from Bethesda Terrace and—*

'Denizen Maddox – this is the FutureLife Cryonics Centre. We have some interesting news for you.'

***

The hologram remained on station for the next hour and explained that his physical injuries had already been repaired and the scanners were running a final check of his neurological, circulatory, glandular, elastographical and digestive systems and bringing his antibodies up to date before the clinic would release him.

Maddox waited impatiently and then the monitors chirped, one after the other. 'That's it, we're through with the tests now, Denizen Maddox,' said the hologram, 'and you'll be pleased to hear that everything conforms to parameters.'

‘That’s swell, *Mister* Hollowman!’ said Maddox, ‘but it’s more than I can say about my belly. How about ordering me a medium rare rib-eye steak with candied jalapenos and fries? A couple of Coors wouldn’t hurt either.’

The hologram smiled. ‘Meat? I’m afraid you’ll need to discuss the menu with the dietician, Denizen. It’s been nice talking to you.’

The airlock behind it opened with a slight thump as ambient air rushed into the room and the projection faded away. Maddox stared at the two white-overalled staff standing at the entrance.

The man spoke first. ‘Welcome to 2077, Denizen Maddox, and congratulations on being our fifth successful recovery! I’m Clinicist Bevan. This is Assistant Thorne. I trust you’re in better shape than when you first came to us?’ The voice and face were the same as that of the hologram.

‘I’m no medic, mister and sister, but I’d say *anything’s* an improvement on being dead unless it’s waking up in Alaska.’

The woman smiled. ‘Well, this is New York so you can consider yourself Lazarus risen now.’ She turned off the systems modules, removed Maddox’s brain activity skull cap and disconnected the ribbon connectors, tubes and clamps from his coverall as Bevan chatted.

‘I can’t say I’ve ever seen your movies, as you call them. We generate our own characters these days. Cheaper, no tantrums and they never age unless we want them to. I hope you’ve got no plans to get back into the acting business; it’s almost history now.’

‘Oh, *yeah?* We’ll see about that, pal.’

Bevan raised his eyebrows and flashed a look at Thorne. ‘Er … OK, Denizen. Shall we see if you can walk?’ He offered Maddox his arm. ‘Sorry, we haven’t got around to levitation yet.’

Maddox ignored the invitation and swung his legs over the edge of the chair. He gingerly lowered his feet to the floor and let them take his weight. Then he took a few uncertain steps, steadied himself and tottered around the room for two minutes.

'Well done, Denizen!' said Thorne. 'Now we need to re-nourish you and run through our induction programmes before your media exposure. A lot has changed during your cryo-preservation, as you can imagine, so there'll be some social adjustment necessary as well as physical.' She opened a storage locker and passed him a package.

'What's this?'

'Lightweight phase-change clothing, it warms you when you're cold and cools you when you're hot. It does more but we'll save that for later. We don't stand on old-fashioned modesty, but you can change in the hygienics station if you wish.'

He took the coverall off in the bathroom and looked at himself in the wall mirror. The reflection pleased him. Although he was several kilos lighter his body didn't seem to be in bad condition for the lay-off. He stepped a little closer and frowned. His nose was off-centre by a few millimetres, both cheeks were indented and a faint stitched scar ran across his forehead like a lid seam and disappeared under his hairline.

A struggle … blinding pain as he brought his hands up to protect his face from another blow … vivid, jagged light … lackness … nothing but blackness …

Bevan tapped on the cubicle door. 'Nearly ready, Denizen Maddox?'

***

Maddox felt mentally battered after his six hours of media introduction to 2077. The science fiction movies of the new millennium had come to life: all road vehicles ran on batteries or inductive rails instead of gasoline, skyscrapers were largely replaced by subterranean storeys, the moon was colonised, scientists manned bases on Mars, denizens took holidays in space hotels, insect and seaweed farms provided protein foods, supercharged ground source heat pumps and solar panels warmed and powered every home, cancer, malaria and a score of diseases had been eliminated by genetic engineering and hundreds of technological breakthroughs had transformed almost everything he'd known.

The re-adjustment guide waved off the immersive display and patted Maddox's shoulder. 'I think that'll do for today, Denizen. It's a lot to absorb, eh? We'll carry on tomorrow if you feel up to it and then there'll be a public reception for you in the Foundation Hall. Right now I'm sure you'd like to relax a little and take a look outside now that you've got an idea of what to expect.'

'Damn right, dude! My yesterday was 58 years ago and I'm still only 49 so I've gotta lot of catching up to do – everything's gonna be changed except me.' Maddox clicked his tongue. 'I guess all the folks I knew aren't around anymore unless you've got them in the freezer too.'

The guide shook his head. 'You're the only one from the entertainment world and we had no response from any bloodline when we announced your imminent return. Even your villa and ranch are gone, but at least they paid for the cryogenics and there should still be enough in your bank account to keep you comfortable for your new future.'

'I guess nearly 60 years interest on a few million bucks helped. Talking about keeping comfortable, your brave new world better be full of pretty girls because my usual playmates will either be great-grandmothers or wearing pine by now.'

'Don't worry about that, Denizen. There'll be more than a few of our young circrosses interested in meeting you.'

'Circuses? Hold up one minute. I'm not gonna be some

fricking fairground attraction for anyone.'

'Cir*crosses*, Denizen Maddox, a circle with a cross on its periphery is the female gender pictograph, just as a circarrow signifies a male.'

'Circrosses, shmircrosses, so much for progresses. I thought I'd left all that baloney behind. And lay off the 'Denizen' stuff, willya? Just call me Roscoe, like my fans do. Or *did,* dammit.'

'That would be most irregular at this stage … Roscoe … but I'm happy to comply in the spirit of affinity. My given name is Austin of the Garfield group.'

Maddox slapped the guide's back. 'Right, Austin of the Garfield group, let's see what I've been missing all these years.'

Austin led Maddox along a corridor and into a circular plant and fountain-dotted concourse with telegenic landscape and wildlife scenery lining the sides. People in corporate jumpsuits hurried along radial passages and music, the like of which Maddox had never heard before, came from every angle. Austin showed him into an elevator.

'This one will take us up to ground level. Are you ready, Roscoe?'

Maddox nodded excitedly. 'Let's go, cowboy!'

The doors opened two minutes later to a bustling atrium and there, spread out before him through walls of glass, was New York. So this was the future! He dashed over and looked around. The few landmarks he recognised between low-rise buildings stood out in perfect clarity against a deep blue skyline; a network of monorails and skybridges was woven above streets teeming with moving walkways and transport pods, shrubs grew on rooftops and greenery lined rows upon rows of balconies. But what caught his attention was a green annular holograph rotating above the city.

Welcome, Roscoe Maddox from 2019. The World's 5th Cryo Success.

In the public eye once more! He had a feeling that his resurrection was going to be more enjoyable than his previous incarnation.

***

He looked at the latest '*Welcome*' holograph sourly. The most recent arrival was a Swedish geneticist who'd pioneered body part regeneration in 2042. Since his own reawakening there'd been nine successful arrivals through cryonic channels, each frozen in their time, like him. His dragonfly-like moment of glory had gone, over in less than six months. A burst of media interviews, guest appearances at dinners and universities, and once again he was old news, an eclipsed star. In the audacious world of 2077 he was short of nothing … except fame.

***

He felt the need for his old routine after a while. It was the only activity that stretched his limits, focused him on beating his own record. He bought an interactive multi-functional fitness suite and after a few weeks he was back to his condition of almost 60 years ago. Now he was ready.

The moon was shrouded in thin cloud as he ran around what remained of Central Park. Only the Metropolitan Museum of Art, Bethesda Terrace, Belvedere Castle, Jacqueline Onassis Reservoir and Boating Lake were readily familiar to him among the BiOrbs, but the perimeter pavements were as firm as they'd ever been. He turned into a tree-lined footpath halfway along East Drive, got his breath back and waited.

***

Maddox woke early, showered, and looked out of the window of his apartment. The holographic headlines flashed in bright red.

Capital Shocked By Murder in Central Park.

He stretched, sat down to his breakfast and smiled. He was back in the limelight again.

One Winter's Day in Untere Ostbrücke

A chill December wind blew across the almost deserted car park and Bergander shivered, despite his overcoat. He leaned on his walking stick and crossed the road to the camp entrance. He didn't stop to read the memorial sign next to the gatehouse. He already knew what it said in its five languages.

UNTERE OSTBRÜCKE KONZENTRATIONSLAGER 1936–1945. This site housed in excess of 655,000 inmates over a nine-year period. Imprisoned here were political dissidents, Jews, Communists, Poles, Russian prisoners of war, gypsies and other elements deemed undesirable by the National Socialist Party. 551,000 never left the camp alive.

He knew all right. First-hand.

VISITING HOURS: 0900–1700, TUESDAY–SUNDAY.

He looked at his watch. Twenty minutes past one. The camp was no longer open all hours but there was time enough for him today. He turned up his collar to fend off a blast of stinging cold that numbed his cheeks and cursed. An old man like himself had no business being out in weather like this. But it had to be done or the re-awakened memories and sweat-drenched nightmares that had plagued him for the last few months would never stop.

The dead weight of Untere Ostbrücke began to press

down on him as he passed through the gate and his heart fluttered. He'd never spoken of his experiences to anyone who'd not been here and even the faces of those who had were indistinct now, eroded by over seven decades. But not their shadows. He braced himself and stepped forward into his past.

The familiar parade ground stretched out before him, flanked by the long administration building. The flagpole was still there in front of the main doors, but this time there was no swastika fluttering from it. He stared at the balcony above the entrance doors where the SS camp *Kommandant* would survey each incoming batch of prisoners, tapping a riding crop against his hand like a liquidator counting assets. A party of nuns hurried towards the gates with their capes flapping behind them. An old couple holding hands were not far behind. There was no one else to be seen. He took a deep breath and went inside. The annexe was filled with photographic displays, documents, dioramas, ragged prison uniforms and sculptures, but he instantly recognised the central corridor stretching the length of the building. He read the signs as he passed each door. *Disinfection Room. Prison Cells. Interrogation Room.* Shards of memory fell into place.

Registration Room. Everything taken from the prisoners had been listed here: clothes, baskets, trunks, books, pens, watches, rings, necklaces, purses, whatever they had. They left the hall with nothing except ill-fitting and well-used camp-issue uniforms.

The next door. *Prisoner's Effects.* The room was empty now except for photographs of those confiscated items. Suitcases stacked to the roof. Wallets. Handbags. Umbrellas. Shoes. Boots. A mountain of spectacles with their lenses reflecting the glare of the flash bulb. Their long-dead owners crowded behind him until he had to turn away. He hurried from the block and into the square as fast as his walking stick would allow.

As soon as he was back into the clean, cold air, he took a hip flask from his pocket, filled the cap with schnapps, emptied it in one swallow and grimaced. This was only the beginning. The prison barracks site sprawled out ahead of him. It was unfamiliar at first. Just one hut, a replica, stood amongst the wilderness of area markers. He looked through the door and pictured the eight hundred prisoners existing in an unheated barrack built for two hundred and fifty; the triple-tiered bunks with three to a bed space sharing one threadbare blanket. The mattresses of lice-infested straw. The smell of unwashed clothes and bodies. The chaos of inmates tumbling through the doors for the twice-daily *Appells* on the parade square.

All Prisoners To Attend Roll Call. Even the corpses of those who had died during the night were lined up in front of the shivering ranks of thin inmates in thin soiled uniforms standing perfectly still for hours in thin weather such as this with their weak breath barely condensing in the bitter air and their skin turning blue. The slightest movement from attention brought the targets a flurry of blows from a rifle butt or baton or boots and they'd join the bodies on the frosted ground. Their fate was settled if they couldn't fall in with the labour party. He'd seen it countless times. *Arbeit Macht Frei …*

Large snowflakes fluttered from the darkening skies and within minutes the hut marker stones were disappearing under a thin white carpet. He looked around. Somewhere to the left had been the kitchen block. He recalled the miserable issues of black bread and scrapings of margarine or jam and rancid leftover scraps from the SS messes that were added to the watery turnip soup. And next to it the hospital hut. He'd seen it filled with hollow-eyed wrecks weak with typhus, dysentery and a hundred other sicknesses. No proper beds. Little medication. Rags for bandages. The patients, if they survived, rarely left in much better condition than when they'd arrived. The doctors and their orderlies were not much more than skeletons themselves.

The snow was thickening on the ground now and covering his hat and shoulders. He followed the path edge markers, unsure of his bearings until he saw a single-storey concrete building standing ahead in a small copse. The camp architecture snapped into place.

Shower Bath read the sign above the entrance. The door at the end of the building opened to the Undressing Room. *'Remove your clothes*,' those prisoners of no use to the *Third Reich* had been told, '*Hang them up ready for when you come back from the shower. Quickly now.'* He trembled in sick anticipation as he walked past the benches and clothes racks, through the open hermetically-sealed door and into the shower chamber with its stained walls and rows of fake showerheads. He closed his eyes and imagined the occupants' last moments. The thud of the door locking bolts. Darkness as the lights were switched off. The screams as Zyklon B pellets rained down the ventilation shafts and began their work. The sobbing and gasping as they blindly scrambled over each other in the gas-saturated air and tried to scratch their way through the walls and locked door as they suffocated.

It seemed his hammering heart must burst through his chest. It was enough. *Enough*. The photographs of naked, twisted bodies and discoloured faces of men, women, children and babies swam past his eyes as he stumbled back through the Undressing Room and into the darkening afternoon. He leaned against a tree for support and fumbled for his hip flask. This time he drained it and waited for the schnapps to steady his nerves and hands. There was only one more path to follow and then he could put everything behind him and pray God wipe this place from his mind forever.

The low-roofed building with its tall chimney was less than two hundred metres away, but between the driving snow and his crumbling joints, it was getting harder to walk. It took him the better part of five minutes to reach the door. He wavered for a moment and stepped inside. Four brick ovens stretched along one side of the *Krematorium*. Their doors were wide open as if still awaiting trade. A faint breeze from the corner of his mind brought back the smell of burning flesh and it suddenly became so ripe that he cupped his hand over his mouth and nose and gagged. He cursed himself. What a damned fool to have come back. What if this pilgrimage only fanned the flames of his night terrors—

'Guten tag, mein Herr.'

Bergander started. A white-haired man stood by the last oven.

'Guten tag,' he replied.

The man slowly walked up to Bergander. 'I think you must be the final visitor for the day,' he said quietly.

There was a trace of accent that Bergander recognised but couldn't immediately identify. 'Perhaps. I've seen no one else,' he agreed. 'I expect the weather is too cold for people to venture far.' He was reluctant to talk, but there were social obligations to respect.

'Most likely … but not too cold for those with a reason to be here, *nicht wahr?'* said the man.

Bergander felt a ripple of unease at the man's remark but didn't respond. He looked at the man's grey suit instead and said, 'Are you a guide?'

'A guide? *Ja*, that is correct.'

The flat and distant replies were too much for Bergander. He wanted to close the conversation politely and be on his way. 'Have you been at Untere Ostbrücke long?'

The guide rubbed his eyes with a finger and thumb and stared at Bergander. '*Ja*, for more years than I care to remember.'

Bergander was now completely unsettled. 'I w-w-was here once.' The words he'd guarded for decades were past his lips before he could stop them.

The lights above them flickered and dimmed. A crystal chill swept through the crematorium. The guide moved closer and pulled up his left jacket sleeve. '*Ja*, I know that, *mein Herr,* I was here at the same time. See, here is my tattoo. But perhaps you don't remember me*?* No, of course not, why should you? I was only one of many. But I remember *you* very well.'

The schnapps rose in Bergander's throat as the guide's body began to shimmer in the half-light and a tall, emaciated young man dressed in a striped prison uniform rolled down his sleeve.

'I've been waiting a long time for you and the others, *Corporal* Bergander. A very long time. We *all* have.'

One by one, an orange glow bloomed from the ovens. Pops and crackles filled the crematorium.

Bergander crashed to the floor as the shadows closed in.

A Beast in the Boot

(Based on a true story. Thanks to Pat Wesson, somewhere in the Western Cape RSA.)

Mervyn wouldn't be needing his car tonight. Malaria has that effect on your social life. The steel skins of Morris Minors were fortunately more resistant to mosquitoes than that of their owners so there was no reason why this particular vehicle should languish in the Kashangani Hospital car park while Mervyn sweated, shivered and shook himself through the next two or three days.

'Mr Cilliers? He's in Room Three,' said the nurse. 'I think you'll find he's rather poorly. Is it urgent?'

Urgent? Well, yes, I suppose it was. There was a party tonight at the Bindalani customs point, thirty miles south, and there was no way of getting there after the engine of my Land Rover had run itself into eternity, thanks to a rock through the sump. Dries van Rensberg and myself had promised two of the new English nurses that we'd show them how the Rhodesian customs department could entertain their guests. Surely Mervyn wouldn't mind giving us the keys to the Morris.

Anyway, I went to Mervyn's private room. The poor chap was comatose and his pillow equally sodden with sweat.

'Just borrowing your car for a while, Mervyn,' I said. 'You don't mind, do you?'

He didn't say anything. He didn't open his eyes either. I

repeated the question. He didn't say anything again. I took his silence as tacit agreement, removed the keys from his locker drawer and left before he could change his mind. I looked at my watch as I pulled out of the car park. It was nearly four o'clock. Ten minutes to get home, fifteen minutes to get cleaned up and ten minutes to get to the nurses' home. We could be on our way by five o'clock if Dries was ready. I rang him when I'd showered. He was. Dries was never behind time when revelry was on the calendar. I picked him up from his bungalow on the way back to the hospital.

'All set for a refined night of Bournvita, bible classes and chamber music, Dries?'

'*Ja,* right, man,' he replied in his thick Transvaal accent. 'The only thing that Bindalani mob knows about refinement is alcohol.' He passed me a cold beer from his rucksack and took two for himself. 'Mervyn didn't mind lending you his car, then?'

'Well, he didn't say I couldn't. Let's pick up the ladies and be on our way. The lights on this thing aren't much better than a glow-worm.'

The girls were waiting for us outside their accommodation block. The taller one, June, was holding a half-bottle of Bells and the other, Trudy, had a bottle of J&B. That was our fuel to Bindalani taken care of. June got up front with me while Dries kept Trudy company in the back. Pretty soon the drinks were going down as quickly as the sun and the girls were starting to lose their British reserve. The Bells and most of the beer were gone by the time we reached the halfway point and the Morris was purring away like the well-oiled machine it was.

The last of the sunlight disappeared then there was nothing to see but a black ribbon of tarmac in the headlight beam, edged with high yellow grass and the occasional thorn tree. June, I thought, looked very attractive in the glow from the speedometer lamp.

And then all I can remember seeing was a pair of close-set eyes glittering in the headlights and a grey shape behind them. We were doing about forty miles an hour and it was too late to brake. I pulled the wheel hard over but hit whatever it was with the left wing. There was a hell of a thump and a loud curse from the back. I pulled up, half off the road, in a cloud of dust.

'*Bliksem!* Spilt my bliddy drink,' exclaimed Dries. 'Went all over my lap, damn it, man!'

'Think yourself lucky it wasn't blood that got spilt,' I said. 'Relax, girls, you can stay off duty.' I took Mervyn's torch from the glove compartment and got out, followed by the others.

The wing wasn't a pretty sight. Nor was the creature lying awkwardly in the grass. I recognised it immediately: it was an adult, four and a half stones at least and lying quite still. A trickle of blood ran from its nose and its eyes were closed. It can't have felt a thing. Well, not much, anyway. We gathered around.

'Gosh, what is it?' asked Trudy.

Dries prodded it with his foot. 'Dead.' He had a peculiar sense of humour.

'A Chacma baboon,' I said. 'I didn't see the ruddy thing in this light.'

'Looks rather like Frankie Howerd,' said June.

She had a point. Baboons do tend to have long and mournful faces when they've been struck by half a ton of British steel.

'What're we going to do with it?' I said. 'And more to the point, what about this bloody great dent in the wing?'

'*Ag*, man, that'll knock out easy enough. Don't get your *broekies* in a knot,' said Dries dismissively and quite wrongly. 'Let's take the thing to Bindalani, its head should look *lekker* mounted on the wall.'

Trudy snorted. 'Are you serious? It's probably full of fleas and things.'

'You're a nurse. You should be used to that. Let's get it into the car and be on our way,' said Dries. 'Give me a hand, hey.'

So we dragged the baboon out of the scrub. Trudy opened the boot and we stuffed the limp shape inside. Dries dusted his hands and slammed the lid as I shone the torch over the crumpled wing again. One headlight was broken and so was the sidelight. The wing was pushed back almost onto the tyre. Well, there was no point in dwelling on it. What was done was done. I'd think about that tomorrow.

We hopped back in and set off again, this time a little slower. I didn't have much choice: as I said earlier, the lights were pretty feeble to begin with and with only one headlamp left I thought it wise to limit our speed to fifteen mph or so. The next time it could be an elephant we hit.

Bindalani Customs Post 1 Mile. Turn Left Ahead For Housing Complex read the sign about three drinks later. It was now as dark as the inside of a mole's wallet and I was sweating like crazy, despite the open windows and ventilator fan.

'Bliddy hot,' said Dries as we turned off the tarmac. 'Makes a man thirsty. Get a move on, there's a good chap.'

I pressed the accelerator a little more. We bumped our way down the sand track and hit a pothole that would have been seen if the near-side lamp hadn't been lying in small pieces ten miles ago. The suspension bottomed and there was a horrible groaning sound from the rear.

'Never mind, tough things, these Morrises,' said Dries, 'nothing to worry about.'

Not for him, there wasn't. A minute later the lights of the customs post appeared. It was still open and would be until eight o'clock. There were about fifteen or so officers based here who were responsible for the entire Bindalani District, which was about the size of Devon and Somerset combined. But if their past record was to be considered, they'd be responsible for very little by midnight. They were drinkers to a man and the party would really be taking off when the last three officers locked the gates and got stuck in.

We pulled up outside the Mess. A group of customs officers and guests were lounging around the thatched bar with glasses in their hands. They greeted us with roars of approval as we got out.

'And about time as well, you old reprobates,' shouted someone. 'Acquaint us with these lovely girls, won't you?'

We jealously made introductions, ordered some drinks and caught up with the latest rumours and scandals.

'You'll never guess what happened to us on the way over,' I said when our turn came.

The circle drew closer. 'Well, hardly. We weren't there, *were* we?' This was from a gauche beanpole I recalled as Cutts, recently posted from Chirundu.

'We knocked a ruddy great Chacma down and killed it. It made a real mess of the left wing.'

'It's in the boot,' chipped in Dries. 'We thought you might like it as a trophy.'

'Marvellous stuff! Let's have a look–see,' said the superintendent. 'That's just the sort of thing to improve the Mess display.'

Everyone trooped over to see our prize.

'… The next thing I knew was this almighty thump and a grey blur flying past us,' I said as I opened the boot, 'and then—'

'RUUUARRRRGH.'

We all leapt back as a snarling Chacma baboon lurched at us from the darkness. I got a faceful of its rancid breath, threw myself back and slammed the boot lid. There was a dreadful howl from inside. I'd probably trapped its fingers.

'Bloody hell!' I said, 'I thought it was dead.' I looked

around. There was no one within ten yards of me. Someone in the shadows laughed nervously. The sounds from inside the boot increased. The onlookers gradually filtered back when they were certain of not being mauled.

'It seems rather angry,' said Cutts. 'Perhaps you'd better take it away, old man.'

I didn't like this much. There was no way I was going to open the boot again, not with that bundle of malice waiting to revenge itself. 'Not flipping likely. Someone else can do the honours.'

'Perhaps we should kill it,' suggested somebody.

'*We*?'

'Well someone's got to do it in case it attacks one of the villagers,' said a swaying senior hand. He pointed to Cutts. 'And I'm detailing *you*.'

'Me! How, for Christ's sake?' protested Cutts.

'With a shotgun. Both barrels should do it. Unless you're afraid, of course …'

'Afraid? Me? Of course I'm not afraid; don't be ridiculous,' muttered Cutts.

There were drunken shouts of encouragement as he fetched the weapon from the armoury. I grudgingly volunteered to help.

'Right, listen. I'll open the lid and get out of the way, sharpish. As soon as he climbs out, let him have it. Don't miss, for God's sake, otherwise we'll have a very cross primate to deal with.'

'All right,' he replied uncertainly, 'let's get on with it.'

The others melted into the security of the bar area as we approached the boot.

'Ready?' I noticed Cutts was sweating badly.

He nodded. I stood by the rear wing, leaned over and pushed the boot release button. The lid was barely open six inches when he poked the shotgun into the gap and let off both barrels together.

BAROOOM. There was a hideous shriek, a burst of thrashing inside and then silence.

Cutts cautiously lifted the boot open. A cloud of blue smoke drifted out, followed by the smell of powder and scorched fur. 'Got it!' he said.

I could see the tattered corpse in the light from the bar. It was a horrible sight; there was blood, brains, bone and gristle everywhere. Worse still, there was a hole in the back seat big enough for a child to crawl through and smouldering stuffing protruded from the leather.

'You silly bugger,' I cried. 'Why didn't you wait until it was outside? *Look what you've done to the car!'*

'I thought it best not to take chances, old man. Anyway, if you were that concerned about it, why didn't *you* take the gun?'

He had me there. Everyone bravely crowded round and offered congratulations. Cutts, who was now a hero, shrugged nonchalantly and accepted a filled whisky glass. Torches were shone into the boot. There would clearly be no trophy for the Mess walls: the shots had obliterated half the unfortunate creature's head and the pelt was little more than a primate's string vest.

The two garden boys were called, given a beer apiece and told to dispose of the remains. The party went on.

***

After breakfast, Dries and the two girls decided to find alternative transport back to Kashangani. I couldn't blame them after looking at the state of Mervyn's car.

I parked the Morris in the same place from which it was taken. The ripe odour of the bygone baboon drifted through the gaping hole in the rear seat; heaven-knows what it was going to smell like when the sun got into stride. I flicked a gobbet of something pink and hairy from the back of the gear stick, locked the door, bought a few things from a trader's stall and wandered into the hospital.

'How's Mr Cilliers?' I asked the nurse.

'Still poorly, but I think the worst is over now. He's been sleeping since I came on shift this morning.'

'I'm glad to hear he's improved. Can I just pop in with these?'

She looked at the bag of fruit and soft drinks. 'Of course, I'll tell him you brought them when he wakes up.'

'No need. I'd really prefer to remain anonymous,' I told her.

She shrugged and went back to her reports.

Mervyn did look much better. For the present, anyway. I put the keys back into his locker and left.

Population Implosion

The Population Stability Officer ran his cursor down the column of qualifying checkboxes on page 2 of the Family Planning Application. There was no reason to turn the request down; the Gender Balance for the area even permitted parents the choice of sex as the projected shortfalls had been made up in the latest bi-monthly review.

He looked up at the sound of drumming on his desktop and frowned. The candidate reddened and lifted his fingers. The PSO nodded and went back to the application. Magnus Goodheart 621. Address: Area Code Lon/54/LG742a. Occupation: Elevator Service Engineer. Age: 27. Genetic Code: B1(c) K36. Notes: 12% probability of inherited rheumatoid arthritis. Predicted male pattern baldness. No previous applications for Libido Initiation.

He scrolled to Goodheart 621's consort. Name: Calla. Age: 25. Occupation: Cyber Sales. Genetic Code: A4(a) L72. No predicted health reduction.

'Well, Goodheart Union,' he said, 'I'm pleased to say that you've fulfilled the primary offspring requirements.'

The pair beamed and held each other's hands.

'The next step will be a DataCurator Procreation Course to study at home. When you're confident with its methods, you'll be given the appropriate Libido Initiation injections, which will prime your reproductive senses and enable mating to take place. The treatment will give a fertility window of between seven and twelve days.' He paused for a moment and smiled. 'So it's up to you to utilise the time as constructively as possible.'

The Goodheart Union smiled back.

'I'd suggest you follow your Medical Examiner's advice regarding optimum biorhythmic cycles and take a two-week break from work when the time is right. I must warn you now that there can be *no* Initiation extension if the results are unsatisfactory. However, that's very unlikely, given proper application. Now, are there any questions?'

F-Mate Goodheart 621 nodded. 'What if conception is successful and the results are twins?'

'You'll be permitted to retain both,' said the PSO, 'but you will *not* qualify for the second and final Libido scheme.'

M-Mate Goodheart 621 raised his hand.' As we're both new to the process, what if we find we're unable to propagate due to a physical problem?'

The PSO sighed. 'As I said earlier, M-Mate Goodheart, you have only a certain window in which to perform your duties. If difficulties *do* occur, contact your Medical Examiner immediately for advice. I must stress that we no longer support artificial insemination. All reproductive acts must be carried out physically in the limited time we allow nature to be the arbiter of such matters. F-Mate Goodheart, you wish to say something further? No? In that case I'll go ahead with your application and confirm the gender choice with our Embryology Arrangement administrators.'

***

Magnus and Calla were lying in the sleeping compartment of their 19th-floor Accommodule. A Planning Department DataCurator link displayed its contents on the wall screen. They read the sexual mechanism and physical interface introduction in embarrassed silence, then Magnus swiped through the pages until he came to the graphics section and selected *The Optimum Positions for Mating*.

'My, my!' exclaimed Calla after a while. 'To think that only ninety years ago, people did *this* whenever they wished?'

'Yes,' said Magnus, 'it does look rather … umm … undignified, doesn't it? And evidently they did it for pleasure as well, although it does seem hard to believe. I mean, just look at their expressions.'

'He must be squashing the poor woman. No wonder she's got that funny look on her face.'

'I'll be more careful, dear,' promised Magnus and advanced the tutorial. 'Ugh, look at *these* two! I saw some dogs doing that in the park last week.'

Calla's lips curled in distaste. 'How are *we* going to do it? Not like that, I hope?'

'Certainly not! I couldn't possibly behave in that manner. And what about *this*?'

Calla looked at the next set through her fingers and blushed. 'And I thought we were living in a civilised society,' she said hotly. 'Out of the question.'

'Quite right,' said Magnus. 'Shall we skip this section for now?'

They read the maternity and paternity instructions until the lights were dimmed at ten o'clock. Magnus closed the DataCurator, reached for Calla's hand and shook it.

'I'm so pleased that the Social Planners selected you to be my partner, Calla.'

'And you mine,' she said. 'I can't imagine being bonded to anyone else.'

***

Magnus rolled his sleeve down as he walked out of the Libido Initiation Clinic cubicle and grinned at Calla. 'Well, that wasn't as bad as I expected. How was yours?'

'I didn't even feel the needles go in!' She stood up and twined her fingers around his. 'I'm so excited that we're on our way and parenting isn't just a dream now, but … well … I can't help feeling apprehensive at the same time. Do you think that's normal?'

'I don't know, Calla. It won't be me hosting Dirk so I've got no idea if it's a natural reaction or not. I suppose anything fresh is bound to be unsettling at first, but at least our health audits and gestation courses will tell us what to expect as we go along. After all, the social scientists have almost a hundred years of breeding studies behind them so we can trust their advice.' Magnus kissed her cheek. 'What I *do* know for certain is that our son will make our bonding even stronger.'

'You're right, of course. I'm worrying over nothing.' Calla flushed and patted away the perspiration that suddenly dotted her forehead. 'Er, can we go home now please, Magnus? I'm starting to feel quite strange …'

***

Dirk Goodheart 622 was seven years old when his parents decided to introduce a sister – statistics permitting – to the Unit. An application was made and the Goodheart Union was eventually called to appear before the Population Stability Department's Reviewing Officer. The reassessment interview passed satisfactorily and their final child was approved for the current demography accounting period.

Magnus and Calla sent their son on a character-building course, took two weeks holiday and rolled throughout their Accommodule in a sexual swansong. On the thirteenth morning, Calla awoke, showered away the last traces of passion and made breakfast. A red-eyed Magnus joined her twenty minutes later. They shook hands and recalled Dirk from his adventure school when they'd finished eating. Then they waited happily.

They made an appointment with their Medical Examiner when there was no sign of pregnancy after the second month. He carried out his tests and gave them the news they'd been dreading. There would be no little sister for Dirk. And no more Libido Restoration. *Ever.*

Calla didn't stop crying for two days.

***

The Goodheart Unit was watching a 2D film from the 2020s on the wall screen. Dirk laughed at the ancient petrol-driven cars and Calla was amused by the quaint clothing and furniture. Magnus's CommUniK chimed six times. He swiped the *Urgent* channel and sighed as he read the message.

'Sorry, I've got a call-out. The Parliament Towers service lift is out of order and has to be repaired this evening.'

Calla sniffed. 'Oh, no. So much for us having Christmas Day together. Will it take long?'

'I don't know, probably not. I'll be as quick as I can.'

Dirk tugged his sleeve. 'Please may I come with you, Father? I've never been inside a Parliament building before.'

Magnus nodded. It was a good opportunity for the boy to see where legislation was passed that affected every man, woman, child and pet in the country.

'Why not! Get into something warm while I pair my tool kit with their system and we'll be off.'

They arrived at the Parliament MagLev terminal at eight o'clock and crossed into the assembly court. Scores of politicians and their partners and guests were spilling from their transport and heading for the Chambers Complex. A doorman directed Magnus to the reception area, where a harassed-looking man was staring at his watch.

'Are you the lift engineer?' he said, managing to sound both accusing and thankful at the same time.

Magnus showed his company identitE card.

'Good. The lift's stuck halfway between the basement storerooms and second sub-level. There are important packages in it for the party upstairs. Can you fix it?'

Magnus told the man it wouldn't cause him any problems and followed him to the service lift control panel. He opened the sliding doors within seconds and shone his flashlight down the narrow shaft. Two or three small parcels seemed to be wedged between the edge of the lift floor and the wall. He muttered about the careless loading that had disturbed his evening, over-rode the circuit breaker and sent the lift down a few centimetres. The jam cleared itself. Then Magnus pressed the 'Up' button and the lift rose smoothly. Small foil sachets cascaded from a lacerated parcel as it drew level with the hatch. He picked it up and examined the label. *Compliments of the Season and Best Wishes to Lord and Lady Bellingham Ffaulkes, West Kent Constituency.*

'Hey, look at these,' said Dirk.

Magnus looked down at the torn sachets Dirk was holding

'Balloons, Father! Lots and lots of them.'

'So there are,' said Magnus. 'It looks like somebody's going to be having a very merry Christmas.'

Give ... and Take

(Two sides of a tarnished coin.)

GIVE ...

He was just about to pull away from the border post and take the metalled road to Mangazi. It was the longer way but it avoided the terrible patchwork of sand and crumbling tarmac that may or may not have been passable in the rainy season.

'Halt.'

He looked at his rear view mirror, sighed and turned the engine off. A border guard, one of those sheltering in the shade of the customs building, strolled towards him with a cigarette in his hand. Obviously there was some kind of lubrication problem … the man's palm had not been greased. He slid the window forward and waited.

'What's the matter?'

The guard, a sergeant, looked at him through Ray-Ban sunglasses that he couldn't have afforded on his intermittent wage.

'Your brake light is not working. It is an offence.'

The driver stared at the sergeant and took in his ragged tiger-striped jungle uniform. The jacket was too big by at least two sizes. Two grenades hung from the breast pockets by their handles and an eighteen-inch panga with a splintered handle swung from his hips on a webbing belt. He was wearing the type of Doc Marten boots usually seen on backpackers. They were laced with string. An AK47 rifle was slung from his shoulder.

'My brake light? *Really*? It was working just fine on the other side of the border.' He knew what was coming next.

'It is an offence, a very serious offence. You must be fined for this breach.'

The driver's temper began to rise; eight years in Africa had stretched his patience to an invisible thread. He opened the door, climbed out, reached under the seat and brought out a tyre lever. The sergeant watched idly as the driver held the Land Rover's brake pedal down and wedged the tyre lever under the accelerator and clutch, locking the brakes on.

'Let's see now, shall we?' The driver strode through the sand and stood at the rear of the vehicle. Both brake lights were on, clearly visible even in the hard African sun.

'So what's the problem?' he said as the sergeant stood beside him. He smelled of stale sweat and cigarettes.

'They were not working,' he stated heavily. 'It is an occasional fault. It is against the law to use an unsafe vehicle in my country.'

The driver looked at the clattering convoy of cars, bush taxis and buses filtering past him on their route to punctures and mechanical disasters. Many had bald tyres, collapsed suspension and dented body panels. Some had no windscreen wipers. Some had no windscreens. Most were grotesquely overloaded and several were belching clouds of blue smoke from their exhausts.

'What about these, then,' he said. 'You call *these* safe?'

'What are you doing in my country, *mzungu*?'

The driver took a deep breath, held it for a few moments and released it, slowly, controlled. '*Look.* I've cleared immigration and customs. My documents are in order and stamped. I'm here as a technical adviser on a water supply project. I've been helping *your* government for five months.'

'You have broken the law,' repeated the sergeant. He

unslung his rifle. 'Give me twenty dollars.'

The driver bristled. Half of bloody Africa was like this.

'*No way*. There's nothing the matter with this vehicle and you damned well know it.'

The sergeant grinned unpleasantly. He swung the butt of his rifle. Shards of amber plastic fell into the sand.

'See,' he said, 'the light does not work.'

'You moron, that's the indicator.'

'*Aaah, I see*. Now we have two offences to consider. Give me forty dollars.'

The driver exploded despite the AK47 in the sergeant's hands. 'I'm bloody well sick of your begging and corruption. Everywhere I go it's the same – money, money, money. You hate the *wazungu*, don't you? You want them out of your country, *don't you*? Well, if you don't want us here, why don't you give back all our technology, *eh?* The electricity, the clean water supplies, the sewerage system, the hospitals, the roads, the cars, the aeroplanes, the telephones, the televisions, the radios, the cameras. Even your clothes and weapons. A mighty fine sight you'd look standing outside your border post mud hut in animal skins *and a bloody spear*.'

He slammed his fist against the vehicle's bodywork. 'You're quick enough to hold out your hands for aid when your crops fail or your rivers overflow or when you need food and tents and medicine. And where does most of that money go? Where does it go? *I* fucking well know where – into the pockets of greedy hyenas like *you*.'

The sergeant leaned against the Land Rover, stretched and lit a Marlboro.

'Give me forty dollars,' he said.

***

… and *TAKE*.

‘What the *fokken* hell do you think you’re doing in my outhouse?’

The skinny black boy, hardly into his teens, whirled around at the shout and dropped a half-eaten banana on the dusty floor. He froze as he saw the shotgun in the farmer’s hands.

‘I asked you what you were doing. Get over there, *now. Move.*’

The farmer jerked the gun towards the end wall of the outhouse, away from the open doors. He swore when he saw the splintered crate and the banana skins on the floor. There was blood on the broken strips of wood where the boy had used his fingers to get to the fruit.

The boy flinched and slid along the corrugated steel wall as the twin barrels followed him. There was an explosion of squawks, dust and feathers as a dozen hens were shunted aside by the boy’s ankles. He half-fell, recovered and jammed his body into the corner of the building. His lower lip began to tremble and his eyes glistened with tears.

The farmer drew his foot back and kicked an oil funnel at the boy. It missed his head by a hand’s width. He flinched as it clattered against a wall stanchion and fell to the ground.

‘What else have you got of mine, you thieving little rat? Empty your pockets, quick time. *Chop-chop.*’

The boy reached into the pockets of the dirty grey raincoat he was wearing and began to empty the contents onto the floor: a banana, a bent kitchen knife, a rusted guitar string fashioned into a snare, two small coins and a pair of cheap, broken sunglasses.

‘Inside pockets and shorts.’

The boy looked at the ground but didn’t move.

The farmer’s eyes narrowed. ‘Do as you’re fokken well told or you’ll get the beating of your miserable life.’

A fat tear ran down the boy’s cheek. It left a dark trail against his dusty skin.

'Christ's sake – do as I tell you.'

The boy unfastened the raincoat's frayed belt and only button.

'*Open* the fokken thing. You deaf as well as stupid?'

The boy shook his head from side to side.

Click.

He looked up at the sound of the shotgun being cocked. His eyes were full of tears now. The farmer raised the gun to his shoulder. The boy pulled the coat lapels back and let the garment fall to the floor. He was naked except for a pair of home-made sandals. His ribs showed up in the half-light like railway sleepers pushing through his skin.

The skinny black boy and the middle-aged white farmer with a paunch hanging over the waistband of his shorts locked eyes. The gun was lowered inch by inch. And then the laughter started a cruel, vicious laugh that filled the outhouse and the boy's entire world. The farmer was looking at the boy's dirty, naked, undernourished body, with its cuts and keloids and faint wisps of pubic hair. And the longer he looked, the more he laughed.

The boy slowly and with quiet dignity bent his knees, picked up the shabby raincoat and put it on. The farmer's face darkened. He looked at the crates of bananas stacked against the far wall and walked over to the boy.

'You still hungry?'

The boy looked at him uncertainly. 'Yes, *baas*.'

The farmer uncocked the gun and put it onto a case. As he turned back, his hand shot out like a chameleon's tongue and jerked the boy out of the corner and onto the floor. He tried to scramble away, but the farmer's grip was too fierce. The back of his head was slammed against the floor.

'OK, well fokken eat this, then.'

The banana that had been in his pocket was rammed into his mouth. The white flesh burst through the green skin as the farmer squeezed it like toothpaste with his big, meaty hands. The boy gasped and spluttered. His bloody and lacerated fingers clawed at the farmer's wrists. They were torn away. The crushed fruit was pulled from his mouth and smeared over his face, in his eyes, his nose, his ears, his hair.

At once, the choking grip and swearing stopped. The farmer leapt to his feet and kicked the boy. The boot's lace eyelets ripped the back of his thigh and drew a tramline of blood. The boy had wet himself and the farmer's shorts were damp where he'd sprayed him. The farmer lashed out again, but this time the boy scrambled clear and darted from the barn. He raced for the hole in the fence with his wet coat tails flapping and never once looked back as the raucous laughter followed him, echoing round and round in his skull.

No Time Like the Present

Newt sat on the patio, absent-mindedly swirling a scotch around in his glass as he looked out over Todos Santos Bay. It was peaceful, the way Christmas Day ought to be in Lower California, or any place, for that matter. The sun was warm on his face and he closed his eyes for a moment, savouring the subdued crash of the waves and the distant cries of wheeling birds. He was satisfied with the world.

'Grandpa, Grandpa, come and see what Uncle Wesley's bought for me!'

Newt sighed, not unkindly, and put down his glass. His grandson stood excitedly at the sliding door leading to the house.

'What's that, young feller?'

'Aw, Grandpa, you gotta come in and see it. It's on the computer.'

'Be right with you, Rusty, just let an old man get his bones together.'

He stood a little stiffly and followed his grandson into the house. The rest of the family and relatives were relaxing in the lounge watching a movie or sleeping off their turkey lunch and highballs. Rusty led him into his bedroom and pointed to the computer screen on his desk.

'Well, what do you think, Grandpa?'

It was the pilot's view of a cockpit, a vintage single-engine military machine by the look of it. Needles sat at various positions on the instrument faces, the paintwork on the panel and sidewalls was worn, revealing shining aluminium underneath, and switches and levers seemed to be scattered haphazardly about the compartment, just like the real thing, like any machine built for war. The old man reached into his shirt pocket and took out his spectacles.

'Not very familiar to me, Rusty, what is it?'

The boy sat down in front of the screen, moved the chair to one side slightly and pressed a button on the keyboard.

'External view, Grandpa.'

Before the boy had finished speaking, Newt had identified the fighter. He'd seen literally hundreds of them. Its aggressive shape and swept-back canopy sent a chill through him.

'Focke Wulf 190.'

'*Wow*, Grandpa, you got it first time!'

Newt could equally-well have identified an Me109, an Me110, or even the jet-engined Me262, but unlike Rusty, his knowledge was first-hand. He swallowed and didn't answer.

'Watch this,' continued the boy. He grabbed the joystick and pressed another key. He was back in the cockpit. A score of specks appeared in the blue cloudless sky ahead of him. Within seconds, they were revealed as silver and olive drab bombers, each identified by red boxes: B-17, B-17, B-17, B-24, B-24, B-17. He adjusted the throttle, pulled back on the stick and soared above the formation. Small puffs of black appeared in the distance. *Flak*. He scanned the sky with the hat switch, eased the power back and rammed the nose down. A formation of bombers filled the windscreen. Tramlines of orange tracer flicked back at him from the gunners. *Whuuuf ... whuuuuuf.* The lead B-17 filled his gun sight.

'Die, *schweinhunds*. Rusty O'Donnell, scourge of the skies, is on your ass!' He pressed the joystick trigger. A salvo of rockets sped towards the B-17. It was gone in an orange-red ball of flame and oily black smoke. '*Yee-haa!* Scratch one bomber, plenty more where they came from.'

Newt sat down heavily on the edge of his grandson's bed. He felt slightly sick.

'Wanna go, Grandpa? It's really good fun!'

He shook his head weakly. 'No thanks, Rusty, these computers are too quick for an old man like me.'

The boy swivelled his chair around. 'Say, Grandpa, weren't you in the air force in the big war? Uncle Wesley said you were a pilot in England and that you got medals and things.'

'Aw, we all got medals. I got mine for saving the lives of a thousand men.'

'*A thousand men*! Wow, what did you do?' The boy was captivated.

'I shot the cook, that's what I did, I shot the cook.'

'Gee, Grandpa, you nearly had me believing you there. Did you really kill anybody or shoot anyone down?'

'Well, not personally. I was flying B-17s, like you've got on that machine there, and they were full of bombs so we weren't out on some picnic. I guess I was helping the bombardier to kill people, though.'

The boy turned away from the computer. The squadrons of B-17 Flying Fortresses and B-24 Liberators droned towards their electronic targets, safe from further attack.

'What was it like, Grandpa? I mean, were there lots of fighters after you? Did airplanes really explode like that? Did you ever have to jump for it?'

What was it like ...

'And the target for today, gentlemen, is ... Schweinfurt.'

The aircrew groaned as the briefing officer drew back the curtain from the European map ...

'Well, one of the worst bits was the wait to find out what the target was. You kind of wanted to know and not, at the same time. Some targets were easier than others; the ones we dreaded were places like Essen, Regensberg, Munich and Nuremberg. All of our bombing was done in daylight, not like the British, who generally did their missions at night.'

We could see exactly what was going on, the Germans attacking us, the Fortresses going down. It was pretty cold at twenty-three thousand feet, but that didn't stop us from sweating when the fighters came in. The Luftwaffe boys were pretty good and they sure had plenty of targets to choose from. Then again, we had upwards of twelve Browning point fives to warn 'em off.

The interphone was full of chatter – Focke Wulfs, four at 3 o'clock low, two Messerschmitts coming in, 7 o'clock level, B-17 going down at 11 o'clock high, that sort of thing. The white parachutes were our boys; the German 'chutes were kind of yellow-brown, but the white ones outnumbered them by plenty. As well as the interphone, there was the noise of the engines and the pounding of the machine guns. The top turret gunner was also the flight engineer; he was just behind us. We could smell the cordite even through our oxygen masks.

Those masks were a punishment for keeping us alive; they were cold and clammy and uncomfortable. Sometimes, we had to squeeze the economisers to break up the ice crystals in case they blocked the flow. When we took the masks off after a mission, the marks would stay on our cheeks and noses for upwards of an hour.

The waist gunners on the early ships probably had it worst of all, standing for hours at an open gun position, swinging around sixty pounds of Browning at about four targets at once and losing their feet on the empty cases. If any of those guys took a glove off for something, they'd get nipped by frostbite. Touch anything metal and they'd stick to it, like glue. Somebody would have to urinate on their fingers to free them.

'Were you ever frightened, Grandpa?'

Frightened ...?

One day, he saw two B-17s collide before they'd even reached the English Channel. An almighty flash, a jolt as turbulence from the explosion hit them, almost flicking their airplane onto a wingtip. Twenty men gone in less time than it takes to blink. The fighters had started to feast upon them long before they reached Germany. FW190s and Me109s launched their attacks from airfields in occupied France and Belgium. They had twenty-millimetre cannons as well as machine guns, and some had rockets that came hissing towards you like something out of hell. A hit from one of those things could tear a wing or tail plane clean off. They knew that the best approaches were from head-on or well above; there was less defensive firepower available from these quick-hit techniques.

Sometimes they'd foul up and crash into the Forts; that was a horrible sight to see. Then there was the flak, small clouds of black cotton wool stretching into the distance; each one was packed with everything guaranteed to hurt you. One 88mm shell in the bomb bay or fuel tanks and that was it – just scraps of skin and aluminium littering the fields. We were obliged to stay in tight formation so we couldn't exactly take evasive action. There was too much danger of collision and once we were on the final run-up to the target we were committed to an exact course and speed so the bombardier could do his job properly. I was a co-pilot. All I could do was sit and watch as the Luftwaffe came barrelling in. Lord, I'd have given anything to be able to do something except watch our ships get picked off. I must have seen at least ten Forts go down over Schweinfurt that day.

Sometimes the crews, or at least some of them, bailed out. Some of them fell clean through the formation before pulling their ripcords to avoid getting hit by anything; some of them did get hit and killed for sure. Then there were those whose 'chutes didn't open, or they got blown clean out of their ships without them.

'Yeah, I was plenty frightened. I was only a boy of twenty who should have been working in an automobile repair shop or something and going to the movies with pretty girls who looked like Betty Grable.'

'Did you know anybody who got killed, Grandpa?'

On that raid, over sixty bombers were lost. Each was crewed by ten men. The navigator got killed by a burst of flak and the bombardier lost four fingers and was blinded for two months. The entire Plexiglass nose cone was blown off. It sent a howling gale through the airplane and slowed us down considerably, as well. We'd just dropped our bombs and were turning for home. We were attacked by Messerschmitts three or four times between Schweinfurt and the English Channel. Number Two engine got shot up, the top turret stopped working and we lost half of our rudder. The left waist gunner caught a bullet in his throat and the tail gunner was hit in the foot. When we came in for landing, the left landing gear wouldn't come down so we had to retract the other one and put her down on her belly. The ball turret gunner refused to fly again after that mission. The crew chief told me the next day that they'd counted over two hundred bullet holes in Seattle Sally, which was the name of our ship.

'I guess I knew a few who didn't come back. Maybe they ended up in a prisoner of war camp somewhere.'

'At least you could sleep at night time, Grandpa, not like the British air force.'

Sleep ...

It was almost ridiculous. We'd get back from Germany after seeing airplanes blow up or go down in flames; guys we knew. We were buzzing with nervous energy, the sheer relief of having made it back through hell. Every bullet and cannon shell and lump of flak had our name on it, or so it seemed at the time. Some of us had dead engines and dead instruments and dead radios and dead crew members. We'd crash land or jump out over the field. We'd see our buddies being lifted into ambulances or washed out of their compartments with a hosepipe and that night we'd be in one of those English pubs, drinking beer or maybe we'd go to the cinema with a girl.

We'd hit the sack, dog tired, but it wasn't easy to sleep. The noise and the sights came back like a motion picture: the fighters and explosions and falling bodies and flames and flak, hearing your crewmates screaming. You'd get off eventually but then someone's nightmare would wake you up again, or your own would. A lot of the boys developed nervous twitches or ulcers. One navigator locked up at a briefing; it was like there was nobody inside him. He just stared without seeing anything. He got taken to hospital and we never saw him again after that.

'That's right. The Germans never got much sleep though, not with us by day and the RAF by night.'

'What were your medals for, Grandpa?'

'Told you, Rusty, they're for nothing, just campaign medals.'

It was our seventeenth mission: Stuttgart. We were attacked by an Me109; didn't even see him, came screaming out of the sun. Bill Abbott, the first pilot, he got hit in the chest and thighs. The engineer patched him up and moved him back to the radio position. We had to give him two shots of morphine to keep him quiet. The prop governor on Number One engine went into maximum revs, we got a fuel leak, Number Two engine started to misfire and the elevator trim cables were shot away. We were losing height all the time; I just managed to put it down on the first English field I saw. I picked up a couple of shell splinters in my arm and face so I got the Purple Heart for that. They gave me the Distinguished Flying Cross as well, but I was only doing my job and I was thinking about myself more than the others when I brought the ship back. The medal would have meant more if Bill had survived.

'Sounds like you had a pretty quiet war, Grandpa.'

Newt looked out of the window, away from the boy. 'Yeah, I guess you could say that, Rusty. I'd take that game of yours anytime; it sure seems better than the real thing.'

Suspended Sentence

'Buenos tardes, Warden Muñoz.'

Muñoz looked up from his desk. *'Señor* Cerrillo! *Buenos tardes*, they told me you were coming tonight. It's good to see you again, but I'd rather it weren't always in such circumstances.'

'I wish this was a social call too, *amigo*.' Cerrillo looked at the list in his hand. 'Villegas, Calderon and Morales?'

The warden pointed to the ceiling. 'First on the left. The others are empty but no doubt they'll be full after the next purge. May the good Lord give you strength in these difficult times.'

The sound of Cerrillo's boots echoed throughout the prison as he climbed the stone steps to the condemned cell. Three men lying on mattresses stared at him through the bars. One of them flicked his middle finger at him.

'Well, well, well, if it's not the Avenging Angel himself. Come to measure our collars for the drop, have you?'

Cerrillo shook his head. 'You're wrong. I'm not here to size you up. I've come with a solution.'

'A solution? For what? Short necks and long waits?'

'Hear me out for a minute. Believe it or not, I'm no less a patriot than any member of your Freedom Movement and hanging you on Martinez's orders doesn't sit well with me. I'm not the only one in public office who wants him overthrown and every one of his bent ministers and generals would look better filling up these cells rather than you. We know there's plenty of support for a revolution behind closed doors in every town, city and village in the country, but until the groups are properly co-ordinated it'll stay as it is – just talk. Right now they're a long way from *any* sort of cohesion.' Cerrillo stepped closer. '*But* … what would be the effect if the three guerrillas were to publicly denounce the government and the rest of Martinez's maggots before their executions tomorrow?'

The men looked at each other incredulously. Villegas tapped his head. 'Is this guy serious? I wonder what he'd say if he were on *this* side of the bars?'

'Words are cheap,' said Morales bitterly. 'He wouldn't be so brave, *that's* for sure.'

'Think about it, *senores*. Wouldn't your deaths be the inspiration for Panaguans to consolidate and fight for democracy rather than living like whipped dogs?'

Calderon got up and stared at the hangman. *'Eh!* You're spouting some mighty fine words for someone who's not going to get strung up, mate! What kind of solution is *that*, for Christ's sake?'

Cerrillo glanced over his shoulder and then back to the men. 'You're not going to be hanged.'

'You're talking in riddles, damn it,' growled Morales. 'You just said that we're going to the gallows. Or is it to be a garrotting instead?'

'No, I'm not going to kill you, nor is anyone. When the traps open you'll fall onto woolsacks instead of swinging on the end of a rope. Our doctor will certify your deaths, we'll bury three empty boxes, smuggle you to a safe house in the mountains and bring you back to take your place among Panagua's heroes once the revolution's over. How does that solution sound?'

The colour returned to Morales' drawn face. He grinned and looked at his two companions. 'Well, *I* like it! Tell us more, *Señor* Cerrillo.'

***

Two thousand men stood in the *Plaza Seis de Marzo,* flanked by five hundred armed soldiers. More were being herded in at gunpoint. The clock on the church spire showed seven minutes to mid-day. The blazing sun squeezed every scrap of vitality from the air. Even the doves nestling in the belfry were silent. A section of sweating guards stood at attention on the gallows platform with their rifles ready. Four minutes ticked by. A drummer commenced a dismal metronomic beat and then the three handcuffed men were led up the steps, followed by a priest and captain. A low moan charged the square.

'*Silence!*' The officer took his pistol from its holster, but the angry murmuring continued. He fired into the air. The doves took off in a frightened cloud and the people waited in sick and silent anticipation.

At two minutes to mid-day the three men were pushed onto the trapdoors and the guards fastened their ankles. A doctor entered the rear door to the enclosed drop with his surgical bag. The captain walked along the platform and turned to face the resentful crowd.

'*Citizens.* You are here today to witness the execution of three criminals who have been found guilty of anarchy after a fair trial. A spokesman will be allowed a short speech to express remorse for their actions before the sentences are carried out.'

Morales and Villegas nodded to Calderon. The crowd edged toward the platform and the soldiers looked around anxiously.

'Fellow Panaguans ... for once we agree with the government and admit that we're sorry for our actions.'

The square's stunned silence was broken five seconds

later.

'Yes, we're very sorry that they weren't strong enough to be successful. But if we must hang for our principles and our country, then what greater way to go to God?' His voice hardened. 'But when we're gone, *compañeros,* you too will die inside as surely as Martinez placing a rope around *your* necks if you allow yourselves to be crushed by this bastard regime any longer. Every one of you standing here and every patriot in Panagua is a small link in the chain of freedom and once you join them together it will be strong enough to tear down—'

The officer sensed the swing in the crowd's mood. '*Enough.* Begin the executions.'

The escort stepped forward and pulled hoods over the faces of the three men. Cerrillo appeared from behind his screen and signalled for the nooses to be put around their necks. The sound of the bell reverberated twelve times between the walls of *Plaza Seis de Marzo*. Before the last peal had faded away the crowd began to hum, slowly and serrated at first until the tune of Panagua's national anthem filled the square. A pure voice soared above it all.

'O land of ours, with beauty filled, and people proud and brave,
We follow you with heart and soul, from cradle to the grave,
O land of ours, we love thee so, from mountains to the sea,
As so you care, we succour you, and we shall both be free,
O land of ours, we—'

Machine gun fire ripped across the square and showered the crowd with shards of stone as bullets ricocheted from the walls.

'Get on with it, get on with it.'

The prisoners braced themselves. 'See you shortly, *chicos*,' whispered Villegas, just as the traps operated by Cerrillo crashed open.

Then Hernan Calderon, Orestes Morales and Jaime Villegas plummeted eight feet and died instantly of broken necks.

***

Cerrillo was back inside the jail before the bodies were taken down. He entered the paymaster's office where the customary full glass of whisky sat alongside the executioner's purse. Angry roars filled the air as the square emptied. Cerrillo picked up the whisky and swallowed it in one.

'What's the matter, *Señor* Cerrillo? The job getting too much for you?'

He ignored the grinning officer, signed for his wage and slowly walked to the Catholic chapel. He pushed the door open. The priest was kneeling at the altar. Cerrillo stood in the aisle, searching for words.

'Yes, Vicente, I know you are there. What do you wish of me?'

'Forgiveness for what I have done, Father Ortiz.'

The priest stood up and turned around. 'Forgiveness from whom? From their mothers and fathers? Sisters and brothers? Sons and daughters? From every single person in the crowd? From Hernan? From Jaime? From Orestes? From me? From God?'

'From myself, Father.'

The priest walked up to Cerrillo and squeezed his shoulder. 'Come, Vicente, I feel you have much to tell me.'

He sat Cerrillo down in his study and poured them both a brandy. 'Whenever you're ready, Vicente, there's no need for a confessional.'

Cerrillo's hand trembled as he picked up his glass. 'Last night I visited those poor souls in the condemned cell and I lied to them, Father, *I lied*. I told them the drop would end on sacks of wool. I told them they'd be taken to the mountains and kept there safely. I told them to stand on the gallows and inspire Panagua with their bravery and last words. All the time they believed they'd be saved and I betrayed them. I *used* them to rally the people. How would they have died if I hadn't promised their freedom?'

Father Ortiz swirled the brandy around in his glass for a few moments. 'I think they would have died in the same courageous manner. Look, Vicente, the outcome would have been the same either way and it's to your credit that you eased their passage to the Kingdom of Heaven, so there's no call to torture yourself. Their names will live on in the hearts of our people forever, so what better legacy could there be? What went on in the jail last night will be our secret. No good will come of revealing it. The Lord will forgive you for your best intentions and I'm sure the three men would too. You alone can forgive yourself.'

Cerrillo sighed. 'Perhaps you're right, Father, but I don't know if I did the wrong thing for the right reasons or the right thing for the wrong reasons.'

'Well, whatever you decide, you can't change anything now. What's done is done and I think we'll see the effect of Hernan Calderon's address on the streets before long. So you'll be right, however you look at it.'

'I hope so, Father.' Cerrillo put his wage on the table, shook the priest's hand and went out into the street. Father Ortiz watched him cross the deserted square, emptied the purse into the Orphans Relief box, said a prayer for the troubled soul of Vicente Cerrillo and sat down to prepare his sermon for the Sunday Mass.

***

The memories of the executions were still glowing white hot in the minds of the Panaguan people a week later. Cerrillo woke up to the sound of shouting and gunfire. He opened his shutters and looked down at the hundreds of flag-waving civilians running through the streets. A handful of bloodied soldiers lay in the road and some of the armed crowd pursued the remainder of their squad. Another soldier sprawled on the pavement and disappeared under a jeering flurry of boots, clubs and rifle butts. Cerrillo gripped the window ledge. So, what Father Ortiz had forecast was true! His heart lifted.

But it stopped five minutes later when he was dragged downstairs, thrown against the wall and executed by a Panaguan Freedom Movement firing squad.

The Look

Angela's getting annoyed. It's the third time she's caught him looking over and it's obvious what's on his mind. Donna's lying half-asleep on her sun lounger and doesn't know she's being eyed by some middle-aged, degenerate Don Juan with sun-bleached hair and Hawaiian shorts.

She's protective of her daughter but jealous of her figure at the same time. She knows damn well that she can't get away with a one-piece, never mind a bikini. To begin with, even her shorts don't cover up the orange peel on her thighs and the red spider's webs behind her knees. And they don't hide her spreading hips and bum either. Her six-year-old passport photo doesn't show the grey hair that's diluting the brown if she doesn't keep on top of it, the wrinkles beginning to crack her face, the bags packed for a long holiday under her eyes and the threat of a double chin. *I never thought I'd end up like this when I was Donna's age*, she thinks. *I was quite a looker in those days. Never went short of boyfriends. Even auditioned for a modelling session with Seventies Girl.* She feels the bitterness rising like the tonic bubbles in her vodka. Maybe a man would have kept her looking and feeling younger, but there hasn't been one of those in over three years. What chance has she got now? She's not only over the hill, damned soon she's going to be over the pill as well.

Unbeatable and Unbelievable Prices for Your Balearic

Break said the leaflet lying on the doormat amongst the bills and flyers. 'Come on, Mum,' said Donna, 'we haven't been away since you got divorced. Do you good. Let's go after I've done my O-levels.'

So here's Angela. Sitting by the pool. All the rage in her relaxed pink shorts, white T-shirt and sandals. Having the time of her life. Another drink or two before lunch, she decides. Donna's still on her first Coke. The ice has melted and the twist of lemon on the rim has curled up in the sun. She catches the waiter's eye and points to her empty glass. He nods and brings another drink from the bar at the end of the pool. She scribbles her signature on the tab. *Numero del Cuarto 248. Articulo 6 – Vodka Tonica*, it says.

She sees that the creep on the other side of the pool has stopped staring and gone back to his magazine. *Prat.* Half the vodka goes down in one gulp and it does its work well. *Never used to drink much before Nick left,* she thinks. Two or three glasses of red on a Saturday night and a small sherry at the monthly Avon party. There wasn't a hole in her life then. Damned men. They're all a bunch of lying, cheating tossers with their brains between their legs and nothing between their ears. And the skinny tramp he left me for was as thick as her make-up, but it chrome-plated his ego that she was five years younger than him. *They'd both better hope to God that my wishes never come true.*

The pool area is starting to fill up now; she sees three or four couples holding hands and smiling at everybody. Aw, honeymooners. Sweet as the icing on their wedding cake and twice as sickening. Just wait until those stars in your eyes turn into the crud you find in the corners when you wake up in the morning. You'll soon learn, you stupid tarts. Mark my words, you'll soon …

The sun burns a hole in her unconsciousness. She wakes up. The glare from the pool makes her squint. She has the beginnings of a headache. Her skin feels tight. There's a sour taste in her mouth as well. She reaches out for her drink. It's warm. And there's a fly in it.

She feels the kindling of fury begin to smoulder. Then she sees the lecher. He's moved to a shaded lounger about ten feet away. And he's looking over again. The kindling ignites with a sudden flash. A chair falls into the pool as she shoves her table aside.

'You dirty pervert!' she screams into his face. 'Can't my daughter lie in the sun without the likes of you leering and slobbering all over her? Why don't you crawl back to your room and watch the porn channel instead.'

People at their tables and sunbeds look around. Donna grabs her arm and tries to pull her back. Angela elbows her away. As she's floundering for a spiteful finale, he stands up. She'll never forget his flattened expression. And she won't forget every well-articulated syllable either.

'Excuse me, madam, but actually it was *you* I was interested in, not this young lady. It seems I've made a terrible mistake. Good day and enjoy the rest of your holiday.'

***

Angela hears the door open. She turns over and looks at Donna, silhouetted against the light from the corridor.

'Are you coming down for something to eat, Mum? The restaurant closes at eleven.'

She turns the bedside light on. 'I'm not hungry.'

Donna closes the door and sits on the edge of her own bed. Angela knows she's weighing her words before she says anything else, afraid of yet another tirade. She speaks after a minute or so. 'You haven't eaten anything since breakfast.'

No, but I drank plenty to make up, didn't I? Angela admits to herself. Then she says: 'I can't show my face after what happened this afternoon. It'll be all over the hotel.

Maybe it would be better if we left.'

'Oh, Mum! We saved hard for this holiday and we've only been here for three days. Don't say that.'

'I made a complete idiot of myself by the pool. How can I hold my head up after that?'

Donna gets up, sits next to her mother, reaches out and holds her hand. 'You were thinking about me when you shouted at him. It wasn't your fault.'

Angela knows better. She knows that her drunken outburst was a venomous snakebite fuelled by long-standing frustration, hurt, resentment and the catalyst of vodka. But wasn't drink the antidote as well, a buffer against all the pain the world could throw at her? And she could do with a drink now. The mini-bar was restocked when they were at the pool and it's only four steps away.

'It *was* my fault, Donna; I know you're only trying to make me feel better. And it wasn't even you he was looking at. It was *me*. Why do I always ruin things for myself?' Her eyes fill with tears. 'Sometimes I can't see the point of going on. It's been so long since anything good happened in my life. I just want to be happy again. I want someone to hold me and tell me he loves me and that things are going to be all right.'

Now the trickle of tears becomes a stinging flood. She can't stop them. They pour from her like the bottle that fills her glass every morning when she wakes up. She slumps into Donna's outstretched arms. Holds her tightly. Then Donna's crying too.

'I love you, Mum. I can't bear to see you like this.'

'I love you too, Donna.'

They lie together, washing the pain away in gulping sobs. After a while, Donna wipes the tears from her mother's cheeks with her finger. Angela kisses her, stands up and goes to the bathroom. She looks at the puffy, red-rimmed eyes reflected in the mirror, fills the sink with cold water and rinses her face, wishing she could cleanse the ugliness she feels inside. Then she blows her nose, tidies her hair and goes back to the bedroom.

'Shall we get something to eat, then?' she says to her daughter, more brightly than she feels.

Donna smiles weakly. 'Hungry work, this crying.'

They take the lift downstairs, cross the foyer and walk into the restaurant. It's almost empty. A guitarist is playing a soft Spanish melody near the bar and three couples sit around candle-lit tables. A waiter greets them and leads them towards a window table overlooking the swimming pool.

Angela stops suddenly. Donna follows her stare. The man sitting alone at a table in the corner sees them. He flinches and looks down.

And then Angela is walking towards him.

'Mum, don't start anything! *Please*.'

'Excuse me,' says Angela quietly.

The man looks up warily.

'I … I … want to apologise for my behaviour this afternoon,' she says. 'I'm very sorry for what I said. I'm afraid I had too much to drink and—'

The man raises his palms. 'No, please, don't worry about it. A drink or two in this heat can go straight to one's head. A slight misunderstanding, that's all.'

'You're being very good about this,' says Angela. 'I'm sure I caused you no end of embarrassment. Whatever must those people have thought?'

The man shrugs. 'It will all be forgotten about by tomorrow.' He smiles and changes the subject. 'How long are you staying?'

'Another week,' says Angela, 'and then it's back to Norwich.'

'Ah, I know the area well. I used to do a lot of sailing on the Broads. Perhaps I should introduce myself.' He stands up and offers his hand. 'Anthony.'

‘Angela,’ says Angela, ‘and this is my daughter, Donna.’

‘I can see where she gets her looks,’ says Anthony. ‘Are you eating?’

Angela nods.

‘In that case,’ he says, ‘perhaps you’d care to join me. I’d appreciate your company.’

Angela feels Donna’s hand on the small of her back, and it’s nudging her towards the table. ‘That’s very kind of you, Anthony. We’d like that very much.’

Anthony studies the wine list while they read the menus. ‘What would you ladies like to drink?’

Angela and Donna look at each other at the same time.

Wish You Were Here

Ricky decides on khaki chinos, a blue polo shirt and tan brogues. Then he carefully teases his hair into fashionable unkemptness, dabs eau de cologne in tactical locations and waits for seven o'clock. He wonders what she's into as he marinates his lust with another vodka and tonic. She didn't give a lot away about herself last night. It's the first time he's been picked up by a woman in a bar and he's feeling smug.

The doorbell rings right on the hour. He smooths his shirt down, looks at himself in the hallway mirror, opens the door and takes her in with one greedy swallow of his eyes. His revs go up. Curly shoulder-length auburn hair above Bugatti-blue eyeliner and Maserati-red lipstick. Well-filled white blouse. Black knee-length skirt over dark tights … or maybe something better. She's nut-tingling hot for forty-something and no mistake. There's a holdall over her shoulder.

'Jacqueline! You look great.'

She smiles at him and runs her finger along his cheek. 'Hi, Ricky! I like to look my best for tall, handsome brutes like you.'

He laughs and shows her to the lounge. 'Can I get you something to drink? Red or white wine, rum, schnapps, vodka or lager?'

She puts her bag on the coffee table and takes out a half-bottle of whisky. 'A red wine for me, please. This for *you*.'

It's a top brand scotch. 'Aw, Jacqui! You shouldn't have, but thanks. I'll be right back,' he says, noticing her fingering the top button of her blouse.

He goes into the kitchen, opens the wine and takes two glasses from the cupboard. He almost drops the bottle when he returns. She's standing there in her underwear. Black lacy bra and matching panties. Stockings, suspenders, high heels. He can't believe his luck. The game's kicking off before the whistle blew. The guys at work are going to love hearing about this one.

They kiss and caress for a minute or two until Ricky's excitement comes between them. Jacqueline steps back a little, grins and runs her fingertips along the evidence.

'How about some lubrication before playtime, tiger?'

He fills her glass and as he's pouring whisky into his, she nudges the bottom of the bottle. It's nearly three fingers full.

'Drink,' she says firmly. 'A nice big swallow for Jacqueline and you might get one back if you're a good boy.'

Ricky is very partial to lipstick on his dipstick so he throws back half the neat scotch in one go. The inside of his nose burns like pepper and his eyes water. He's not used to drinking whisky like that.

'*Ooooh*, well done, Ricky,' she breathes. She stares at his crotch and licks her lips. 'Now take me to your bed and I'll give you an experience you'll never forget. Bring the bottle as well.'

Ricky's in a sexual thrall. She knows what she wants and he's going to be in on it in less time than it takes to bake a pizza. He opens the bedroom door and she follows him in with her wine in one hand and the bag in the other. She puts her glass down on the bedside table and pushes his towards his mouth.

'Finish the nice medicine off for Jacqui.'

The whisky doesn't burn quite so much this time, but it's gone to his head in a rush. His groin is smouldering though.

He notices faint bruises under her bra straps and wonders if she likes her sex rough. It's not his idea of fun and he hopes she doesn't ask him to oblige.

She takes his tumbler and pours another whisky for him. There are two double measures in there at least. 'One more and then we can get down to business,' she says. 'Bottoms up. *All* of it.'

Ricky doesn't want to do this, but then again, he doesn't want to miss out on a wild session once she's gotten over her odd preliminaries. This time his body complains. He chokes and whisky sprays from between his lips and dribbles onto his shirt.

'Never mind,' says Jacqueline in a soothing voice. 'Get your things off and let's see what you've got for me.'

Jacqueline opens the holdall as he's struggling to get his fly undone because of the altered topography. She takes out a battery-powered CD player and turns it on. Pink Floyd. He doesn't mind, it's good music to shag to, but he's getting a little anxious as she rummages through the bag. He's concerned it might be crocodile clips, spiked collars and cattle prods. Or maybe nappies and a dummy. What he doesn't expect, when he's standing there naked with an angry erection, is a grey suit, silk shirt and chintz tie to be laid out on the bed.

'Jacqui likes her lovers to look smart before she screws them,' she says and points to the clothes.

Strange fucking evening this is turning out to be, he thinks, as his head starts swimming in the deep end, but it clears pretty quickly when Jacqueline reaches behind her back, unclips her bra and thrusts her breasts towards him. So the shirt, trousers and jacket go on.

'What about the tie?' suggests Jacqueline as she traces small circles on his chest with her finger.

Ricky tries to do a neat job of fastening it but fails miserably.

Jacqueline takes over. 'No, this one doesn't suit you anyway. Let's find you another.' She takes a handful of ties from the bag and chooses one with green and black diagonal stripes. This time she fastens it around his neck herself.

'Yes, that's much better.' She stands back, steps out of her panties and brushes her finger across his groin. 'You're looking a bit weary, Ricky. Do you want to lie down for a while?'

And Ricky *is* a little fuzzy. The heavy jolts of whisky on top of the earlier vodkas have made sure of that. So they go to the bed and Jacqueline puts him to sleep nicely with her hands and mouth after some reciprocal foreplay.

When Ricky wakes up, he doesn't like what's happening. *No way, rosé*. This is because his wrists are fastened to the bed legs with neckties and there's a gag around his mouth. The clothing beside him reeks of whisky. Jacqueline – who is most definitely not sweet Jacqui anymore – is astride him with a Stanley knife in her hand. She's wearing her clothes again and her eyes are burning pools of hate.

She pinches his cheek with the other hand. *'You drunken fucking bastard,'* she hisses.

He grunts in pain and surprise and tries to buck her off but finds that his ankles are tied to the bed as well. The knife blade flashes in front of his eyes. It cuts through his drunkenness, but he can't believe this is happening.

'Keep still, you disgusting little maggot.'

But it's difficult to be still when the knife starts to trace a path down his chest. It's easy to sweat, though.

'You needle-dicked twat.' He feels the blade drawing lightly across his stomach.

'You mental fucking pygmy.' She's straddling his knees now and holding a tuft of pubic hair between two fingers. He watches as she yanks it like a garden weed and saws it away from his belly. He bites his quivering lip. The blade slides down further. It's at the base of his penis now. He cries out

under the gag. He can't stop himself.

'Shut your fucking mouth you spineless dickhead unless you want to piss sitting down for the rest of your pathetic life.'

He can shut it, but he can't stop the sobs as the knife follows the contours of his penis: along the top, underneath, and then slowly over his testicles. She grips his scrotum as if it were the neck of a chicken about to be slaughtered. The flat of the blade pushes hard against his contracting balls. His eyes roll wildly, and whisky, acrid and sour, stings the back of his throat. He clamps his buttocks together. His screams are muffled by the gag. He pisses himself.

Wish You Were Here swirls through her laughter as she cuts halfway through one of the wrist ties and climbs from the bed.

***

She's home and safely asleep long before her husband lurches into the house from the casino, full of scotch and simmering violence. She's made sure his grey suit is hidden away until she can get it cleaned tomorrow. He may want to wear it to work on Monday. The shirt is in the washing machine. And as for his ties – well, she can afford to leave them at her various assignations.

She's got plenty more of the same in the boot of her car.

Kalaf

The Belgian's day began badly. An hour to refuel his aircraft by buckets because the airstrip's pump was broken again and another delay because the freight was nearly two hours late for some unexplained reason. The oppressive humidity was already stealing lift from the wings as he set course for Isilu and he knew the regular mid-afternoon equatorial rains were going to batter him before he was halfway there. *Just another day in Africa,* he thought.

Then the abrupt silence was like an electric shock that stalled his heart in an instant. The propeller stopped turning and began to slowly windmill in the airflow. He snapped out of his surprise, pushed the nose down to maintain his airspeed and looked around the instrument panel. The magneto switch was in its correct position. The fuel gauges indicated that both tanks were more than half full. The fuel cut-off was in the ON position, the carburettor heat set on COLD and the fuel selector was feeding both tanks. He switched on the electric fuel pump and tried to re-start the engine. The propeller revolved uselessly every time. He dredged up every curse he wouldn't use in refined company. Engine failure was every pilot's nightmare in the Congo … the rainforests stretched for hundreds of kilometres with barely a break in their thirty-metre canopies; it was almost certain death to come down on them and even if he survived the crash there would be little chance of escape from the dark, unfriendly floor. He pressed the primer and engaged the starter again. The engine coughed, spluttered and backfired but refused to pick up. That was the last card in his pack … it must be contaminated fuel from the airstrip blocking the filter. Damn it. Damn it. *Damn it.* Without all the luck in this god-forsaken country, it was going to kill him. The altimeter needle slid below a thousand feet. He tightened his straps and flinched as the green nightmare reached up for him.

***

The Belgian woke to a hammering headache, a dull, sweating malaise and the sound of excited chatter. He opened his eyes and was completely disorientated. Instead of the fan-cooled bedroom of his bungalow in Stanleyville, he was lying in a humid leaf hut with several loin-clothed Africans squatting around him. He tried to sit up, but pain ricocheted from one side of his skull to the other and brought waves of nausea with it. When the throbbing receded, he propped himself up on his elbows and looked around uncertainly.

The man closest to him spoke first. *'Salamu, bwana.'*

'Greetings to you also, *bwana*. Where the hell am I?' The Belgian's croaked Kiswahili was as good as his French.

The man shrugged. 'Where is *anyone* in the rainforest? There aren't any roads or signs like your fast cities. This is no place for a *mzungu* – we're where we are, but you're not where you should be.'

The Belgian tried to sort through the kaleidoscope of memories since he'd taken off from the airstrip, but they remained a splintered mystery. He looked at the man's cicatriced chest, blue facial tattoos and teeth that had been filed to points like the jaws of a gin trap. This was not the rainforest he knew anything of other than watching it slide past his wings from two thousand metres.

'I'm damned if I know how I got here – the last thing I remember is flying my aircraft to Isilu.' His swollen nose grated when he touched it and a plug of dried blood and mucus came away in his fingers as he tried to clear a blocked nostril. There was a tender lump on his forehead as big as a plum and another above his ear. He rubbed his jaw and found a gap where at least two lower teeth were missing; he had a heavy stubble, his stomach felt as if nothing had touched its sides for several days, his face and arms were cross-hatched in scratches and it seemed there was no part of his body that didn't ache, burn or itch with stings and insect bites. 'Now I'm lying here talking to you. Everything between this and that's a complete mystery. I must have come down in the forest somewhere – maybe it was the weather, maybe my engine stopped, maybe I got lost and ran out of fuel, who knows! All I *do* know is that I'm damned lucky to have survived a crash in this sort of terrain. Pilots that go missing here have never been seen again. Did your hunters find any wreckage?'

'No, *bwana*, we've seen nothing of your machine. Its secret may lie within the trees forever, as yours almost did. It's fortunate that our hunters found you in time.' He said something to one of the boys standing in the entrance. The child disappeared and returned a minute later with a bowl.

The headman muttered something over the contents and passed it to the Belgian. 'Here, this will help you recover.'

The Belgian sipped the amber liquid cautiously and raised his eyebrows. *'Aai!* What *is* this stuff?'

'*Kalaf* – the forest's gift to those who lie within its arms. It has great healing powers.'

'Well, if it works as good as it tastes I'll be fixed up in no time.' The pilot finished the *kalaf* in three swallows and lay back down. Its warmth spread through his body like a drop of ink in a glass of water and he was asleep within a minute.

***

The Belgian's headache was gone when he woke up to the smell of cooking meat, but his weakness still had the better of him and the remnants of a dozen vivid dreams swirled through his mind and faded away. He got to his knees and crawled to the hut's entrance. The sun was directly overhead the clearing and the heat was stifling. The camp was no more than ten huts in a circle and a cooking fire in the centre with women peeling cassava roots, men talking and a gaggle of children playing around them. He stood up and stepped out of the hut unsteadily. A woman noticed him and shouted to one of the men.

'Teefo! The *mzungu* is awake.'

Teefo stopped what he was doing and came over to the Belgian. It was the chief.

'Habari! How are you?'

'Habari. I'm a hundred times better after that potion of yours, thanks. I barely had the energy to lift my head yesterday.'

'Yesterday? You've been asleep for two days.'

'Two days!' The Belgian shook his head. 'You're kidding me?'

'No, *bwana*, it's true. The *kalaf* was much occupied with defeating the fever. You're over the worst of it now and it's time to put some flesh back on your bones.'

Only the Belgian's bunched hand held up what was left of his trousers and rows of ribs showed through the tears in his shirt. He scratched his chest and grimaced. 'It'd make a blasted change from things feeding on *me*. Listen, I'm very grateful for everything you've done, Teefo. I'd have been dead for sure if your men hadn't found me.' He shook his head ruefully. 'My family and friends probably think I already am.'

'It's the way of the forest, *bwana*. Give your thanks to the tree spirits instead, it was they who were watching over you.' Teefo nodded towards the men. 'Look, see how they favour our hunters when we respect them. Now there'll be enough to fill our bellies tonight. Even yours!'

The Belgian recognised a duiker's skull and pelt next to them. 'I'll be thankful for whatever you can spare.'

'Think nothing of it. I'll bring you some more *kalaf* and then you can rest until it's ready.'

***

Day by day, the Belgian filled out and his energy slowly returned with the help of the *kalaf.* After two weeks he was exercising in the area around the camp and feeling almost ready to travel. He discussed it with the chief.

'How far are we from the edge of the forest, Teefo?'

Teefo thought for a moment. 'Not less than a week's travel and even then there are no roads to take you anywhere. The fastest way back to your world is by the Bangala river ferry and it would take two days to reach it.'

'I guess that's the way for me, then. How do I get there?'

'With us. We've got animal skins to trade at Bangala so we can go whenever you feel up to it.'

The Belgian put his hand on Teefo's shoulder. 'I'm very grateful for all the trouble you've gone through on my account. I promise I'll find some way of making it up to you all when I get home.'

Teefo shook his head. 'It's not necessary, *bwana.* The forest's roots are our roots and we are guided by them.'

***

A blanket of humidity settled onto the camp after the heavy afternoon rain. The tribe built up the fire and within minutes the heat of the blaze drove them back to the doorways of their huts, where they sat until the light faded. Before long the enclosure was lit by writhing flames and the still air became alive with the forest's screeches, piercing calls and grunts.

Teefo slipped into his hut after a while and returned with a pot and a bowl of *kalaf* for the Belgian. The mixture was even more intoxicating than usual and within a few minutes he was pleasantly stupefied. A branch cracked loudly in the fire and Teefo squatted in front of him.

'If it would please you, I have a tale to relate. It is renowned among our people and concerns the beast whose roar turns bowels to water: Mbadaba – *the Leopard God*.'

The Belgian had spent many years in Africa and enjoyed these convoluted semi-moralistic folk tales. He lay back and listened to the story.

'It was many moons ago, in the time of my father's father's father. There lived a traveller, Letuku, wishful of crossing the Great Forest to visit The Mountain That Thunders. But Letuku was vain and sought no permission from the forest gods and of this consequence became lost. For many days he was without sustenance, rivers shrank away and fruits refused to grow.

'High above, Baki, the night owl passed by.

'O, wise and wonderful owl, guide me from this terrible place,' implored the foolish traveller, but the owl was without mercy, for not only had Letuku failed to seek permission to enter the forest, but he had brought no gifts for the mighty tree spirits. And so the traveller continued even deeper into the forest and became even further lost; he could see no stars to plot his path, for the trees clasped each other and their leaves became as a green cloud.

'Presently he came across Diyoka, the snake, and beseeched him for the knowledge to leave this accursed place. And Diyoka was also without compassion, for Letuku had angered the gods by the manner of his coming.

'I am humble and therefore there are no obstacles in my

path,' said the snake and slithered away.

'After many days, the traveller became little more than a skeleton and even the insects found him not worthy of food, yet he plunged even deeper into the forest. It came to pass that Mbadaba, the leopard god, became exceedingly angered by the impudence of the wayward traveller and sought to put an end to this intrusion.

'Mbadaba pursued Letuku, who had irritated him so, but the traveller, by virtue of his thin body, was able to elude the leopard god by slipping inside a cave, whose width did not permit Mbadaba to enter.

'Mbadaba roared and scratched, but Letuku was safe inside his refuge. While the leopard god raged, Letuku cast his eyes around the cave and there, in great quantities, lay succulent fruits, nuts, meats and gourds of cool water. Letuku fell upon these victuals and gorged himself until his hunger was satisfied.

'For ten days and ten nights, Mbadaba waited outside the cave but the traveller would not leave, for there was food and water aplenty. At length, Letuku wished to explore his surroundings but was afraid to do so, for he had no fire with which to see his way. Instead, to pass the time, the traveller took to provoking Mbadaba, making much of that the leopard could not catch a lowly mortal despite his status as a god. Mbadaba remained silent.

'And that very night, it chanced that a spear of moonlight penetrated the thickness of the forest canopy and shone directly into the cave. Letuku picked up an empty bowl and caught the beam inside.

'At last I have light,' he cried, 'and am now able to leave this place.'

The traveller ran to the cave entrance and pointed the bowl at Mbadaba, shining the light into his eyes.

'Farewell, impotent god, for I am now rested and replete and so must make my way to The Mountain That Thunders.'

'And, to torment the leopard god even further, Letuku threw a bone, striking him upon the head.

'Mbadaba said nothing but slowly walked away. Letuku shook with laughter at this weakness as he collected food and water for his journey. When he was done, he pointed the moonlight bowl into the darkness of the cave and went on his way. After a short time he became alarmed to see two glowing green eyes in the darkness ahead.

'Who goes there?' he cried fearfully.

'It is I, Mbadaba, the leopard god, whom you sought to mock,' roared the mighty beast.

'At this, the traveller dropped his provisions and ran back to the mouth of the cave, afraid for his life. And Mbadaba padded after him, content in the knowledge that Letuku, after many days of feasting, would not be able to pass through the small entrance to make his escape.

'And so the forest took revenge upon a traveller who had no right to enter its domain and Letuku, for his many days of gluttony, made an even better meal for Mbadaba.'

Teefo refilled the Belgian's bowl. 'I hope you found our tale entertaining, *bwana*.'

The Belgian sat up and took a mouthful of *kalaf.* 'You tell a good story, Teefo. I enjoyed it very much. You know, there's always something to be learned—' The bowl fell from his fingers. It was as if every muscle and nerve in his body was disconnecting from his brain, second by second. He stared at the headman and tried to speak, but the words were seizing in his throat.

'The *kalaf.* God damn … it … Teefo … why?'

The chief emptied the pot onto the ground and looked at him impassively. 'The medicine of the forest brought you back to life, *mzungu*, and now its gift must be passed on. It is the way.'

All at once it seemed a giant hand had closed around the Belgian's chest. Its fingers tightened at every intake of breath; he cried out, but the creeping paralysis overtook his vocal cords, strangled the screams to a grunt, then to a faint rasp and finally to an impotent silence that was no rage against the rib-cracking grip. His heart fought on against the pressure, pumping useless flat blood to his organs and as the last traces of oxygen fed his brain he saw the women add more wood to the fire and the men gather around him with their knives ready.

He thought of Mbadaba and Letuku and then his world faded to black.

Staying Alive?

'Eh, *what*? Speak up, can't you?'

'For Christ's sake, McCrudle, *I said* the television crew will be here at three o'clock. I told you this morning, *didn't I*?'

'I don't know, Doctor Abendstern, I don't remember. What do they want?'

'Look, what's the date today?'

'The what?'

Dr Abendstern turned the amplifier up by two decibels.

'The *date*.'

McCrudle sat up and squinted at his daily status screen. 'May the twentieth. Sounds familiar.' He chewed on his lip for a while. 'It's my birthday. Yeah, well ain't that the cat's pyjamas …'

'It certainly is for this clinic. We've kept you alive to be a hundred and fifty. Twenty-five years older than anyone else. That's why the television people are coming.'

'No one asked *me* if I wanted to be displayed like some monkey in a zoo, dammit.'

'It's not asking much, McCrudle. Frankly, we'd expect a little more gratitude for our efforts instead of your constant griping. Have you any idea just how much time and money it costs to keep you running?'

'Keep me running? When was the last time you said that to your automobile, Doctor?'

‘Don’t be ridiculous – my Maserati’s a mechanical device, not a Homo Sapiens.’

‘Oh, is that so? Let me see … your world’s oldest man seems to be rigged with a brain pacemaker, a mechanical heart, a synthetic windpipe, an artificial bladder, someone else’s kidneys, liver and lungs, hearing implants, vision enhancers, dentures, replacement hips, replacement knees and Christ knows what else I’m connected to. No, sir. I’d say I’m a closer relative to your jalopy than my own mother. The only damned reason I haven’t got cancer is that there ain’t nothing left for it to take a liking to. Why, it’s a wonder that—’

McCrudle blinked twice and sank into a deep sleep. Dr Abendstern took his finger off the tranquiliser dispenser button and turned to the nurse.

‘Bring him back at 14:45. Oh, and give him a shave before NBC arrive. We must have him looking his best for the evening news.’

***

McCrudle was propped up against a pair of pillows at 14:50. The silver stubble on his chin had disappeared and the dozen or so hairs on his head were tidily arranged like broad-gauge railway tracks. He watched the nurses as they hung coloured streamers over the screen frame and planted birthday cards where they could be seen by the cameras. Birthday cards … from whom? All his family and friends had died half a lifetime ago. He didn’t know anybody outside of his little room.

The door opened and Dr Abendstern walked in, followed by a woman with a microphone and a cameraman. He nodded to one of the nurses. She took a box from the side locker and put it on McCrudle’s bed table. Dr Abendstern grinned into the camera.

‘On behalf of everyone at The Silver Cloud Clinic – and everyone in the world, I’m sure – I’d like to wish Elmer McCrudle a very happy 150th birthday and hope there’ll be many more to follow!’

Everybody clapped and Dr Abendstern lifted a cake from the box. The nurse handed out paper plates and glasses whilst another opened a bottle of wine.

‘None for our guest of honour, I’m afraid,’ said Dr Abendstern, ‘Mr McCrudle is on a strict diet for his health’s sake.’

McCrudle watched as Dr Abendstern, the NBC crew and the three nurses ate their pieces of cake and drank their wine.

‘Would you like to talk to Mr McCrudle now, Wilma?’ said Dr Abendstern when the party was over.

The interviewer dabbed her lips with a serviette, nodded to the cameraman and stood by the side of McCrudle’s bed.

‘It’s indeed an honour to speak to the world’s oldest man, Mr McCrudle,’ she said. ‘You must have seen a thousand changes in your life?’

‘Eh?’

‘I said, you must have seen a thousand changes in your lifetime, Mr McCrudle?’

McCrudle leaned forward. ‘I dare say.’

‘And what was the most significant event for you over, say, the last fifty years?’

‘I’ve got no idea, young lady. I can’t even remember what I did this morning.’

‘You seem to have kept your sense of humour, sir! Tell me, what would you like as a birthday present?’

McCrudle looked at the umbilical cord connecting him to a bank of sensors, condensers, alarms, balms, probes, strobes, oximeters, toximeters, repeaters, heaters, scanners, planners and dispensers.

‘I reckon a power cut would do me just fine.’

I.F.O.

The sound would stay with Schecter forever. The crash of flesh and bone bursting through his roof, through the bedroom and through the kitchen ceiling before finally ending up as a ragged and bleeding heap on the floor. If he hadn't left the stove where he'd been waiting for the coffee pot to boil and looked out of the window to investigate the noise of distant gunfire and jet airplanes screeching through the night, it might well have fallen upon him instead. Then there would have been two bodies for the pathologist to analyse. But Schecter was a medium-height white Caucasian, straight-haired and red-blooded. The medical examiner would have seen plenty of those.

He jumped back at the thunderclap and then the ceiling collapsed, spilling his bed, closet, floorboards, battens and roof tiles onto the kitchen floor and table. Sparks drizzled from a swinging light fitting before its fuse blew and then the room was in darkness.

'Christ on a cross! What the hell was that?'

Schecter stumbled across the debris and felt around for the flashlight he kept hanging next to the fuse box. The beam was diffused by dust hanging in the air and detritus from the wrecked bedroom continued to fall from the hole. He shone the flashlight around and cursed at the damage. Maybe one of those military airplanes had come apart and of all the thousands of acres in Chaves County, the goddamn thing had decided to fall on his house. Then he stiffened as it lit up a human shape lying on its side, partially shrouded by the upended bed, mattress, blankets and sheets. It was a corpse, without doubt. No one could survive the impact of punching straight through a roof, rafters and hard wooden floors. He stepped forward and primed himself to confirm what he already knew.

It was *impossible* – his eyes must be playing tricks. The body looked to be ten or eleven feet long, judging by the green-coveralled leg that protruded from the tangled bedding. No one of that size could fit into an airplane cockpit. Then he saw two glistening pink bones piercing the thigh. Classic compound fractures, he noted automatically, despite his shock. But these bones, of equal thickness, ran parallel to each other, unlike anything he'd ever seen.

His chest tightened and it seemed a physical ball of fear in his throat was about to choke him. He was no stranger to mutilated bodies after nearly four years in action as an army medic in Europe and the Pacific, but moving even an inch closer fought every instinct. The trembling flashlight illuminated what appeared to be purple blood seeping into the floorboard gaps and an earthy odour like cumin rose from it. His heart bounced against his ribs as he pulled the sheets away. And then he screamed as he'd never screamed before.

***

'*Mister Schecter? Mister Schecter*? It's Scott Geary and Arlen Zelatsky from the government.'

Two men, silhouetted against the pale dawn, stood at the doorway of the farmhouse. The first man spoke into a walkie-talkie.

'Beethoven Two – this is Mozart.'

'Mozart – Beethoven Two, receiving you strength three. Go ahead, Scott.'

'Uh, Roco, we've located some major wreckage at the Schecter farm, about ten miles north of Artesia on the Roswell road. He's a crusty sonofabitch according to the sheriff, runs the place alone since his father died and isn't partial to strangers. We've been knocking on his door for ten minutes but can't get an answer. I'll squawk you again when we've had a word with him.'

'Copy that. We'd better ask the air force to set up a command post on his land right away. I guess we'll need a couple of helicopters, some armed guards to keep the area secured and an ambulance or two. *Say again*, you're fading. *The what?* The press? Tell them we're investigating a flying accident or something. Anything, just keep them away. Over and out.'

Geary rattled the door handle again, stepped back and shouted at an open second-floor window. 'Mister Schecter – it's Scott Geary and Arlen Zelatsky from the government. Can we talk to you for a minute, please?'

He waited for a while. There was silence except for the sound of farm animals going about their early-morning routine. Zelatsky rapped on the door with his flashlight.

'Mister Schecter, open up, please. *Mister Schecter*?'

Nothing. He glanced at his partner and nodded. The door jamb splintered and gave way under the weight of Geary's shoulder.

'Mister Schecter, we're—'

Zelatsky's words disappeared in a deafening blast. The two men threw themselves onto the floor. The door teetered on its lower hinge and crashed down beside them.

'*Don't shoot*, for Christ's sake, Mister Schecter, *don't shoot*,' screamed Geary. He wiped a stream of blood from his face and eyes, '*We're with the government, we're friends*.'

There was a low sob from the darkness of the house. 'Take it away, take the goddamned thing away. Oh God, *somebody help me.*'

Geary and Zelatsky stepped over the remnants of the door and shone their flashlights around the ruined kitchen and passage. Powder smoke hung in a blue haze. Geary blinked disbelievingly and stepped back as his beam illuminated a shape lying on the floor next to a purple-mottled bedsheet. His head began to spin. He grabbed the doorpost before his knees gave way. Zelatsky doubled over and began to vomit.

Another shape cowered in the darkened living room with a smoking shotgun in its hands. It whimpered like a child. Geary swallowed hard, grabbed his radio and stumbled into the daylight. 'Roco … tell them we've found one.'

***

'We're going to give you a small injection to make you sleep, Mister Schecter. Just close your eyes and we'll have you in hospital in no time. There's a helicopter on its way right now.'

Schecter lay on the stretcher, quivering like a tuning fork. His eyes were wide open, fixed on a point well beyond the sight of anyone else. Bloody marks showed where he'd bitten clean through his lower lip. One of the air force medical sergeants tightened the straps.

'That's the deepest case of shock I've ever seen. He's just about cataleptic.'

'That could be a good thing,' said Geary as a group of men in white one-piece suits and full helmets gathered outside the farmhouse door. Two of them carried Geiger counters. A few twisted pieces of metallic wreckage littered the untended garden.

The sergeant wiped Schecter's forearm with a swab. 'What did he see to turn him into a cabbage like this?'

'You don't want to know, you really don't want to know,' said Geary, 'and I'd suggest that none of you mention this to anybody. If you want to keep your pensions, that is,' he added.

The sergeant grimaced, held a hypodermic up to the light and depressed the plunger until the correct quantity of sedative remained. 'That should do it,' he said as he injected Schecter. 'You won't hear a peep out of him now. Or me, come to that. Listen out, sounds like the cavalry's coming!'

The *thwap–thwap* of two helicopters seemed to fill the morning as they touched down in the stubbled field next to Schecter's house. The medics slid Schecter's stretcher into the station wagon ambulance, slammed the door and raced off towards the Sikorskis.

Geary walked over to his vehicle. Zelatsky was sitting in the passenger seat. He was white-faced and trembling.

'Got a smoke there, Arlen?' Geary had quit two years previously, but now seemed a reasonable time to light another one.

They both took a cigarette, but Zelatsky's hands were shaking so badly that Geary had to take the lighter from him. His own were not much steadier. He pulled hard on the cigarette and leaned back in the seat. 'So, now we know for sure,' he said eventually.

Zelatsky's voice was little more than a croak. 'Keeping it quiet's going to be a mission. *Christ*, I still can't believe it!'

Geary ground his cigarette out in the ashtray. 'Well, as far as we know, only Schecter's seen one other than us and the rest of the team. If anyone finds more wreckage before we do, we'll say it was a mid-air collision between one of our fighters and a light airplane. It wouldn't be the first time.' He nodded towards the farmer's kitchen. 'Let's just hope it was alone.'

'Alone …' said Zelatsky. 'We thought we were alone, once.'

***

Geary held out his hand. 'How are you doing, Mister Schecter?'

Schecter looked up from his hospital bed suspiciously. 'How am I doing? How the hell would *I* know? No one tells me anything here.' He shook hands anyway, despite the wariness in his eyes and voice. 'Now, if you don't mind me asking, who might you be?'

'Oh, I'm sorry, Mr Schecter, Scott Geary from the Federal Aviation Administration Accident Investigation Branch. Mind if I sit down?'

'It's free, as far as I know. So how can I help you, Mister Geary? My head's not been right for a while. I didn't even know who I was when I woke up. Come to that, I don't even know how long I've been here. Like I say, no one tells me anything.'

'Well, I was wondering if you could tell me anything about the Cessna?'

Schecter stared at the ceiling for a while. It seemed to Geary as if there was nobody behind the blank eyes. 'The *Cessna*?' he repeated eventually. '*What C*essna?'

'The *crash*, Mister Schecter. A Cessna single-engine airplane collided with an air force Shooting Star jet a week ago. It seems the pilot wasn't qualified to fly at night and he entered a restricted area. The jet pilot got out, but the Cessna came apart in the air. The civilian pilot came clean through your roof along with bits of airplane. He was killed instantly of course. We found you the next morning huddled in your house and badly shocked. We've had teams of investigators crawling over your land for clues; hopefully, everything's back as it should be by now. Don't worry about your animals, we've got someone looking them.'

'Sure better be. Say, don't I know you from someplace? You look a little familiar.'

'That's possible, sir. I was out at your farm when the medics arrived.'

'Thought so, it's not often I forget a face, except my ex-wife's.'

Geary laughed. 'I wish my memory was like that.'

'When you work a farm by yourself you can't afford to forget anything. Tell me, who was the fella who came through the roof?'

'The Cessna pilot? Oh, a guy called Rubens from Montana. He was delivering it to a customer in Durango or some place.'

'That so?' Schecter's face took on a distant look. 'Wasn't anything odd about him, was there?'

'Odd? How do you mean, *odd?'*

'Well, I keep getting these flashbacks … they're kind of in my mind for an instant, but the more I chase them, the further away they go. There was a god-almighty crash. I remember that much. I keep hearing it, even now.'

'What is it you see, exactly, Mr Schecter?'

'Dammit – I've *just said* I don't know. There's something really peculiar about it. That's all I can say. Sometimes it comes to me in a dream, but as soon as I wake up, it's gone, just like the flashbacks.'

'OK, Mr Schecter, no problem. You were in the living room when the airplane fell onto your house, right?'

'Yes, I was – *no, no,* I was in the kitchen; I remember now. I was looking out of the window to see what the ruckus was. There was the sound of those new-fangled jets screaming around not too far away and gunfire.'

'Gunfire?'

'Yeah, fifty calibre or so. I did four years in the army so the sound of shooting isn't exactly strange to me.'

'How far away was this gunfire, can you remember?'

Schecter closed his eyes for a moment. 'Not easy to tell at night-time. I'd say it was probably out north, Roswell, maybe, and high up.'

'That ties in with what the air force say. They had a

fighter squadron doing practice night interception and gunnery on the target ranges around about that time.'

'That what it was? I've never heard them doing it before and I've been here since early '46.'

'That so! Anything else you remember, Mr Schecter?'

The farmer frowned and rubbed his chin thoughtfully. 'There's something, god-dammit, but it won't come. Must be the drugs they've been giving me. *Jeez,* I've hardly had a clear thought since I woke up.'

'All right, Mr Schecter, thanks for your time. If anything does come back to you, here's my office telephone number.'

Schecter took the piece of paper. 'Who's going to pay for the damage?'

Geary stood up and straightened his jacket. 'It's all arranged, Mr Schecter, government insurance liability. Get better soon, eh?'

***

The air force doctor closed the door behind them and motioned for him to sit.

'So how can I help your department, Mr Geary?'

Geary leaned back in the chair and touched the side of his face. The medical sergeant at Schecter's farm had removed half a dozen shotgun pellets from his cheek and it was still tender. One had just missed his eye.

'We're still trying to find out what happened in the crash. Schecter seems to be the only civilian witness to the event, but he doesn't appear to remember much about it, which, as far as I'm concerned, is good. Some things he *does* remember, though, which *isn't* good.'

The doctor looked at Geary oddly. 'That's fairly common in an accident or traumatic experience. Sometimes the events are recalled later, sometimes not. In Schecter's case, we have five days of amnesia; his conscious mind remembers virtually nothing of the incident. He was heavily sedated when he arrived, mumbling something about aliens in his house. He's been having terrible nightmares ever since, waking up screaming and crying. We've had to put him on heavy medication to keep him calm.'

'Aliens! He's been drinking too much of that New Mex moonshine.'

'Ha, either that or not enough!'

Geary was silent for a moment. Then he took his identity and security clearance cards from his pocket and pushed them over the desk towards the doctor. 'Time to stop beating around the boonies. Look, Major, certain things happened at Schecter's place that aren't best publicised; they'd only spread alarm and unnecessary panic. I have it from the highest authority that any treatment that will help Schecter forget what he saw will be sanctioned. I believe that lobotomy was mentioned as a possible cure for his – shall we say – psychosis and hallucinations.'

The doctor looked at the project identity documents and clicked his tongue. 'That's pretty serious stuff, Mr Geary.'

'So was what happened to Schecter. It's imperative that what he saw doesn't go any further. That's why we need guaranteed silence.'

'I suppose this conversation isn't happening, Mr Geary?'

'Conversation? What conversation, Major?'

***

The social worker waved to the ambulance driver and joined Schecter as he walked unsteadily up the path to his house. He didn't remember the door being panelled. Or blue, come to that. He stepped inside and was disorientated for a moment. There was linoleum on the floor instead of bare wooden boards and rugs and he didn't recognise any of the kitchen furniture. The ceiling looked different too. Ripples of unease suddenly ran through him. Goddammit, what was happening? A man should feel safe in his own home. He felt a hand on his shoulder.

'Are you all right, Mr Schecter?'

'Uh … yeah, I'm fine, Maylene. Someone's made a few alterations while I've been away and it doesn't look much like it did before.' He stared at the wall for a few seconds. 'Well, I guess it hasn't got any right to if an airplane fell through the roof, but I don't remember any of that, only what the government man told me. Anyway, how about I fix us a cup of joe before I see what else they've done?'

'My father always said a good cup of coffee makes even a bad day right, Mr Schecter.'

'Well, I don't know about that, but it doesn't hurt any, that's for sure.' He opened a wall cupboard. It was empty. He rubbed his chin for a moment, shook his head and looked into the next one. Cups, plates and tableware. 'Damnation … where's the coffee pot?' He bent down and opened a base cabinet. A breath of cumin hit him like a fist.

Maylene rushed for the telephone. The operator could barely hear her for the screaming in the background.

A Closing Door

The air was fat with the scent of newly-cut grass and only the occasional click of scythe blades against stone, distant sorrowing of sheep and creak of early-evening bats parted its silence.

But John Saymore, standing at the parlour window that overlooked the meadows of Bittesthorpe, took in none of this: all he saw was the cleric making his way back to the rectory. Once the black-cloaked figure was absorbed by the dusk he sighed and climbed the stairs to his son's bedroom. The candlelight threw his shadow against the wall, making him many times bigger than he felt inside. As before, the boy was lying unconscious. The coverlet had been thrown off and his arms and one leg were draped over the sides of the cot. John took his kerchief and wiped the lank hair that clung to his son's face, listened to the faint rasps that followed the feeble rise and fall of his chest, held his hand and cried softly at first and then in great gulping sobs. All the physick's promises, infusions, leechings and bleedings had been for nothing and now the departing cleric's prayers seemed as final as a closing door. Matthew was dying. He knew it as surely as night followed day.

***

A faraway bell tower chimed. Eight … nine … ten times. The room seemed stark and cold despite the warmth of the

August evening; even the flickering candle gave him no comfort. All at once he desperately needed to hear a voice, to see the light and feel the warmth of a blazing fire, but he was loath to leave, afraid that his son might pass alone, condemned by the sickness like his mother. He held Matthew for a while longer and went down to the scullery. His manservant was sitting at the table. He looked up as John poured himself a noggin of rum.

'What news, master?'

'I … I fear God will be calling him very soon, Gilbert.'

Gilbert beat the sides of his fists against the table top. 'The boy has barely lived. *Where* is the lord's compassion? What says the good book – ask and thou shalt receive? Then where went our prayers? There was no lack of them and neither were they spoken in whisper.'

'Alas, it grieves me to have no answer. It is said that He works in mysterious ways. There may be some purpose that escapes our understanding.'

'Indeed so,' said Gilbert after a moment, 'but mayhap one of His mysterious ways will allow some intervention by the hand of man.'

'By the hand of man? What do you mean? How can we cast off this accursed ague when all others have failed?' John waited for a response, but his servant said nothing. 'If you have something to say, then pray say it – this is no time for riddles.'

Gilbert stood up. 'Very well, master, so I shall. There is a woman … Margaret Spenser of Lutterworth. I have heard it said she can remedy all manner of ills.'

'*All* manner of ills?'

'You surely know of Thomas Reeve?'

'Taverner Reeve of the Lamb's Head in Allethorpe?'

'Aye, him. Some five summers ago his daughter fell gravely ill with fever. She lay at the foot of death itself and none could aid her, neither the bloodletters nor the agents of

God. By fortune or otherwise, Margaret came to pass through the parish and laid hands and potions upon the girl in private. Before a week was gone she was free of her bed and is now of fine health and betrothed to Fletcher the baker.'

John rubbed his chin thoughtfully. 'Now that you relate it, I do believe I heard something of the like.' Then he frowned. '*Wait*. This Margaret – is she not also known as Margaret the Solitary? Would she be of witchcraft, perchance? Answer me truthfully, man.'

Gilbert shuffled his feet. 'Well … some have muttered such across their empty tankards, but there is no proof she has done harm to either man or beast. It is to the contrary, but tattletales cannot be silenced, nor rumours halted. Was not our Lord Jesus also accused of sorcery?'

'Then you say it is no more than idle talk?' The flat look in John's eyes was suddenly gone. 'Will she save my boy?'

'I can promise nothing, master, but she can surely do no less than the physick or the priest. Margaret is known to kin of mine in Lutterworth, do you desire that I seek her help?'

John strode back and forth across the flagstones. After a few moments, he stopped abruptly at the table. He nodded once, then twice more. 'Yes. *Yes*, I must take what I can. Make haste, bring to me this Margaret and you shall both be well rewarded for the life of my son.'

'Master, for her, I cannot speak, but for myself the only gift I need will be Matthew standing here with us, hale and hearty.'

John embraced him. 'Oh, Gilbert, my friend and faithful servant, I shall be forever in your debt! Take Surefoot and my saddle and ride as if your life depended on it.'

Gilbert took his jerkin from the back of the door. 'Not my life, master – Matthew's.'

***

John watched at the stable gate as Gilbert rode off into the moonlight. Lutterworth lay some five leagues distant in the county of Leicestershire. It would be a punishing journey for both him and the horse under the cloak of night. 'Godspeed,' he whispered, 'pray bring comfort before Matthew's spirit founders.'

When he could no longer see his servant, he returned to the scullery, poured himself another noggin and sat down in his fireside chair. For the first time in over a week, he felt the heavy hands of worry lighten on his shoulders. The fluttering flames and shadows that danced on the walls and floor soothed him even more and he was fast asleep before the rum was even half finished.

***

He awoke with a start as the burning logs in the grate collapsed in a shower of sparks. For a moment all was well with him and then he remembered his dying son. He threw off his short-lived comfort and lurched upstairs to the boy's bedroom.

Matthew was lying as John had seen him last. His breathing was still shallow and rapid and even in the soft moonlight, sweat showed on his face and chest. John lit a new candle with his tinderbox, sat on the chair beside the cot and prayed and prayed. Just before dawn, Matthew opened his eyes and flew into a storm of coughing. Blood dribbled onto the pillow from the side of his mouth; he reached for his father, tried to speak, and then slid back into unconsciousness. John beat his temples and wept.

***

Just before midday, John was woken in his chair by rapping on the cottage door. His eyelids were like lead as he opened the bedroom window and looked down.

‘Who is that? Is it you, Gilbert?’ he called hoarsely.

A handful of men stepped out from the porch and looked up.

‘No, it is not Gilbert, whoever he might be,’ cried a rough-looking creature, ‘it is William Tynan.’

‘William Tynan? You are not of this parish. What ails thee?’

‘Would thee be John Saymore?’

‘That I am,’ concurred John uneasily.

‘That is well, for we have apprehended Margaret the Solitary crossing into this county.’ He pointed to a ragged shape lying at the end of the path next to the strangers’ horses.

A chill rippled down John’s spine. ‘Margaret the Solitary?’

‘Aye, none other. She and her companion sought refreshment in our village and fled when she was recognised. We pursued them for a league until their horse fell. The man is dead. His neck was broken like a twig, but we have the woman, though she be grievously hurt about the arms and face.’

His accomplices looked at each other and laughed.

‘We spoke with her at length,’ continued Tynan, ‘and in due course she confessed to witchery.’

John clung to the window frame as his knees sagged.

Tynan waved his fist in the air. ‘Aye, confessed all, Justice Saymore, and we are demanding her prosecution this very day.’

The Big Squeeze

(Lopsided Larssen, P.I)

Wun Tu was waiting for me when I turned up at the office. I hadn't seen him for a while, not since I'd helped get Vinnie Di Sorderli and his protection racketeers a ten-year stretch for extortion and tax evasion. After that I lived on free Chinese chow until I started to change color. As usual, his face didn't let on what was going on inside his head. He made the Sphinx look like the village idiot after a shot of laughing gas. He put his hands together like he was going to pray to Buddha and bowed.

'Ah, Mistah Larssen – long time no see. How you keeping?'

I bowed back and noticed my shoes needed cleaning. 'Hi, Wun,' I said. 'I'm just about keeping out of debt. What brings you out of the restaurant?'

His face dropped by a thirty-second of an inch. He took a letter out of his pocket and passed it to me. I passed it back. It was in Chinese.

'Oops – very sorry, Mistah Larssen; that from my brother in Shanghai.' He gave me another one. It made better sense, but it was probably worse news.

Dear Customer. We can now offer you a very special insurance scheme. You pay up and your place will not get burned down/blown up/flooded/infested with cockroaches (delete as applicable). You will be contacted by one of our specially-trained advisors within the next few days. Be warned – there are many deaf people in this city who have lost valued property. Assuring you of our personal attention at all times. Take very good care.

It looked as if someone was putting his big feet into Di Sorderli's shoes.

'Come through my letter slot this morning, Mistah Larssen, along with cut-price holiday brochure and double-glazing special.'

All of his mail was extortion or fraud, by the sound of it. I got up and held the letter against the sunlight that was streaming through the Sleuth Booth window. There were no watermarks on the paper, but there were two greasy paw prints on it near the bottom. I sniffed them. The faint smell reminded me of something.

Wun Tu looked at me with eyebrows that had lifted the distance a micrometer might not have detected. I patted his shoulder. 'Don't worry, Wun Tu, leave it with me for a while,' I said. 'Be sure to let me know if you get any more unsolicited mail or unwelcome visitors.'

'Thank you, Mistah Larssen,' he said, 'you welcome anytime at the Chinese Wall. Not cost you nothing.'

I watched him through my office window as he walked down the block towards 51st. He must have been a worried man despite his inscrutability. He had four kids, a wife and two lots of parents to look after, never mind his three brothers and one cousin from Canton. Any more expense might well break him.

Kate breezed in with a mug of instant. I diluted it with an ounce of Jack, put my feet on the desk and sat back.

'Wun Tu got troubles?' asked Kate as she touched up her lips with a stick of something redder than my eyes.

'Yep, someone's trying to put the squeeze on him again.'

Kate frowned, which didn't suit her. She liked Wun Tu. Everybody liked Wun Tu; he'd made it the hard way and didn't deserve some cheap punk leaning on him with an insurance policy he couldn't afford to turn down.

'Any new boys in town?' I asked her.

'Nothing I've heard of, let me make a call to Mississippi Minnie.'

Mississippi Minnie was a retired nun who'd done twenty years with Girls Town and was as hard a cookie as they came. She'd once sapped Don Ationes of the Rafia for not taking his homberg off when he'd dropped into her office with a ten grand contribution towards the upkeep of the place. Chief O'Flanagan of the NYPD was just as frightened of her. His nose had a hard left turn on his face thanks to him being late for the Girls School fifteenth anniversary gala. More than once she'd cracked someone's skull, on both sides of the law, for back-lipping her. She had a voice like a drill sergeant, a grip like a one-armed man hanging off the Empire State Building lightning rod and a heart of twenty-carat gold once you'd chipped away the granite. Her information network would have made Edgar J. Hoover green with envy.

I took a wander down to Seamus's Sweat Shop, a sauna-cum-gymnasium on the corner of the block. I found him in the bloodstained arena that he called a boxing ring. He was tying a pair of sparring gloves onto a jasper with a face that looked as if he'd tried to shave with a salami slicer.

'Hiya, Lopsy, how's tricks?' He had a voice that sounded as though he used gravel and broken glass as a mixer for his drinks, but today it was quieter than usual.

'Fair to middling, Seamus, how's yours?'

He jumped out of the ring and threw me a light punch on the shoulder. I stepped back for the count of nine, then launched a climbing right cross at his jaw. As usual, he blocked me with a paw the size of an elephant's foot and laughed his Irishman's laugh.

'Will you be wanting medical attention for your injury, Mr Larssen?'

'That's why I came, you big galoot,' I said. 'Don't spare it. I can take the pain.'

He opened a footlocker, took out two glasses and a bottle of something that looked like cold tea but wasn't, and poured a couple of slugs that could have put WC Fields onto the ropes.

We swapped banter for ten minutes or so. Then I said: 'Is your insurance up to date on the Sweat Shop, Seamus?'

His eyes took on a worried look. 'Meaning what, Lopsy?'

'Meaning, have you received any offers of expensive policies that guarantee against arson, explosions, structural failures and other unlikely catastrophes?'

He reached inside the footlocker again, took out a typewritten letter and handed it to me. It was a carbon of the one Wun Tu had shown me.

'Found it under the door when I opened up this morning. I've been doing my best to forget it until I get home.'

Seamus was a big man who could look after himself with one arm in a sling. But muscles weren't going to be any good against this sort of fight. 'What are you going to do about it?'

He took a long shot of his home-brewed whisky. 'What can I do, Lopsy? If I don't cough, everything I've worked for over the last ten years is going to collapse around my ears. Sure, my insurance company will pay up if I get one or two accidents, but then my premiums'll go through the roof. Maybe I should just give these guys what they're asking. I've got a family to feed. This place gets torched if I call the cops in and then there'll be nothing on their plates but air.'

The gym echoed with the sound of the ugly joey pummelling a punchbag. Seamus swirled his whisky nervously around the glass. I could imagine how he felt.

How many others were worrying their heads about these letters

I gave him my card. 'Ring me when these punks get in contact again, Seamus. Maybe I can put the pinch on them before their grip gets too big.'

He looked at the card and nodded. I finished my drink and left him.

I wasn't counting on getting a call.

***

Kate was typing up a letter to the bank when I got back. The pawnshop Olivetti must have been bored with hammering out the same words every other day.

'Any joy from Mississippi Minnie, kitten?' I asked.

'She's put her menaces on the terraces. If there's anything going on she'll have the griff before the end of the week.'

That was typical of Minnie – it was already Friday. I went into the office, carefully measured out a full tumbler of Jack and made my feet comfortable on the desk. Eventually my eyes got tired of looking at the wall and pulled their shutters down.

Kate woke me at some time much later. My eyelids creaked open.

'Sorry to bother you when you're busy, Lopsy. Minnie's got word on the racket. She says to drop by around six.'

I looked at my watch – a quarter after four. It was a two-hour run to Girls Town on Staten Island. Maybe half that in something that wasn't my Lincoln. I picked up my hat and took a drive.

Girls Town was an old army bootcamp looking out at Brooklyn. I pulled up outside the main block and took the stairs to her first-floor office. The door was open. She was arm-wrestling with the janitor, watched by a handful of her girls. She looked up.

'Hello, lunkhead. I'll be with you in a second or two.'

I heard the janitor's bones crunch and then his knuckles hit the desk with an almighty crack. He got up from the chair, threw her a greenback and pushed past me. His hand was jammed into his armpit and if he wasn't close to crying, then my name was Pierre MacYamaguchi.

'Maybe next time, Lester,' she cackled as he disappeared into the passageway. She clicked her fingers and the girls vanished.

Minnie shoved the greenback into a note-packed jar and waved me towards a chair. 'Just keeping the bank balance up, Lopsy. So what's going on under the skin of The Big Apple?'

She poured a couple of shots of Kentucky as I filled her in on the latest get-rich-quick dodge. She slid one over the desk. 'Well,' she said, 'according to my sweet little sniffers, a Corsican shark who goes by the name of Corky Vandaletto is throwing his pebbles in the protection pond. Who's he been putting the squeeze on?'

I told her about Wun Tu and Seamus. 'Probably a whole bunch more, too, Minnie. How come this weasel's never tickled my ears before?'

'Ever heard of Jersey?' she asked.

'Jersey? Sure I've heard of Jersey – who hasn't? It's just below Newark. I was there on the Masher Molloy fraud case last month.'

'Ignoramus,' she said. 'Jersey in the Channel Islands, part of Britain.'

What the heck was an ignoramus? It sounded like some African water-bound mammal. 'OK,' I said, 'What's the connection?'

'He had a beach refreshment concession, but the authorities ran him off the island for adulterating the ice cream with goat milk.'

‘Sounds like a nasty piece of work. But what’s the tie-up with Wun Tu and Seamus?’

‘How would I know?’ said Minnie, ‘that’s what you get paid to find out. Speaking of which, there’s a ten-buck handling charge for what I’ve just told you. No checks, please, especially one of yours.’

I dug deep into my pocket and pushed a brace of fives over the table.

‘Girls Town thanks you for your very generous contribution.’ Now finish your drink and beat it. I’ve got a hundred waifs to look after.’

I got up and stuck my lips on her cheek. ‘Thanks, Minnie, I’ll be seeing you.’

‘If I’d known you couldn’t afford a razor, I’d have given you discount. Mind how you go.’

I dropped into La Cantina on 51st when I got back and washed the air from my mouth with a Manhattan Skullslammer. What was the link between ice cream, Oriental chow, and gymnasiums? This Corky Vandaletto sure had his grubby mitts in some peculiar pies. I gave my think tank the rest of the evening off and filled the vacant spaces with shock-absorbing fluid. I had a grumbling feeling that tomorrow was going to be a busy day.

***

It was. For the fire department, anyway. A delicatessen, a Lithuanian knitting club and a Portuguese Poets coffee shop had mysteriously burned down by the time I got into the office at noon. The New York immigrants’ news grapevine moved quicker than brushfire. Seamus was there to tell me all about it. His face was longer than a giraffe’s neck.

‘I’m going to pay up, Lopsy,’ he said when he was through. ‘If I don’t, the Sweat Shop’s going to get a damn sight hotter.’

I couldn't blame him. The cops were going to bang their heads hard against a wall of silence. No one was going to talk, that was for sure. I poured us both some lunch and puzzled for a while. Sherlock Holmes was supposed to have two-pipe solutions to his cases. I didn't have a fancy smoking tool like that so I made do with a toothmug full of something just as soothing.

'Got any boxing gloves in my size?' I asked Seamus when Jack started to give me the count of ten.

He gave me a puzzled look. 'Got 'em in any size except for ankle grabbers and Goliath. Why's that?'

So I told him.

***

I got into the Sweat Shop around eleven on Sunday morning. Seamus's punchbags were as hard as a bank manager's heart and I worked up a bigger sweat in five minutes than I had in running a block and a half to catch Luigi's Liquor Store before it closed last night. It had been a choice between buying gas for the automobile or gas for me; three bucks fifty-five doesn't stretch as far as it used to and my pockets were as empty as the Lincoln's tank.

A six-five bruiser drooling like a Pitbull terrier over a kitten offered me a sawbuck if I'd spar with him for a quarter of an hour, but I figured I wouldn't live to spend it so I turned him down on the grounds that he wouldn't get his money's worth. Five minutes later he boppered a fifty-pound punchbag clean out of its ceiling hook.

I kept an eye on Seamus's office as I worked out; I could see him through the half-glassed walls behind his desk. Just as I was about to do a press-up, a pair of swarthy palookas in suits and hombergs strolled into the gym and looked around. Unless their left armpits had excitable lymph glands, they were packing pieces. It didn't take half a moron to figure out that these two were the insurance salesmen. Seamus looked up from his desk at the same time they got to his office doorway. Even from twenty feet, I could see the dismay on his face. I wiped my mug with a towel and took a hike towards the shower room. Then I pulled my togs on and went back. They were standing in front of his desk as I crept past the door. One of them was a handsome Herbert with blue jowls and the other, judging by his features, looked like he'd once been an amateur – and very unsuccessful – parachute tester. When I had their backs to me, I ducked down and pressed my ear against the thin office panelling. They were selling their premiums. It wasn't good listening material.

'So, Mr Hannahan, have you taken the time to consider our selected customer policy? We hear there've been a few unfortunate accidents in the locality lately.'

Seamus was quiet for a few moments. 'I'll not be having a lot of choice, will I? How much are you asking?'

The other voice said: 'A very sensible decision indeed. For a building of this size, I'd say fifty bucks a week should cover all eventualities.'

'Fifty bucks! Sweet Mary above – there's no way I can pay that.'

'Not being very considerate, are you, Mr Hannahan? I don't think you're aware of how much effort we've got to make to ensure your building is kept safe.'

There was a crash as something hit the floor and a strangled ring. I guessed the telephone wouldn't be making any more calls for a while.

'Oh, gee, that was unfortunate,' said the first voice.

'And so easily avoided,' sniggered the other. 'Are you sure you wouldn't like to reconsider?'

'Two hundred a month will kill me,' said Seamus, 'I'm barely making enough to survive as it is.'

'We're not unreasonable. We'll give you another couple

of days to come up with the right answer,' said the first one. 'We'll be back on Tuesday, let's say ten o'clock. Meanwhile, here's our calling card.'

I snuck a quick look over the panelling and watched as the parachute tester dragged the foresight of his gat over Seamus's polished desk.

'Have a good day,' laughed Bluejowls.

I ducked down, waited until the footsteps had died away, waved to Seamus through the office window and went after the two punks. They were disappearing around the corner of the block heading east as I pushed the door open. That two hours working out must have had some benefit because, within a minute, I was right behind them. I could hear them laughing, the two-bit jerks. After five minutes, they stopped off at a joint called Pietro's Pizza Parlor. Some Italian New Yorker in need of an enforced insurance policy, no doubt.

I crossed the road, settled myself into the window seat of a third-rate bar and ordered a first-rate Jack from an uninterested waitress with enough ladders in her stockings to reach the top of the Chrysler Building. The petty cash was sure taking a hammering lately. There was still no sign of the two salesmen by the time a third Jack had slid down my gullet. Pietro was either very helpful or very unhelpful. Just then, my view of the Pizza Parlor was interrupted by a delivery truck being parked right in front of its entrance. That was just what I didn't want. Then I noticed a very odd thing – the driver and his assistant were lugging boxes into Pietro's Pizza Parlor and bringing others out. This went on for maybe ten minutes. What was going on? Then I remembered something about Wun Tu's insurance invitation. I finished my drink, fed the phone booth five cents and called Kate. It didn't take long to get the dope. It was time to stick my beak into the nut basket.

There were ten or so diners inside the restaurant getting stuck into pizzas the size of Cadillac hubcaps. A waiter appeared as I looked around and thrust a menu at me.

'Can I help you, *signor*?'

'Yeah, my Lincoln needs two new wheel bearings and a carburetor tune and I think my geyser needs de-scaling.'

'Uh?' he said.

'Well, you did ask, pal,' I said. 'Is Corky around or is he out on business?'

His face was eclipsed by suspicion. 'Who wants to know?'

'No one,' I said. 'Have you got tossed salad on the menu?'

'*Si*, naturally.'

'With a dressing of the Family *Oleaceae,* genus *Olea,* classification *Olea europaea,* variety *europaea,* of course?'

That got him. His face darkened for a moment. 'I am just the waiter,' he said, not quite so cocky now.

Just then the kitchen doors opened and a waitress hurried out, pushing a trolley stacked to the gunwales with desserts. I could see my two salesmen friends inside, having what was obviously a social jaw with the truck delivery men and a dude with a chef's hat like The Leaning Tower of Pisa.

This was getting as clear as a Swedish motion picture. And then I remembered something.

***

Kate was fending off the rent collector when I arrived at the Sleuth Booth on Monday morning. He was a small man, which almost put him on a conversational level with her chest. As I hid behind the filing cabinet, I heard him say he'd be back tomorrow morning. I guessed it wasn't because he was expecting the lucre – he was hoping Kate would be wearing something even more revealing.

'Thanks for stalling his motor, kitten,' I said. 'It'd be kind of difficult working from a sidewalk.'

'I might get a regular income selling matches and newspapers, though,' she grumbled. 'How did you get on with the extortion racket? I heard a few places were hit over the weekend.'

I lit up a Camel to give my lungs some early morning exercise. My eyeballs could have done with a set of safety straps. I hadn't coughed like that since Luigi had given me December's liquor credit tab. 'Promising, maybe we'll break it today. What have you got on glycerine?'

'Glycerine?' Kate thought for a second or two. 'Glycys Keros, a by-product of animal and vegetable fats and oils. Colorless, viscid and sweet-tasting. A hygroscopic trihydric alcohol with a specific gravity of 1.265 boils at 290 degrees Centigrade. Used, among other things, for paints, cosmetics, toothpaste, solvents and explosives in conjunction with nitric and sulphuric acids.'

'Just as I thought,' I said.

I took a walk to the end of the block. A swarthy beggar with silver stubble was sitting on the corner. He looked more down on his luck than me. The placard around his neck said: Please Help A Blind Man With A Wive And Fambly To Suport. I fumbled in my pocket and lobbed a nickel into his collection tin.

He lifted his dark glasses and stared pointedly at my contribution. '*Qué es ésta* you cheap bum! I no accept nothing below a quarter these days.'

'Aw – are all those little coins too heavy to lug to the bank, *hombre?*'

'You damn right,' he laughed. 'You keeping well, *Señor* Larssen?'

'Well, you know how it is, Paco. When it ain't raining, it's pouring. Been down south lately?'

'Sure! I visit my little *senorita* only last month. She sure know how to keep an old man young.'

'Yeah, you look pretty good for sixty, you rogue. No

trouble with the revolutionaries?'

Paco spat a stream of tobacco juice at two flies being intimate on the side of his collection tin. They slid to the sidewalk in a brown ball. 'No, not since the government troops find their weapons stash. They out for revenge, as sure as my wife would be if she find out I no visit my sick nephew.'

He quickly lowered his dark glasses as a party of blue-rinsed biddies came around the corner. '*Vamos, hombre*; here come my next cigar and bottle of tequila. See you around.'

I killed some time in Glinka's Department Store watching the ladies shopping in the lingerie section until I was asked to leave. Then I took a stroll to the downbeat bar opposite Pietro's Pizza Parlor, drank a four-course lunch at my window seat and sat back to see what was developing.

Sure enough, another delivery truck pulled up across the street and a pair of heavily mustachioed and unsavoury-looking characters jumped out, opened the back doors and disappeared into Pietro's. Someone had left a couple of quarters on the next table. I guessed they were an appreciation of outstanding sub-standard service as there were at least three separate sets of used glasses on the dirty tablecloth. I took them before they corroded away and made two calls in the booth. I stepped outside and waited. If I wasn't mistaken, Monday was going to start the week off with a bang.

Seamus steamed along the sidewalk twenty minutes later with half a dozen tracksuited gorillas in his slipstream. Their biceps were bigger than my thighs and none of them had any use for a necktie; their heads sprouted straight from their shoulders. Wun Tu arrived with two of his brothers as Seamus trotted towards me. I put them all in the big picture and I swear Seamus's pals were slavering in anticipation.

'Ready?'

Wun Tu and his clan nodded. Seamus's mob began to paw the ground like bulls seeing a smirking matador. We crossed the street and marched into Pietro's Pizza Parlor. The joint was packed with lunchtime scoffers. They all looked up as we stood by the kitchen doors.

'Right, folks, the restaurant's closed,' I bawled. 'You're all in danger of becoming seriously ill, don't eat another bite, go home quickly, take a dose of Epsom Salts and if you're lucky, you won't need to call a physician or funeral parlor advance booking clerk.'

There was uproar. Tables and chairs were overturned, plates and glasses smashed on the floor, people screamed. A burly waiter pushed through the fleeing patrons and jabbed his finger at me. *'Diffamazione!* What's this you say? There nothing wrong with food at Pietro's – who you think you are, frighten my customer like this?'

One of Seamus's friends reached out, curled his fingers around the honcho's neck and lifted him up until his feet were clear of the floor. 'You're not looking too well, buster - perhaps you'd better sleep it off.' He clenched his other hand and slammed it on top of the air-dancer's nut. He went down and twittering birds fluttered up.

The kitchen doors burst open and twenty or so assorted staff flew into the room, some brandishing rolling pins and tenderising mallets. The Sweat Shop gang grinned and began rubbing their hands. Pietro's mob looked at each other nervously. Wun Tu and his brothers opened the action with a dazzling ten-second display of wu shu. Seven of the mob kept the first waiter company on the floor. Not wanting to be left out, Seamus and his pugilists joined in and seconds later the floor was full of shouting, punching, wriggling and bleeding figures. Seamus was on his knees, pummelling the amateur parachute tester with one hand while the other was steadily throttling Bluejowls. He didn't need any help, for sure.

Then I saw someone in a lemon suit making a dash for the fire exit. That, I figured, would be Corky Vandaletto or somebody else. Either way, he was obviously one of the big cogs in the machine. I snatched a bottle of Chianti from the wine rack and lobbed it at the back of his head. It was a good shot from thirty paces. The bottle ricocheted from his nut and caught a kitchen hand between the eyes, knocking them both off their feet at the same time. If this had been the Central Park Fair, I'd have won a pair of dying goldfish. I jumped over the pile of squirming bodies and grabbed whoever was in the lemon suit before he came to his senses. His eyes were rolling in their sockets like ball bearings in a saucer and the lump on his sconce would make sure he didn't sleep on his back for the next day or few.

Meanwhile, the scrap was coming to an end; Wun Tu was sporting a promising shiner, while Seamus's only injuries appeared to be his knuckles. All the other good guys were on their feet except for one of the Sweat Shop boys, who was kneeling groggily across the two unconscious truck men and a bottle of grappa.

I was just about to open the bar for a victory drink when Lieutenant Kochleer and his bunch of flatfeet rushed into the restaurant.

'I might have guessed you'd be painting somewhere in the middle of a bad picture, Larssen – what's going on with the sleeping beauties?'

I jerked my thumb towards the groaning herbert that may have been Corky Vandaletto, Pietro, or probably both. 'You'd better ask the gentleman in the canary suit and I'm sure President Cuervo of Salivia will be very interested in what he's got to say as well.'

***

That night we had a small party in the back room of the

Great Wall of China.

'Spill the haricots, Lopsy,' said Seamus through a mouthful of Bombay Duck. 'What put you on the scent of Vandaletto and his bunch of desperados?'

'Well, it didn't take long for it all to add up. *Los Luchadores de la Libertad de los Granjeros de la Lechería De Salivia,* otherwise known to the FBI as The Salivian Dairy Freedom Fighters, were employing Corky Vandaletto to supply them with explosives to blow up the State-run creameries. With his Alimentation and Organic Chemistry degree from the Ajaccio School of Higher Learning, Corky was producing the nitro-glycerine from olive oil supplied by the Californian plantations, using Pietro's Pizza Parlor as a front and shipping it across the border to the revolutionaries. He was receiving his payment in rebel Salivian Romano cheese, thereby avoiding the 70% tax levied on certain imported Italian dairy products under the '53 Kincaid Pungent Goods Act. Who knows how long he'd have gotten away with it if he hadn't moved into the protection racket to finance his Toggenburg and Cashmere goat cross-breeding experiments. The olive oil stains on Wun Tu's demand got me thinking.'

Seamus raised his glass to me and took a thick envelope from his pocket. 'As a token of our appreciation for screwing the lid down on Corky and his henchmen, Lopsy, the immigrant retail community would like you to accept this. We're all very grateful.'

I took the envelope and opened it. There was five hundred bucks in twenties. That would cover all the Sleuth Booth's bills and Kate's wages for the next two months. There was also a wad of credit tokens from Abe's Delicatessen to Ziegler's Zener Diode Manufacturing Co, including one from Luigi's Liquor Store, value not exceeding $20.00. Strangely, that was exactly what I already owed them.

I poured three shots of rye. Wun Tu didn't drink, so Seamus and I shared his glass, poured him another and shared that one too.

It was going to be a long night.

Mistress Quickly's Barnacle

The damned man first appeared at the Yacht Club one Sunday afternoon in June. North of six feet tall. Fair wavy hair. Grey eyes. Sparkling teeth. Tanned. A jaw Superman would be jealous of. Brown deck shoes. Grey Sta-Prest trousers. White roll-neck sweater. Blue brass-buttoned blazer. The uniform of a sailing poseur. Surrounded by women. And he had his arm around Felix's wife.

Felix crossed the bar area and scowled at the intruder, who slowly freed his hand from her waist.

'Ah, you must be Celia's lucky husband. *Je suis* Greg Villiers, it's such a pleasure for you to meet me.' He offered his hand.

Felix's grip was little more than a light kiss of fingers. 'Delighted, I'm sure.' He turned to his wife. 'Are you ready, Celia?'

She held up her glass. 'I'm only halfway down, darling. Give me a few more minutes. Greg's been telling us all about his travels. It's been so interesting.'

'Has it really? So, Mr Villiers, what brings you to a dull place like this?'

Greg chuckled. 'I've just got back from cruising the Med, old chap, thought I'd spend a few days in the Sceptred Isles while the hull is being scraped.' He looked around at his admirers. 'I'm getting mine done at the same time. One must move smoothly in foreign waters, you know.'

‘Greg’s invited us all to an onboard cocktail party tonight,’ cried Celia.

‘I say, how terribly thrilling. Haven’t you forgotten we’ve got an appointment with Quentin and Alicia at the Bridge Club tonight?’

Celia pouted. ‘*Oh, darling*, I’m sure we can give bridge a miss, just this once.’

‘I’m rather partial to a few rubbers myself, actually,’ said Greg. ‘Perhaps we can get together sometime.’

Felix ignored the innuendo and took Celia’s hand. ‘Yes, perhaps. Now if you’ll excuse us, we must be off.’

He was irritated by the Villiers character and the short journey to their detached house on the outskirts of Fordingley passed in wintry silence. Celia gripped Felix’s arm as they pulled up outside the garage.

‘I do believe you’re being childishly jealous, darling.’

‘*Childishly jealous*!’ You were openly flirting with each other in full view of my friends and colleagues.’

‘Oh, Felix dear, don’t be so silly; he’s just very good company, no more than that. Perhaps you should have taken more time to get to know him instead of being so hostile.’

Felix snorted. ‘No need. I can tell a cuckolding fraud when I see one. The man’s an oily charlatan and I’d prefer that we *didn’t* socialise with him if you don’t mind.’

***

For almost a week they saw nothing of Greg Villiers and then, on Saturday morning, the telephone rang. Celia answered the call as Felix was cleaning his bowling shoes.

‘Why, Greg, it’s lovely to hear from you. I’m so sorry we couldn’t make it to the party. How are you and how is the boat?’ She tilted her head and twirled the cord with her index finger as she listened, unaware that Felix was now standing in the hallway behind her. ‘Yes, we’d be delighted, I’m sure,' she purred after a while. 'Let me phone you back. What's your number?'

She wrote his details on the scribble pad. 'Thank you, Greg, darling, talk to you soon. *Byeee.*'

Felix noticed she was dreamily embroidering his name with her pen. 'And *what* would you be delighted about? How did he get our number anyway?'

Celia whirled around in surprise. 'Oh, for heaven's sake, Felix, Greg's just being sociable. What *is* the matter with you? He got our number from the bar secretary and only called to see if you'd like to join him in a small club race around the bay.'

Felix's mood lifted instantly. This was more like it! He was no mean hand at yacht racing and the thought of humiliating Greg in public was very tempting.

'Yes, dear, of course, it would be churlish to refuse. Ring him back and tell him I look forward to it.'

He dug out his sailing rig in delicious anticipation.

***

Greg met them at the marina, resplendent in a Musto waterproof suit and rakishly-angled yachting cap. He waved to the fleet of feminine admirers sitting on the clubhouse patio.

'Ah, Felix, so glad you could make it. Hello, Celia, it's *very* nice to see you again.'

Celia glowed. 'You too, Greg. Good luck in the race.'

'I've no need to resort to fortune, my dear, but thank you anyway. I booked a pair of National Solos if that's OK with you, Felix. They should make things rather competitive in this blow.'

Felix glanced at the sea conditions and shrugged. 'Whatever, Greg, it's all the same to me.'

Celia wrapped herself up against the wind, took Felix's

binoculars and joined the wives while the dozen or so club members readied their dinghies.

Greg waved his hand. 'Four circuits, dog-leg at the outer marker buoy, last one back buys the G and Ts.'

***

Greg rubbed his hands together. 'Make mine a double, old man. Tough luck, I'd have come back and fished you out, but the Commodore was closer. Never mind, it's the taking part, not the winning, wouldn't you agree!'

Celia patted Felix's shoulder. 'Oh, darling, and you were doing *so* well too. Greg was never more than fifty yards ahead. It was such a pity that you capsized on the second lap. Let me get your dry things from the car.'

Felix changed into his spare set of clothing in a fury while Greg and Celia went into the clubhouse. He was never going to live this one down, at least while Greg-damned-Villiers was in town. It was proven moments later when Felix joined him at the bar and ordered the drinks.

'Bottoms up,' he cried, reminding everyone of Felix's ducking.

Felix bit his lip in rage but tried to act a good sport. 'Yes, cheers, well done on a good win.' He reached into his pockets to pay for the round, but they were empty. He checked again and realised his wallet was in the car along with his sodden clothing.

Greg noted his furious rummaging and pulled a wad of twenty-pound notes from his jacket. 'Finding yourself somewhat impecunious, old chap? Allow me to bail you out.'

Felix cringed inside. Somebody was going to have to do something about this bloody man.

***

Just as all bullies are not cowards, so are all braggarts not lying incompetents, as Felix discovered over the next few evenings. Greg proceeded to trounce him at chess, tennis, croquet and backgammon. His only redemption came when he narrowly avoided a thrashing at pool after Greg sank the black before his remaining ball. And to make his humiliation worse, these crushings were witnessed not only by his wife but by several influential members of the club. And Celia's applause for the winner always seemed rather sustained for his liking.

It wasn't cuckoldry. Yet. But, as Felix found out, he wasn't the only one to face such behaviour at the hands of Greg Villiers. The problem was not so much what the scoundrel did, for to the eye of a neutral onlooker, he did nothing except play the part of a jolly good egg. Greg the Egg. But this egg was up for poaching and the poaching was of other men's wives.

It was three weeks after his embarrassing ducking that Felix confided his troubles to Charles Sharp, a solicitor acquaintance. Charles was the recent owner of a twenty-two-foot sloop and had taken to weighing his personal anchor in a scruffy harbour-side bar each evening to ingratiate himself with those who sailed for a living. Smelling of *eau de cologne* instead of *eau de mer* did nothing to improve his sea-going credibility, but he was accepted under good-humoured sufferance and permitted to buy grizzled amphibians a tot of rum or a pint in exchange for some extremely fishy maritime tales. It was here that Felix occasionally met him for a drink or two after work. It wasn't long before the issue of Greg Villiers came up. Charles wrinkled his nose as if a foul odour had filled the bar.

'Villiers, appalling fellow, no decorum whatsoever. Should be drummed out of the club. Absolute bloody disgrace. Can't think how he ever got in to begin with. Bypassed all the temporary membership rules. Specially approved by the Commodore. Greased a palm or two, I'll wager. Social bloody virus.'

Charles spoke as if he were communicating in Morse code and sometimes made as much sense, but on this occasion, Felix thoroughly agreed with him. But there was more.

'Confounded chap had the gall to make improper suggestions to my wife, damn him. Soon put him right on that. Rascal tried to make me feel guilty. Claimed he'd been misunderstood. Almost had me believing him. Not the only one. Came on strong with Reggie's fiancée too. Complete bounder. Should be keelhauled.'

Felix wasn't surprised. Greg Villiers' moral rigging was as slack as a spinnaker in The Doldrums. The man was a menace, but without the Kryptonite to neutralise him, they were powerless. Until the subject of the Regatta Ball came up.

***

The Commodore, Rear Admiral St John-Weatherall, OBE, DSO, DSC and Bar (Retired) opened the festivities at noon and throughout the day, handicap races, the latest sailing craft designs, various naval displays and several charity performances kept the guests happy.

At seven o'clock, the ball proper started with music by the Royal Marines Band. Celia looked very attractive in a low-cut taffeta dress and Charles' fragrant wife, Henrietta, dazzled the men with her revealing Prada gown and inspired muted comments from the feline members of the club. And neither Felix nor Charles appeared to mind the undisguised overtures of a certain person toward their respective partners. Rather, they plied him with brandy, champagne and *bonhomie*. The world eventually took on a very rosy tint for Greg Villiers.

Just before eleven, as the band launched into a rendition of 'The Power of Love', Greg was interrupted in mid-innuendo by an insistent ringing in his jacket. After making his apologies to Celia, he slipped out of the marquee and answered his mobile phone. A voice as sultry as the summer night whispered sweetness and coarseness in his ear. He listened as intently as the blood pounding in his ears would allow. Then he looked at his watch, grinned and strode towards the clubhouse, snorting like a bronco after his inhalation of electronic catnip. He found the right door, went inside, carried out clothing adjustments, sniffed his armpits and eagerly awaited the arrival of Henrietta Sharp.

Felix was filling two champagne glasses when the dance was interrupted by a PA announcement.

'Urgent telephone call for the commodore in the conference room.'

Commodore St John-Weatherall apologised to his dancing partner and made his way to the club, wondering what could be important enough to disturb him. He was an unruffled veteran of two wars, three sinkings, several unfounded scandals and countless diplomatic crises in the service of the realm. But none of these prepared him for the sight of a naked figure in a testosterone-charged frenzy blinking in the sudden light as he pushed the conference room door open.

***

The *Mistress Quickly* slipped her moorings and throbbed her way into the dawn before the multitude of hangovers of the night before were even aware of their own existence. The sunrise was not even half the hue of the captain's face as it cast its rays over Fordingley. Felix had slept soundly. Celia not quite so. Charles and Henrietta, extremely well.

Greg Villiers not at all.

Reduce to Produce

Word has it that your past life goes through your mind in a flash when dying of unnatural causes. This could well have been the case in my meaningless husband's demise for I seem to have miswired the kitchen brass light switch (£4.50, special offer, one week only!) that I'd bought this morning at his demand. I wasn't actually present when this terminal incident occurred but when the potting shed was plunged into darkness, probably during a *Car SOS* commercial break, I knew he'd moved on to a far better place. Well, for me, anyway. I picked up a torch and trudged back to the bungalow.

I wasn't overcome with remorse, as I was six months after exchanging marriage vows. Nor did I telephone 999 as I'd so often felt like doing during our nineteen years of matrimonial misery. I took a screwdriver from my pocket, disassembled the switch, put the offending live wire where it rightly belonged, re-set the circuit breakers and poured myself a rigid gin instead. Then I sat down in his armchair, next to the coffee table littered with his collection of 1960s Dinky Morris Minors. It was the work of an instant to send them crashing to the floor with the back of my hand.

The gin tasted exceedingly good.

***

The following morning, which arrived much later than

expected due to half a bottle of Gordon's, brought with it the problem of refuse disposal: a 5' 4" eight-stone crotchety assortment of fluids and minerals called Malcolm.

A garden burial was clearly out of the question; that would be the first place the police would look, should anyone become inquisitive about his disappearance. Central heating precluded fiery destruction and the removal of his body on the pillion seat of a Triumph Bonneville (occasionally jumps out of third gear under hard acceleration, otherwise in reasonable condition for the year) was plainly Not Going To Work, especially on that sharp left-hander just past the Post Office. What was to be done? Malcolm lay on the bathroom floor where I'd dragged him from the kitchen. It was very inconvenient. I took a stroll in the garden to clear my head.

Summer was just around the corner and my roses were doing very well, thank you. I had high hopes for the county show trophy. Last year's third place had whetted my appetite; not only that, but I wished to wipe that look from Major Gribble's supercilious face. The Major *always* won first prize. The solution came to me as I filled a watering can from the greenhouse tap. Such simplicity and two clichéd birds killed with one stone.

I bought the items at half a dozen different shops in the nearby town of Beauchamp Pending to avoid suspicion. The Triumph only broke down twice so I was back in time for the afternoon. I began after another gin. First was the hacksaw and angle grinder, then the mincer; one of those handy gadgets that can be clamped to a bench with a wing nut, finishing with the four food processors. It was all over within three days, with the liquidisers working side by side to the strains of Heart, Spinal Tap, Stiff Little Fingers, Blood, Sweat & Tears and Elbow. By the end of that time Malcolm consisted of no more than powdered bone and several litres of semi-liquid fertiliser in coral-pink, according to the

Homebase colour chart.

I tested the concoction on a small corner of the garden. It worked even better than I dared hope for. I was initially concerned about his atomised crabby streak until I saw the weeds flourishing out of all proportion to my roses. These were summarily dealt with and despatched to flame.

As I was retired, time was now all mine at last. I spent long days in the greenhouse experimenting with what I came to call the Vertiliser on account of its rapid growth properties. The optimum mix, I discovered, was seven parts water to three parts Malcolm, with a dash of Thrip-Gone Xtra.

I poured a little of my ex-husband onto the flowerbeds every second day. Within six weeks they were an inferno of colour with roses and carnations the size of cauliflowers. Amazingly, they progressed from plain reds, whites, and pinks to a variety of blues, purples, greens, yellows, and even black. The more concentrated the Vertiliser, the more intense the colours. I wondered how Malcolm would have viewed himself.

My excitement grew as quickly as my flowers. The county show was less than a month away and rumours in The Beast and Biped snug bar suggested that Major Gribble was once again cultivating some prize-winning blooms. I caught him one evening over a gin and tonic. He said very little under the terms of the Geneva Convention except that for me the war was over. Not by a long chalk, I told myself, not with the secret weapon in *my* armoury. I was so confident of victory that both the local press and television were anonymously informed well in advance of the showdown.

The vicar, a regular judge at the show, paid an unexpected visit one afternoon, purportedly just passing. I invited him in for a drink. The lounge curtains remained closed, blocking his view of the back garden. He was leaking curiosity.

'I hear you expect to do well in the county show next month,' he said, once the usual flaccid pleasantries had been used up.

'Yes,' I said.

He sipped his sherry and tried another tack. 'What will you be entering – something new or sticking to last year's selection?'

'Yes,' I said again.

'Careless talk costs lives, eh?'

'Very true,' I said, despite being both propagandist and defender.

'And how is Mr Peebles? I haven't seen him at matins lately.'

'He's gone to ground for a while,' I told him.

The vicar eventually realised that he was going to leave with no more than he'd arrived with, other than 60 ml of Harvey's Bristol Cream. He stood up and buttoned his jacket. 'Well, I must dash, Mrs Peebles, see you at the show.'

'Yes,' I said. 'I'm looking forward to the result.'

***

The village was awash with excitement. It was Thursday and the county show was due to start on the following Saturday. I'd twice seen Major Gribble on one of his reconnaissance missions, rubbernecking as he strolled past my bungalow. Ten feet of shade netting camouflaged my biological weapons; my secret was safe, short of drone or Hubble Telescope surveillance. I checked my stock. Malcolm (concentrated) was now down to little more than two litres; Malcolm (diluted), was spreading through my flower beds in his coat of many colours like some massive, finely delineated bruise. He now manifested himself in orange, turquoise, gold and brown, as well as his previous hues. His buds were the size of dinner plates and the roses, carnations, tulips, begonias and the like, spanned no less than satellite dishes with their petals unfurled. And the odd thing is, they seemed to know exactly when their next meal was coming. Only seconds after stepping from the greenhouse with my Vertiliser-filled watering can, the multicultural ranks would pivot their heads in my direction and nod expectantly. Some were more aggressively pleased and bobbed their heads so alarmingly that I feared for their structural integrity.

I thought about the show. Even though I was confident of victory, there was the problem of transportation. My Triumph was clearly out of the question; there was barely space for a sack of potatoes on the pillion seat, never mind the four examples that I intended to display. A bottle of Navy Neaters rum acquired the use of Shadrack, the retired milkman, and his soft-top electric float. It would serve admirably as a Triffid taxi. It was booked for Saturday morning, eight o'clock sharp.

I went over my specimens like a glutton in a cake shop; I simply couldn't decide which ones to pick. In the end, they decided for me. They stretched their petals as if yawning and turned in my direction: a green carnation merging into vivid gold, a purple rose edged in lilac, another in royal blue and, my *piece de resistance*, a cherry-red begonia gently fading to ultra-feminine pink. I couldn't have made a better conscious choice.

***

Even with Shadrack's help the relocation of my Vertilised plants was going to be something of a mission. They each weighed sixteen kilos and stood almost two metres tall once I'd transferred them into clay pots. Shadrack arrived at seven minutes past nine on the dot, already stupefied by an early issue of naval rum. He squinted at my show entries and grabbed a nearby rose stem for support.

'Wot's them then, lovely?' he slurred and yelped as a prickle the size of a toothpick pierced his palm.

'Those,' I informed him, 'are the agents of Major Gribble's downfall.'

'Never min' Major Gribble's Asians,' he wailed as his heavily-influenced blood dripped onto the soil, 'what about my hand?'

The ground twitched for a moment like an immature earthquake. Shadrack looked down. A brown root as thick as my thumb burst from the soil and coiled itself around his foot, followed by a dozen more. His expression was an interesting mixture of horror and disbelief as the roots spiralled up to his waist and pulled him to the ground. My two show roses leaned over in the manner of gymnasts touching their toes and their previously defensive prickles now went about sucking blood and nutrients from his squirming body. Overall, he accepted the business of being murdered rather quietly. Scarcely a peep passed his lips. Perhaps the tendril twisting around his neck supplied some form of mute decorum to his passing. Shouting and screaming is so very undignified; one should never be remembered for such.

Within two minutes of being throttled, poor Shadrack had been desiccated by the quivering plants, just as his milk had once disappeared into my Weetabix. He was now pushing up daisies, both literally and figuratively. Well, that virtually solved the problem of disposal. I applied my angle grinder to the papery Welshman and bottled his slivers for future use. A passing Aid for Africa collector gratefully accepted his green Barbour jacket, Fair Isle pullover and rubber boots for some unsuspecting tribe in the Ituri Rainforest.

I checked my entries once more. The roses were glowing with vitality after their meal. I poured myself a pre-celebratory gin and telephoned the major.

'Yes, Peebles woman, what is it?' he barked.

'Just calling to give you a chance to withdraw from the flower show, Major.'

'*Withdraw?* What on earth are you blathering about?'

'Well, I'm making this offer as a friend. I would hate to see you and your feeble flowers humiliated in public, especially as Bulsetshire Television and *Flower Arranger Monthly* are going to be in attendance.'

'Humiliated! What bloody nonsense,' he thundered, 'it's you who should be withdrawing. What's the basis for this absurd assumption of yours?'

'Why don't you drop by and have a look, Major? It may save you a lot of embarrassment and the trouble of wasting your time and fuel this afternoon.'

'Preposterous, absolutely bloody preposterous. I'll be over within the hour to reduce you to the ranks of non-starters.'

***

I don't know which expression I liked best: the one of utter disbelief as he realised he could never win the competition or the one of terror as a seven-foot-tall rose bush took him in its spiky arms and proceeded to transform him into a shrivelled husk. He'd been through hell in his service for King, Queen and Country, as he'd ranted to the dismayed occupants of The Beast and Biped on a hundred occasions, usually concluding by demanding the return of National Service, flogging, hanging, the Lewis gun and Camp coffee. Well, now he'd been through the mincer too.

I bottled his flimsy remains and stored them next to Shadrack. Then I lifted my plants onto the milk float, lashed the pots down with rope and set off for the county show at twelve miles an hour.

The exhibition tent was an ocean of colour when I arrived, but there was little of any consequence on display compared to my blooms. A platoon of amazed army cadets helped me unload the float and set up my entry. As I made my way to the beer tent, I could hear their officer shouting for some missing recruit.

I, or should I say *Malcolm* and my flowers, won first and second awards that afternoon. A woman from Lesser Brockerly was awarded third rosette for her insignificant selection of dahlias and geraniums, obviously to avoid allegations of favouritism. Oddly, no one could find her when the prizes were awarded.

Well, the outcome of this story is in some part predictable. The baffled Bulsetshire police force is holding four reported disappearances on file and worried villagers no longer stray far without an escort or pitchfork, although attendance at The Beast and Biped has doubled since the tiresome Major Gribble became one of the statistics.

As for me … I've been on Death Row since the supply of Vertiliser, visitors, small garden animals, birds and inquisitive cats dried up. I was fortunate to escape with no more than a light savaging after I caught my blooms indulging in cannibalistic practices and now my telephone line is dead and all escape routes are closely guarded by a bloodthirsty squad of garish super-plant sentries. I'm down to three Lapsang Souchong teabags, a jar of Marmite and half a pack of fish fingers. One way or another it looks as if Malcolm and I will be reunited before too long.

No flowers by request.

Still Life

I looked out of the window. Wafers of cracked ice floated on the nearby boating lake like some oversized transparent jigsaw puzzle and displaced ducks crouched on the glistening grass with their feathers puffed in defence against the crispness. I was glad to be inside. I went back to tidying my studio. Just as I'd finished throwing away empty tubes of paint and congealed bottles of linseed oil there was a rap on the door. I wiped my hands and opened it.

'Good day to you, sir,' was the brusque greeting.

I looked at my visitor. He was ruddy-faced, as slim as he was short and looked to be in his twenties. He was curiously dressed in a shapeless brown suit with high lapels, a flat cap, white shirt, loosely-knotted neckerchief in place of a collar and heavy black boots. And despite the weather he wasn't wearing an overcoat or gloves.

'And a good day to you,' I said. 'How can I help?'

'You're an artist, I believe,' he said. 'Would you be interested in taking on a commission?'

'Well, I'm not too busy at the moment,' I replied, which was more than I cared to admit to myself. 'What would you like me to paint?'

'Me. The face only. It *must* be exact.' His accent and flattened vowels suggested Lincolnshire.

'Naturally,' I said. I wasn't in the habit of painting

matchstick people or colouring blue skies green. That's probably why I had to resort to the occasional overdraft at the bank.

'And the price?'

'Well, that depends upon the size, the medium and how many sittings are required. My last double-sized portrait of a face required four sittings, including the sketch.'

'Yes, quite,' he said. 'But how much?'

'Well, if I use oils, we're probably talking in the region of four hundred pounds—'

'Four hundred pounds. Very well, when can you begin?'

My studio was still a shambles. 'This afternoon,' I replied. 'Would two o'clock be convenient or perhaps tomorrow morning at around nine?'

'Not now? Well, two o' clock would be tolerable. I dare say I can stand waiting a little longer.'

A little longer? I couldn't see what difference five hours was going to make to anyone wanting their portrait painted. Photographic studios and railway station Quick Snap booths are there for the impatient. 'Two o'clock it is. I'll see you later, then. And what name is it?'

'My name? Hanley.' With that, he departed.

I watched him as he strode down the icy path to the pavement. A strange man. Not the sort of client I was used to, but his custom would pay the heating bill so I couldn't complain.

Hanley, I wrote on the back of a new canvas.

***

Hanley was punctual to the second. He was dressed as before, apparently indifferent to the weather.

'Ah, Mr Hanley, come in and warm yourself by the fire before we begin. Can I get you a coffee or a brandy, perhaps?'

He took his cap off and looked around the room before answering. 'Thank you, no. I'm not bothered by the cold.'

I picked up a pencil. 'Very well, then let's get you down on canvas.' Thus began my strangest-ever commission. Perhaps any artist's commission.

I sat him down on a high stool with a back and armrests. 'Make yourself comfortable,' I told him. 'I'll start when you're ready.'

'I *am* ready,' he said.

I can't say as I cared much for his manner. Still, his attitude would no doubt come out in the portrait. I adjusted my easel and studied him before I put pencil to canvas. His sandy hair was unparted and severely cut below temple-level. Despite his small build, he gave the impression of wiry strength and his features lent themselves well to canvas despite a slightly receding chin. I would have to wait for the painting stage before I could carry off his eyes. They were slate grey and as hard as the quartz the rock contained. There was a flash of blue in them that only the palette could capture. I began to draw.

Sometimes silence weighs heavily when I'm working and I like to break a session up into two parts. Not only that, I was wondering about his strange choice of clothing.

'What do you do for a living, Mr Hanley?'

'What do I do? Nothing at the present.'

I added some shading under his high cheekbones. *Too much*. I rubbed a little away, licked my finger and smudged the cross-hatching until it was just so.

'So what *was* your trade, if you don't mind me asking? I'd put you down as a farmer or maybe a builder.' He had a face that had seen more sun and wind than an office provided.

'Well, if that's what you see, I'm not very optimistic as to how the painting's going to turn out.'

'Sorry,' I said, 'it's just that I find it easier to paint if I can build up a mental picture of each of my clients as well as a physical one.'

'I was a deckhand on a coaster,' he said gruffly.

He was obviously unwilling to say anything more so I got back to the business in hand.

'That's it,' I said half an hour later. 'If you'd like to come back next week, let's say Tuesday afternoon, I can start to flesh you out.'

And then, for the first time, he smiled. There was no humour in it whatsoever.

***

He came once a week for the next three weeks and sat unblinkingly for an hour as I gradually transformed him into the second dimension. He remained as tight-lipped as when I had first met him. A right miserable bugger to be truthful.

'There we go,' I told him at the end of the last session. 'Come back next week. It'll be finished and ready for collection. What sort of frame do you have in mind?'

'No frame,' he said in his usual manner.

What on earth was the point of having a portrait painted if you weren't going to display it? But the client is always right even if he's wrong so I let the matter ride. 'Very well, I'll just keep it tacked to the mounting frame, shall I?'

'Just do as you see fit. How much will I be owing you?'

'Four hundred, as we agreed.'

'All right,' he said. 'We'll conclude the matter next week.' He picked up his cap and walked to the door.

I let him out into the bleary afternoon. Flakes of snow the size of guitar plectrums thickened the white carpet that had been laid overnight. He was gone without another word.

***

The painting was finished on Sunday night and I immodestly

patted myself on the back. It really was an excellent likeness; I'd captured Hanley's features and accompanying surly moods from the outset.

The knocker announced his arrival at two o'clock on the following Tuesday. 'Have you finished?' he demanded.

'A good day to you, Mr Hanley. Yes, the portrait *is* finished and unframed as you wished.'

'Right, let's have a look at it, then.'

He crossed the studio floor ahead of me. The canvas was on the easel, covered by a sheet.

'Mr Hanley – meet yourself!' I announced, pulled off the cover and stood there expectantly. The result was disappointing, for me at least. His face remained as impassive as that on the canvas.

'Aye, he said eventually, 'it's a good likeness, it'll do.'

'I'm glad you're satisfied,' I told him, 'I do like an appreciative client.'

'I have a request,' he said. 'I want you to hold the painting here for a while. Here's your fee.' He took a thick brown envelope from his jacket pocket and handed it to me. 'I'm sure you'll be able to deal with the visitors.'

'Visitors? What visitors?'

'There'll be some people interested in the portrait, I assure you. And now I must be on my way. I have something to attend to.'

He strode out of the studio without another word. I followed him but he'd disappeared. He'd been gone for no more than five seconds and now there was no sign of him. It was impossible. I opened the door and looked around. The settled snow on the path was undisturbed; the only prints were the light arrow marks of small birds in search of food. Hanley couldn't have flown away as they did.

As I stood there puzzling, I remembered the envelope in my hand. It seemed rather bulky, but that's what it contained: four hundred pounds in five-pound notes. And not the blue ones of Queen Elizabeth the Second; these were of the type that had gone out of circulation long before I was born. I couldn't believe it.

Well, he wasn't going to get the portrait until he'd paid me properly in a currency acceptable to the NatWest bank. But what if he *never* came back? I would be saddled with an unsellable picture.

He *would* be back, I assured myself eventually, why go to that effort otherwise? But what of these visitors?

***

I was wrong. He never returned and what's more, several of the useless notes were ruined; stiff and stained a reddish brown. It looked very much like dried blood.

'Little Heath Police Station, Sergeant Barton speaking.'

'Oh, good morning. This is Gavin Allen from Lakeview Crescent. Look, I've just been paid for a painting that I did with old five-pound notes, the big ones about the size of a paperback cover and what's more, some of them look like they've got blood on them.'

'Old five-pound notes with blood on them?'

'Yes, that's right. This chap called Hanley wanted his portrait painting so I did it, charged him four hundred pounds and he left before I could check it.'

'Well, sir,' he said slowly, 'didn't you think it a little unwise to let him take the picture without checking the money first? I very much doubt you'll be able to change it at the bank, especially with blood on it. Are you sure it's blood?'

I could imagine the look on his face as he listened to my implausible tale. 'But he didn't take the picture with him, that's why I didn't open the envelope at the time and anyway, he said that some other people might be coming to look at it. He was dressed in old-fashioned clothes.' I was beginning to sound ridiculous. How could the sergeant take me seriously when I was jabbering away like this? And then I said, stupidly: 'There weren't any footprints in the snow when he left, either.'

The sergeant, to his credit, was patient. He was obviously talking to someone who was deranged.

'All right, Mr Allen, someone will be around later. Lakeview Crescent, you said?'

'That's right, Gavin Allen Portraits, last on the right.'

***

A policeman turned up an hour later. It was Sergeant Barton, the man who'd taken my garbled telephone call. I sat him down in the kitchen and made us some tea.

He took the mug, leaned back and grinned. 'So, where's the bloody money?'

His humour broke the ice of my mood in spite of being rooked by Hanley. Even though he hadn't got the painting, he'd still taken many hours of my time and creativity. I brought Sergeant Barton the evidence.

He lifted one of the notes out of the envelope and examined it. 'They certainly go back some time. I'd say this type hasn't been in circulation for at least sixty or seventy years.' He removed a few more by their corners. His face darkened as he came to the first of the stained notes. He put it down on the table and turned it over with his pen.

'Well, it certainly looks like blood. I'll have to take this further. Who did you say this man was?'

'Hanley,' I said. I showed him into my studio and lifted the dust sheet from the canvas. 'This is him. He was always dressed in the same sort of clothes as they used to wear before the war.'

He looked at Hanley closely and chuckled. 'Excellent. That saves us the bother of putting an e-fit together. I'm sure it won't take long to find someone who recognises this character from your painting once we release a photo for the press. Meanwhile, I'll get these notes off to forensics for analysis and see what they come up with.' He glanced at his watch. 'Right, I'll take a statement about this Hanley chap and we'll get the ball rolling.'

So that's what I did, and I felt a complete fool as I read back over it. But it was exactly how it happened.

***

Sergeant Barton returned the following morning with a photographer and he had a few snippets for me. There were three unsolved murders still on the county's books: two were relatively recent, going back to 1983 and 1991 and the third one was a complete mystery. The skeleton of a man had been unearthed in 1995 by a farmer reclaiming a few acres of marshland on the far side of what was now the nearby boating lake. This was the first I'd heard of it; I'd only been living in the area for two years. The skull had been smashed by a heavy object and the fingers of both hands broken. And although little remained of the man, the forensics team had managed to approximate the time of his death, working on the indistinct serial numbers of five banknotes found in a disintegrating wallet. The earliest, according to the Bank of England, had been issued in 1938 and the latest in 1944. So many people, both civilian and military, had disappeared without trace during the war that it proved impossible to identify the man, even through dental records. But murder it had been, for sure. After police investigations came to a dead end, so to speak, the man's remains were buried without a headstone in the west side of the town's churchyard.

The odd thing, Sergeant Barton told me, was that the serial numbers of the notes found in the wallet were part of the batch Hanley had given me.

***

Does Anybody Recognise This Man? read the local newspaper headlines. *Police Puzzle Over Mystery Man From the Past,* trumpeted one, *Riddle Of Local Artist's Curious Portrait and Wartime Cash*, blazed another. Even the local television station sent someone to interview me, which at least gave me some free advertising, but I'd rather that Hanley had taken his commission elsewhere.

***

Well, somebody recognised him; a sprightly old man whom I guessed to be approaching his nineties. He came with a young man who'd driven him down from Spalding after phoning me. The old man blinked furiously behind his glasses when I uncovered the portrait.

'Aye, that's him, that's our Ted,' he wheezed.

'Who's Ted?' I asked. He cocked his ear towards me. I asked him again. He looked at me through rheumy grey-blue eyes.

'My elder brother. Walked on the wrong side of the tracks, did Ted. Broke my mother's heart, God rest her soul. He got mixed up with a bad crowd when he joined the Merchant Navy, the bugger had more than a few run-ins with the bobbies, I can tell you.'

The young man looked at him with interest; he was obviously unaware of the family history.

'Aye, turned out a bad 'un, did our Ted. He jumped ship in 1945 and we never saw him again after that.' He pointed his walking stick at the portrait. 'So where did you get that, young man?'

'I didn't get it anywhere, he sat for me.'

He poked the stick into my ribs. 'Now see here,' he said loudly, 'if Ted were still alive today, he'd be ninety-five, nothing like your picture here and *you're* certainly not old enough to have painted him when he was that age.'

There seemed little point in arguing with him in this mood. 'So what happened to your brother?' I asked when he'd finished prodding me.

He fiddled with his hearing aid and grimaced. I repeated the question.

'All right, all right, I'm not bloody deaf. He got involved in a bank robbery according to local rumour and fell out with the gang over the money. That's the last we ever heard of him.'

The young man stepped closer to the portrait. 'So *that's* my great-uncle!'

I looked at him and his crusty elder; there did seem to be a resemblance between them and the painting. The old man looked to have been short as well, but it's difficult to tell with people of that age.

The old man rapped his stick on the floor. 'Come on, let's be going and leave Ted in peace. There's lamb for tea and bingo tonight.'

'Are you going to tell the police about this?' I said to the young man as I saw them out to their car. 'They're looking for a name to go with the body in the graveyard.'

He closed the passenger door and walked around to the front of the car. The old man was mumbling and tugging at his seat belt. 'It's only right,' he replied. 'I'll do it when great-uncle Charlie's back in the nursing home. It must be a good painting of this Ted if the old duffer recognised him because he doesn't know who I am sometimes. I don't understand all this stuff about sittings though.'

'Nor do I,' I said.'

***

A couple of weeks later the body in the graveyard was exhumed and DNA samples taken from the young man compared favourably with those in the coffin. Nobody except for the participants of those events over 70 years ago – if there are any still alive – will ever know what happened to Ted Hanley. My strange client never returned. But now, thanks to my painting, he's got a headstone and is no longer a nameless man lying in an unmarked grave. And the portrait? I gave it to the young man. The majority of the obsolete four hundred pounds was eventually returned to me; the bloodstained notes were kept as police evidence in the case of Edward (Ted) Hanley, unlawfully killed, decided the coroner, by a person or persons unknown.

They fetched almost eight thousand pounds at an auction. But clients like that I can do without. Even at that profit margin.

Stolen Time

Mswati had known little but poverty for most of his twenty-seven years, much like everyone else in the village. Despite that, he was rich in ideas. He had many schemes, all guaranteed to make him a wealthy man, he claimed. But … they required capital.

There'd been talk of a new school and repair garage in the village downstream. He'd make the bricks and sell them for less than the suppliers in the city. All he needed was nine hundred kwena for a moulding machine. And then there was the motorised fibreglass dinghy. He'd ferry travellers across the fifty-metre-wide river for half the price of the Lebanese trader who lived in a splendid house paid for by his massive profits. This could be his for only K2,400. All he required was a loan, repayable over two years. He'd be prosperous by then. For sure. If only he could scrape together K4,500, he knew of a Volkswagen Kombi that would make an ideal taxi for transporting the villagers to the city. He'd get his money back in six months, without fail.

Mswati's grand plans came to nothing. He couldn't even raise enough money to buy a coat and gumboots for the approaching rainy season, let alone anything else. The Lebanese trader flatly refused to give him a loan after he was foolish enough to mention the motorised dinghy and it was unlikely that the collective wealth of the villagers exceeded two or three thousand kwena so there'd be no loans from that quarter either. His only assets were a few goats, chickens and a sorghum patch, none of which were acceptable security to the men in the city banks with their smart blue suits and flywhisks.

Mswati brooded on this as he strolled home from the cattle post where he'd spent the afternoon drinking palm wine with a friend. As the sky darkened, so did his mood. Life was not good enough. Not good enough at all.

***

Dikunye's cousin, a wealthy importer of Russian trucks and agricultural machinery, had recently died. Many years previously Dikunye had done him a considerable favour and he'd not forgotten it in his will. And now Dikunye was rich to the tune of K20,000.

He travelled to the city for only the third time in his life and collected his inheritance from the lawyer. His eyes grew wider and wider as the bank notes were counted out. The first purchase he made from the legacy was a blue Raleigh bicycle with chrome mudguards and a very pleasing bell. Along with this he bought a saddlebag and a pair of panniers in anticipation of necessities and luxuries.

He became uncomfortable with the unaccustomed noise and bustle of the city after two days and decided to leave for his mud and reed hut, a journey of 45 kilometres. The tarred – but ill-maintained – road would take him most of the way to his village and then a bush track would see him safely home. Dikunye had no understanding of banks and, in any case, there were none within easy travelling distance of his village, so the balance of his windfall was wrapped in a leopard-skin pouch and hidden in one of the panniers. He waved goodbye to his relatives and wobbled away in third gear, muttering about the complicated levers on his handlebars. By the afternoon of the second day he had less than ten kilometres to go.

Was he becoming more tired or was the bicycle holding him back? He dismounted and examined it. A camel thorn protruded from the rear tyre. The rectification of this disaster was beyond him, he had no idea of even how to remove the wheel, much less repair the puncture. So, with darkness approaching, he switched on the battery-powered handlebar lamp and pushed his useless asset along the pitted road.

Meanwhile, the half-drunk Mswati stumbled along the same road and blinked as he saw a bright eye glaring at him in the distance. He sat down and waited to see what this could be. The figure of an old man pushing a heavily-laden bicycle loomed up, silhouetted against the pale blue, pink-streaked sky.

Mswati stood up. 'Greetings, baba,' he said. 'How do you travel?'

Dikunye returned the salutation. 'Greetings, young one. I travelled well and in hope but my bicycle has become lame and delays my way to Lebuka.'

'I am sorry to hear of your misfortune,' said Mswati. 'What are its troubles?'

The old man explained about the tyre. Mswati looked at it and reassured him. 'It is but a small problem, baba. Where is your repair kit?'

'Repair kit? What is that? Forgive me, I know nothing of these matters.'

'It is a box some two fingers in length that contains the tools and sticking plasters for punctures.'

Dikunye thought for a moment. Yes, now he remembered being given such a box by the bicycle salesman. It was blue and black.

Mswati glanced at the bulging saddlebag and panniers. 'Then let us find it and make your machine well.'

The old man rested his bicycle against a termite mound and began to unpack his belongings as Mswati held the lamp. Clothing, tinned food, cooking utensils, hair-restorer, fountain pens, picture books, a finger piano, a corkscrew, a transistor radio and an inflatable pillow littered the sand. Dikunye squinted at the brightness of the lamp.

'I do not see the box.'

'Then let *me* be your eyes,' offered Mswati. His own were suddenly hungry, like those of a hyena. He handed over the lamp, dropped to his knees and rifled through the old man's possessions but saw nothing resembling the puncture repair outfit.

He began to refill the panniers. Then a bulging yellow and black pouch dropped from a mess tin. He picked it up. 'Ah, what is *this?'*

'It is nothing,' declared the old man hotly. 'Let me be on my way.'

Mswati's interest increased ten-fold. He held the pouch out of reach of the old man and unravelled its lace with one finger. The old man was surprisingly agile for one of over fifty summers and tried to snatch his purse back. Mswati grabbed the lamp from his hand and darted to the other side of the termite mound. His heartbeat doubled as he shone the light into the open pouch. There, secured with elastic bands, were bundles of banknotes – at *least* fifteen thousand kwena! He had never in his life known anyone to have so much money.

The old man scrabbled around the mound and lunged for the pouch, all the time hurling abuse at his false Samaritan. A possessive rage filled Mswati's previously good-natured heart. He pushed him away and gripped the pouch as if it were a lifeline. The old man rushed at him again, bursting with wild strength from this injustice.

'You reeking spawn of a pox-ridden baboon, I swear to the gods that you shall never rest if you steal what is mine.'

Mswati threw him aside as the lust for money coursed through his body like snake venom. The old man staggered and fell backwards. There was a *crack* like the snapping of a dead branch and then silence. Mswati stepped away from the mound and shone the lamp onto the ground. The bicycle had fallen over and the old man lay on his back. His neck was bent over the crossbar at a crooked angle and his eyes stared unblinkingly at Mswati. A thrill of dread ran through him as he knelt down beside him and shook his arm. There was no response. His eyes did not move, nor his lips. And neither did his chest.

Mswati dropped the pouch, covered his face with his hands and wept bitterly. He hadn't meant to kill the old one, nor had he intended to steal the money – the sight and feel of it in his hands had summoned a demon that in turn had seized his mind. As he cried, he cursed the events that had brought him to this; the courts would surely send him to jail forever. What was he to do – oh, what was he to do? And then the gulping call of a hippopotamus cleared his brain. *The river.*

Five minutes later the corpse of the old man was carried away in the fast-flowing waters of the Malakutse. Mswati ignored the flat tyre, rammed the old man's scattered belongings back into the saddlebag and side panniers and furiously cycled into the darkness towards the city.

***

Mswati now lived like a king in a land of paupers. He bought the smartest clothes, ate in the classiest restaurants and drank in the most fashionable nightclubs, surrounded by young and shapely admirers. He sold the bicycle and travelled everywhere by taxi. He slept in a proper bed for the first time. And then he started to have terrible nightmares.

He dreamed that no matter where he went: in the streets, in the restaurants, in the nightclubs and in his apartment, he was being followed. The dead man kept pace with him like a playful dog, always a steady three steps behind. His eyes gleamed like the lamp of his bicycle. Mswati began to wake up screaming in sweat-soaked sheets.

After a month in the city he became a walking ghost himself. His once handsome face was now lined and his eyes and cheeks were as hollow as that of a corpse. Waiters looked on in amusement or disgust when he found himself unable to hold his fork steady. His expensive clothing became spattered with food and his drinks rippled as if something had fallen into them. The good-time girls began to find new tables. And all the time he looked fearfully over his shoulder.

He awoke one morning alongside a girl he'd escorted from a bar. The old man stared at him accusingly over her shoulder. He lashed out with his fist and caught the sleeping girl in the eye. He was shunned by every woman in every nightclub after that. He hurled a dinner plate and carafe at the old man in his favourite restaurant and was violently ejected after they struck the owner's wife. The dead man dogged him relentlessly. The ill-gotten money slowly disappeared as he moved from quarter to quarter, trying to escape from his tormentor. And finally he realised he had nowhere to hide.

He sought out the services of a witch doctor on the outskirts of the city. She lit a stick of herbs and listened as he explained about his haunting, although he was careful to change some details of the old man's death. When he'd finished, she asked him for a personal belonging of the dead man. He passed over the leopardskin pouch and she instructed him to return the following morning.

The old man launched a violent assault on Mswati's senses once he boarded the city bus, as if anticipating his banishment. Everywhere he went that evening the ghost was by his side, pushing, pulling, pinching and screaming. Sleep became a hunted beast that outran him.

It was a grey, trembling, red-eyed Mswati who returned for his appointment. He squatted and watched anxiously as the witch doctor murmured incantations and threw her divination bones. Once, twice, three times, the bones rolled across the mat. She looked at them intently and rolled her thumbs against each other but said nothing. Mswati swallowed and felt his heart thudding against his ribs like a tribal drum. The air in the hut grew thick with heat and tension. After a while the witch doctor began to gather up her pieces.

This was too much for Mswati. 'Well?' he demanded, although his voice was little more than a croak.

'The bones have spoken,' she said. 'If you desire, I can surely dispel the spirit that plagues your existence. However, the price will be high.'

Mswati almost cried with relief. He reached for his wallet. 'How much, how much?'

She closed the bone box's lid and held her hand out.

'Eighteen thousand, seven hundred and ninety-five kwena, *you reeking spawn of a pox-ridden baboon.'*

Rising Son

Mitchell was very tired. He was a sick man and could no longer guide, which had been a passion of his as well as an income. His guns were greased and locked away in the cabinet at the back of his bungalow and his equipment gradually gathered a tropical patina of mould and verdigris where it hung in the wardrobe beside his bed. He still wore his slouch hat and the heavy calf-length boots that even now bore the fang marks of the cobra that had nearly ended his life on the hills of the Damodar Valley. He'd been quicker in those days. Not full of morphine.

And then his *mali* had rapped on the verandah door one hot morning in September, a morning that promised to fuel itself on his energy like some invisible parasite and suck the sweat from him until the sun took its persecution elsewhere. Then the crushing humidity of the night would move in to take its place. India was like that.

'Mitchell *sahib*!' His garden boy was perhaps forty years old. Or perhaps fifty. No one knew, least of all him. He leaned his bicycle against the rail. '*Sahib*, a great catastrophe has occurred.'

'What is it, Vish?'

He wrung his hands and his feet danced on the wooden floor. 'Oh, sir, oh, sir – it is *Karan*. He is returned.'

Karan! A shadow passed over Mitchell. 'He's back to his tricks?'

***

Father Colquhoun, the founder of the orphanage, led Mitchell along the rows of paint-chipped and sagging cots. The children, some little more than infants, lay listlessly in the oppressive heat. Their eyes followed him as he walked between the beds, handing out small gifts of toffee and barley sugar. Some took the strange presents without a word. Others smiled and displayed their white teeth like the keys of the unused woodworm-stricken piano that stood at the end of the shabby infirmary with its paint peeling like some awful skin disease. He stopped at a bed beside one of the room's four windows. A yellow rind of tape held the cracked pane together. Mitchell looked at the boy. He was thin, though no more than most of the other orphaned or abandoned children. His black hair was lank on the sweat-stained pillow, but his eyes were bright, not with fever but with intelligence. Mitchell offered him a twist of barley sugar. He accepted it with a smile that seemed to fill his face.

'Who's this mischievous little devil?'

'This is Rajiv. He's just getting over the mumps; it went through the orphanage like wildfire.' Father Colquhoun pinched the boy's nose playfully. He grinned in delight.

'Good morning, Rajiv. I'm pleased to make your acquaintance. How old are you?' Mitchell spoke in Hindi.

'I am pleased to make your acquaintance also, sir. I am no less than eleven years old.'

'Eleven years old! Well, I suppose you can't do too much damage. How would you like to be a guest in my home, Rajiv?'

'Sir, I would like that very much. Is it permitted by the father?'

'Yes, it's permitted by the father,' said Father Colquhoun.

'Then I am most happy to come with you, sir. When must

I return?'

Mitchell looked at the priest and then back to the boy. 'It's not necessary for you to return. You may remain in my house for as long as you wish.'

Father Colquhoun smiled. Rajiv smiled. Mitchell smiled. But of the three, Mitchell smiled most of all.

***

Rajiv was rummaging through the steamer trunk of reference books that Colquhoun had sent from the orphanage library. He chose an atlas, stretched out on the floor and flicked through the pages.

'Father,' he said, for Mitchell was now his father, 'is it true that a voyage to England takes many weeks?'

Mitchell looked over Rajiv's shoulder. The atlas was open at the map of Europe. He knelt beside him and turned the pages until the world was flat and complete. Then he put his finger on the tip of India and traced it across the Arabian and Red Seas, through the Suez Canal and the Mediterranean Sea and north to Britain. 'That's right. This route would take about three or four weeks by steamer. The view can get a little boring at times.'

Rajiv measured the length of Britain between his thumb and forefinger and compared it to the map's pink-shaded areas. 'Your country would fit into India many times over! How is it possible that such a small island can have so large an empire?'

'Britain's always been a sea-faring nation; it's said that no man in England is further than eighty miles from salt water. It's in their blood to seek new places. Many of the world's greatest explorers were English: Walter Raleigh, Francis Drake, Captain Cook, Charles Darwin, Hudson, Frobisher—'

'David Livingstone?'

Mitchell laughed. 'He wouldn't thank you for saying that! Livingstone was from Scotland. We have Wales, Ireland and The Channel Islands, too.' He saw the puzzlement on Rajiv's face and ruffled his hair. 'Don't worry, young man, I'll teach you everything I know and what I don't know you'll find in the trunk.'

***

'He's a fine young man,' said Father Colquhoun as he thumbed through the photograph album. He sipped his whisky and dabbed the sweat from his forehead. His crop of hair was whitened by the passing of four years as well as the ferocious Indian sun. It had also taken its toll on his bluff Irish face; deep wrinkles mapped his skin like the mountain passes to the north.

Mitchell leaned back in his chair. A sudden mid-afternoon breeze signalled the approaching monsoon; the sliced-cane blinds were already trembling and grating against each other. Thunder rumbled in the distant hills. 'He's coming along nicely. I'll miss him.'

'When does he leave?'

'In late October. I booked his passage on the *Kolar Star* last week.'

'Just in time for winter.'

Mitchell laughed. 'Yes, it should be interesting for him. He's looking forward to seeing snow. He'll be disappointed if they don't get any. You know, sometimes I miss the old country, this damned heat wears you down.'

'Stonebridge College, isn't it?'

'Yes, nearly two hundred pounds a year, but he's worth every penny. He'll come back knowing more than me. He's a bright lad.'

Fat drops of rain spattered the verandah steps.

'Tell me, Gerald, why did you choose Rajiv from the

others?'

Very few were privileged to use Mitchell's first name. Colquhoun had known Mitchell from the army: a cynical first lieutenant who attended funerals but never masses or the confessional box.

'I did a terrible thing in Burma. I needed to ease my conscience.'

'Do you want to talk about it?'

His mind drifted back to yet another day in the sapping mosquito-ridden swamp. Two herons burst from the treetops thirty or so yards to their left, shrieking and indignant. Something or someone had disturbed them. Mitchell gave his platoon the arm signal to take cover, unslung his machine gun and edged into the forest as the men waded through the knee-deep water and ducked behind the clumps of semi-submerged mangroves. He crept through the architecture of sprawling roots, trees and shrubs towards where he estimated the birds had been disturbed. The dank air was filled with the peculiar cracking and popping sounds of the mangrove forest and a haze of mosquitoes followed him despite the daylight. He stiffened as he saw a Japanese soldier standing in the dense foliage ten yards away holding a rifle in one hand and loosening his helmet strap with the other. He seemed to be alone. Mitchell crouched behind a knot of roots and waited to be sure. He didn't want to engage in a firefight until he knew the odds were in his favour. The Jap's tunic was unfastened and his puttees and trousers were wet. He'd probably seen or heard the Indian Brigade troops moving through swamp and alarmed the birds when he took cover in the forest. Perhaps he'd been cut off from his unit. Perhaps he was the only survivor of a scrap.

'Mister Mitchell, sir. Mister Mitchell?'

The Japanese soldier wheeled around and dropped to the ground at the sound of Havildar Kumar's shout. Mitchell bit his lip. His sergeant should damned-well have waited in silence until he returned. Then he heard the frantic rattling of a rifle bolt in its breech and equally-frantic cursing. He didn't understand Japanese but he could imagine the man as he either tried to unjam the weapon or chamber a dirty round from a new magazine.

The soldier stood up, fumbled with his rifle for a few seconds and darted towards the swamp, away from the almost impenetrable greenery. So he was alone, after all. Mitchell followed him. He'd hunted deer, boars, bears, tigers and leopards before, but never one of his own kind. He felt a thrill, a strange tingling he'd never known before. The unsuspecting soldier was kneeling beside a mangrove tree at the water's edge, still trying to clear the rifle. *You fool,* thought Mitchell. *It would have made more sense to stay where you were ... even though the outcome is going to be the same.* He shouldered the Thompson, pulled his bayonet from its scabbard and ran through the shallow water. The Jap's narrow eyes flared in surprise as he saw his attacker, he threw his rifle down and reached for his own bayonet, but it was only half-drawn before Mitchell was upon him. The tingling was sensuous now. His bayonet slid through the soldier's throat and grated against his spine. There was no scream, only a rattling gurgle as he fell onto his back. His hands clawed at Mitchell's wrists while his legs thrashed the stagnant water, sending spray high into the air. Mitchell bared his teeth and pushed harder, feeling a burning sense of omnipotence as he took away the life of another human being with his hands, not some remote device forged from steel alloys and automatically machined to within thousandths of an inch on a miller or lathe. He twisted the bayonet and pulled it out. The helmet slipped from the Jap's head and he stopped moving.

Then he was no longer a soldier; he was a conscripted boy of no more than sixteen or seventeen with acne and a paltry beard that sprouted from his face like the spines of a cactus. Bloody foam poured from his sun-chapped lips; his screwed-up eyes opened forlornly, flickered and closed. And then Mitchell was horribly aware of what he'd done and why he'd done it. He knelt down beside the man-boy as he lay in the filthy water that was at first red, then pink as his life trickled away. He held the small hand with its thorn-ripped fingers and dirty, chipped nails and prayed feverishly for the man's god to give him the release that he could not bring himself to provide. The screaming urge was gone, back into the dark recesses of his mind.

It took him two minutes to die: he opened his eyes once more, rasped, his chest subsided and then it was all over. Mitchell lifted the sodden, pathetic body onto drier ground and covered it uselessly in rotting leaves and rotting branches…

'No.'

'All right. But why Rajiv?'

Because of his skinny legs and arms? Because of his wide, imploring eyes? Or perhaps because of his sunken, hairless chest? Did the sum of these subconsciously remind him of a small, wretched figure lying in dirty, bloodied water, slowly slipping into the next world?

'I don't know. He looked as though he might be handy around the bungalow. You know how difficult it is to get proper help these days. How's your whisky?'

'There's a lot more to you than meets the eye, Gerald Mitchell. No matter.' He held his glass out. 'Where did you get the Johnny Walker? The stuff we get from Raighar is like paraffin.'

'I picked up a case in Calcutta last month. I've been feeling a bit run-down lately so I took the train and had some checks done at Doc Rubenstein's clinic.'

'How is the old rascal? Still chasing the nurses and prescribing Mackeson for gangrene and rabies?'

'He hasn't changed much; still the same old lush he was

in the Mess. Soda?'

'Just a squirt. How's the hunting trade? You'd think that folk would have had enough of blood and bullets by now.'

'No, business is good – the animals don't shoot back. I'm thinking of wrapping it up next year though; the older I get, the less I feel like being involved in taking *any* lives. All the same, something's been preying on goats and buffalo calves near the villages downstream so there's probably a bit more work to do before I hang my hat up.'

Colquhoun clicked his tongue. 'What's your money on – tiger or leopard?'

'Could be either. Most likely it'll—'

His words were swallowed in a sizzling hiss of rain. The pea-sized drops hurled themselves against the ground and rebounded before being knocked down again by their followers and then settled, turning the soil into a glistening lake of silt. The view from the verandah was wiped away like chalk from a blackboard.

The two men looked at each other and drank their whisky in silence as the rain hammered on the tin roof.

'Will you stay over?' said Mitchell when the downpour had passed. 'It'll be hard work driving to the convent in this morass.'

'Yes, I will, if you don't mind. I'll tell the Mother Superior I was exorcising a few demons. When do you expect Rajiv back from the village?'

'Oh, he'll be back before dark, he's a sensible lad. It's his turn to cook, so he'd better come back or it's bully beef and biscuits for us.'

'Just like old times, eh?'

'God forbid.'

'I'll have a word with him the next time I'm on my knees. I suppose you're still a lost cause, Gerald?'

'A lost cause for whom? Are you on commission or something? No, nothing's changed.'

'I'll pray for you if I get time.'

'You do that.'

A shape under a wet groundsheet walked towards them, splashing its feet as it went. It stamped on the verandah step and revealed itself to be a gangling boy in khaki shorts and a baggy white vest. A faint moustache decorated his upper lip. His face lit up like sugar thrown onto a fire. He dashed forward and grabbed Father Colquhoun's hand. He danced in excitement as he shook it.

'Oh, Father Colquhoun, it's you. I can't believe it, I can't believe it!'

'*Rajiv*, you scamp. Stand back and let me look at you. My, my, how you've grown!' He looked at Mitchell and grinned. 'Why, in a year or two he'll be wrestling water buffaloes and breaking more than a few hearts.'

Mitchell squeezed Rajiv's shoulder. 'Get yourself dried off and join us. I'm sure you've got a lot to tell Father Colquhoun here.'

The boy skipped into the bungalow, chuckling to himself.

'You know, Mitchell,' said Father Colquhoun, 'for a misanthrope, you're not a bad father.'

'And for a priest, Colquhoun, you're a good drunk. Fill 'em up.'

***

Mitchell hadn't cried since his parents died within months of each other, five years before the war. He didn't cry when his son picked up his bags and walked up the gangplank of the *Kolar Star* although he felt like doing so; the tears came two days later when he read the letter that Rajiv had left on his pillow. The dust and sweat of the journey was still on him as he stretched out on the bed and opened the envelope.

My Dearest Father,

You will never be far from my thoughts even when great

distances separate us and I feel you will be watching over me as I begin my marvellous adventure. I promise you that I shall be diligent in my studies and conduct myself in a manner of which you will be proud. I shall write as often as I can.

Your most respectful and adoring son,

Rajiv Mitchell.

When the tears were done, he put the letter into his left breast pocket, where his heart could feel its warmth. There was another letter in his jacket. Even though every word was etched into his brain, he read it again.

To Dr A. Nasr, The Jamshedpur Clinic: Re Mr Gerald Mitchell. I have prescribed the following medication ... It was signed: *Samuel Rubenstein (Doctor-in-charge). The Maidan Medical Centre, Calcutta.*

He was half asleep when he heard the excited voices. He swung himself from the bed and looked out of the window. The headman was there in his white *dhoti* along with twenty or more villagers. They squeezed themselves onto the verandah, chattering like the langur monkeys that sometimes raided his larder when he was out.

'Mitchell *sahib*, Mitchell *sahib.'*

He grimaced and opened the door. '*Yes*, what's the matter?' He hadn't meant to be so abrupt. The pain was worse than it had been for a while.

The headman waved his hands in the air. The others crowded him, looking over his shoulder. 'The son of Din went for water and a tiger has taken him. Nasim is no more.'

'*When*? When was this?'

'Not more than one hour ago, *sahib*. The tiger is gone into the forest and there is nothing left of Nasim but his sandal.'

Mitchell sighed and rubbed his eyes. 'All right, wait.' He went back inside, unlocked his gun cabinet and took out a rifle and two packets of cartridges. The crowd parted as he pushed his way towards the jeep. 'Where did the tiger take the boy?'

The headman caught up with him. 'Near the place where the women wash the clothes.'

'Right, get in. Four more in the back. Here, hold my rifle.'

They bounced down the sand track that led to the village, two miles to the south. The men in the back were talking angrily.

'I am sorry about the boy. In future, one of you must accompany the water bearers and the *dhobi* women. Who has a rifle?'

'Sanjay, *sahib*.'

'Then Sanjay must guard the river while these people go about their tasks.'

There was nothing but disturbed sand and a patch of sun-dried blood when Mitchell got to the place. Nasim's one-eyed father was kneeling on the ground, beating his thighs with clenched fists. The boy's wailing mother knelt next to him, gripping the sandal in her hands. The other women of the village stood around her silently.

Mitchell checked his rifle, strode through the shallows to the opposite riverbank and headed downstream. After a minute he saw drops of blood and paw prints where the tiger had left the water and disappeared into the dense undergrowth with the boy. He could see by the size of them that the tiger was fully-grown and favoured its left foreleg. It was lame. That was why it had moved to settlements and found easier prey than the grasslands held. It would probably eat when the opportunity arose rather than through necessity. He was wary of following the animal into the tangle alone.

'I'm sorry,' he said when he returned, 'it could be anywhere by now.'

'What are we to do, Mitchell, *sahib*?' said the headman.

Mitchell looked around. 'Build a platform in one of the

trees over there. Tether a goat every evening for a week. If the tiger returns, we'll kill it.'

'But who will supply the goat, *sahib*?'

'*For Christ's sake.* Which is cheaper – a goat or a human life?' The pain was getting worse now. 'I'll be back at sundown.'

He could still hear the woman weeping as he drove away.

***

The goat was being led to the spit of sand by the river as Mitchell arrived at the village. It bleated furiously as if anticipating its fate.

'Where's Sanjay?' he said.

'He is coming,' said the headman.

When Sanjay came with his Lee Enfield he was wearing a khaki shirt. It still had the stripes of a lance corporal on its sleeves. He stood to attention with the butt of the rifle on the ground.

'Reporting for duty, *Sah*,' he shouted.

Mitchell rolled his eyes and sighed. 'Come on then, Sanjay. Let us see what we can see.'

They walked down the sand track, past the palm-thatched huts that looked like thick-stemmed mushrooms and past the frightened faces of the villagers. Mitchell recognised Din, the dead boy's father. He was a hawk-nosed man with a fine moustache. His one eye followed them.

The goat was tethered to a stick in the centre of the sand spit. It was chewing a piece of rotten sugar cane. The two men that had dragged it there put up their hands to Mitchell and walked away quickly. Mitchell climbed the ladder of the hide, and Sanjay passed the rifles, water, and food up and followed him. The hide was solid in the branches of the tree despite its appearance. It was made of bamboo with leaves and grass for camouflage and gave a good view directly ahead and below. The two men arranged their weapons and provisions and settled down as the dusk descended like a gentle mist. They waited all night but the tiger did not return.

'I didn't expect it to come back so soon,' said Mitchell as the darkness retreated. 'It won't be hungry enough to hunt yet, but we'll be ready, if and when it does. We'll do the same tonight.'

Mitchell held the rifles as Sanjay untied the goat. 'Who provided it?'

'Din, *sahib.*'

He slept fitfully until the early afternoon when the pain woke him. There was a brown ribbed bottle on the locker next to his bed. *Not To Be Taken With Alcohol*, it said on the side. He opened it, took two tablets and washed them down with a small whisky.

They tethered the goat again that night. Once again the tiger, Karan, did not appear. It now had a name: it became an individual that the village could collectively hate. After the third night Mitchell passed over the watch to Sanjay. There was no shortage of volunteers to keep him company, for all wanted a part of the glory that would come with the death of the man-eater. Others kept watch in the daytime but Sanjay was careful to select only those who understood the workings of his rifle. There was no sign of Karan after a week and the village slowly returned to its usual routine.

On the day that Mitchell did his last hunting trip with a party of Americans he received a letter from Rajiv. The snow, he said, was jolly marvellous: he'd never eaten water before. He was enjoying his studies and the British way of life. His fellow boarders thought it very amusing that he automatically emptied his shoes before he put them on in case of scorpions and centipedes. He still did it after finding a drawing pin in one, but that, he thought, was the wonderful British sense of humour. Was his father, whom he missed very much, aware that nearly a sixth of the world's population lived in India? No, he hadn't known either until he came to Stonebridge College. Was not education a splendid thing?

Yes, it was, thought Mitchell, *a very splendid thing.* Earlier that day one of his clients had missed a boar at sixty yards with three bullets and then spitefully shot a rhesus monkey as they returned to the jeep. It annoyed Mitchell, but he said nothing. The client was a New York lawyer. They shook hands as they left and the lawyer presented him with a bottle of cheap whisky. He finished Rajiv's letter and opened the bottle. He drank half of it as he locked away his guns and hung his equipment up for the last time. Then he slept all night and most of the next day.

***

Vish, the garden boy, told him that a *dhobi* woman had been attacked by a tiger in the village further down the river as she went about her washing. She had been badly mauled and lost an arm. It was, the villagers suspected, the work of Karan. It was seen to limp as it was chased away. Then two more villagers even further down had disappeared within a week of each other. It seemed that Karan was moving south.

He saw Doc Rubenstein again in May and came back from Calcutta with more whisky, more tablets and more letters for Doctor Nasr. Another person had been taken, this time upriver. It had been seen by a British railway engineer. Probably over four hundred pounds, he said, and about eight feet from nose to tail.

There was wonderful news when he returned from a provisioning trip one morning in August. A post boy was waiting on his verandah with a telegram. He ripped the envelope open.

Dearest Father. Returning five days next month. Friend's father's cargo plane. More to follow. Rajiv.

He signed for the message and gave the boy a handful of coins. The weight was gone from his steps as he walked back into the bungalow and he felt better than he had for a long, long, time. He'd send that drunk Colquhoun a telegram; perhaps he could make it up for a day or two. After all, Rajiv was one of his old boys.

He was very sick the following week. Vish cabled for Doctor Nasr as the *sahib* lay sweating and hollow in his bed.

'Look,' he said, 'I am not a specialist in these matters. I am thinking that you should consider moving to some place where they have the proper facilities to help you. Calcutta or Allahabad, perhaps.'

Mitchell shook his head. 'I don't know how long I've got, neither do the specialists at the Maidan Centre. When I go, I'd prefer it to be here. But I will see Doctor Rubenstein after my boy goes back to England. Now, have you got any stronger tablets than the last lot?'

***

Rajiv's airmail letter arrived a week later.

Dearest Father,

I am flying in an aeroplane called a DC4. The airline is called Asiatic Cargo. It will land at Kalaikunda on the 14th and leave on the 20th. It will take three days to arrive and the same to return. I am looking forward to it as I have never flown before. I will confirm the arrangements by telegram before we leave.

Yours affectionately,

Rajiv.

He wondered about the changes he'd see in his son after eleven months. He'd be tall, probably still wire-thin, and no doubt have the amusing self-confidence that adolescent boys developed when they thought they were men because of a few hairs on their chin and crotch. Perhaps he had a girlfriend. But most likely not, because dark skin was more a novelty than an attraction to the rosy-cheeked daughters of Somerset. Jaspal in the village would be pleased about that, for she was sweet on him, and would be even more so with the kudos of being in the company of a travelled and educated young man.

It saddened Mitchell to think he probably wouldn't live long enough to see Rajiv grow into the fine person he was sure to be. Whatever happened, he suspected India wouldn't be his future; he'd bitten into the apple of Western culture and would probably be ill-contented with the rice of Asia. As for religion, he'd left him to make up his own mind about which spiritual path he should take. His own beliefs had long-since lapsed, but he'd encouraged him to weigh up the many faiths and decide which, if any, were best for him. Rajiv had opted to behave in a decent manner to all people and allow an understanding god to select him instead. Mitchell was pleased with his choice and Father Colquhoun accepted it with equanimity.

***

Mohan Singh, the area police inspector, sat on the verandah. He was drinking tea. Mitchell also drank tea, but his contained whisky. He had respect for other men's religious beliefs; alcohol was repugnant to a Sikh in much the same way that abstinence was repulsive to him. So he poured his Johnny Walker into a cup, out of sight of the inspector.

'This problem with the tiger is growing,' said Singh. His English was excellent. He had been an officer in the Fifteenth Indian Corps and earned distinguished service and conspicuous gallantry awards during the Burma Campaigns. He was much respected.

'It has taken two more people in the last three weeks. He must be held to account.'

‘And you want me to do something?’

Singh put his cup down on the floor and toyed with his magnificent beard. ‘Yes, Mr Mitchell, we could certainly use your assistance. Even the army are afraid to look for him. They fear him as a demon. Ruddy idiots.’

Mitchell sighed. The moment the police jeep had pulled up outside his bungalow he’d known it wouldn’t be a social visit. ‘Inspector, I’m not a well man. My rifles are locked away. I can’t hunt. I’m tired.’

‘I am sorry to hear that, Mr Mitchell.’ But Singh still played with his beard and looked at him expectantly. He wasn’t sorry enough to let the matter rest. ‘The people are saying that you don’t care.’

It was a cheap shot. Mitchell didn’t rise to it. He didn’t say anything for a while. He drank his supercharged tea instead. ‘You’re a first-class shot, Inspector. You killed many Japanese in the war. You have medals for your bravery. Why don’t *you* kill the bloody thing?’

‘I was counting on your help, Mr Mitchell. I am sorry that you cannot be of assistance.’

‘So am I, Inspector, so am I.’

After the inspector had gone, he was sick.

***

The post boy rapped on the open door with a telegram in his hand. It was the same boy as before. ‘It is marked *Urgent*,’ he said to Mitchell. All telegrams were urgent to Mitchell.

He paid the boy and read it on his bed. The pain was growing by the day and the morphine was losing its effectiveness in the doses that Doc Rubenstein had prescribed.

Dearest Father. Arriving Amta train station early on 14th. Your loving son.

Rajiv.

The pain was gone for a while.

***

'You're not looking so good, Gerald.' Father Colquhoun didn't shake the trembling hand as firmly as he would have liked. It was moist and the perspiration transferred Mitchell's weakness like an electrolyte.

'I'm not *feeling* so good. I'm glad to see you again, even if you do drink all my whisky.'

Father Colquhoun opened his bag and brought out a bottle of bourbon. 'Here's your communion wine, you wretched heathen.'

Mitchell took the bottle and looked at the label. 'Where did you steal this from?'

'The Monsignor's mistress left it under my pillow.'

Mitchell slapped the priest on the shoulder. 'You're a good man for all your faults, Michael. Let's drink to everything.'

'Why not? It beats drinking to nothing. Do you want me to come with you to Amta tomorrow? I'll drive you if you wish.'

'Thanks, I'd welcome your company. Rajiv will be excited to see you again.'

'It's you he's coming to see, Gerald, not me.'

Mitchell put his glass down on the table. 'Look, you know that I don't believe in God anymore. I don't know *what* I believe in, but I'm sure that when we die, there's another place, not your fire and brimstone of Hell and smiling angels waiting at St Peter's gates with neatly-clipped wings and harps, but somewhere for people like me who live their life as best as they can without treading on too many toes or stealing from the collection box.' He coughed into his handkerchief. 'What I'm saying is that I've done my best and tried to make up for my mistakes. Is that good enough?'

Father Colquhoun rested his chin between his thumb and first finger and thought for a moment or two. 'A one-step karma?'

'I suppose that's what I mean. Yes.'

'It's a good philosophy. Most religions support that to a certain extent.'

'Do you consider Rajiv to be a good exchange for my sins?'

The priest shrugged. 'Well, I don't know what your sins are. You've never shared a confessional with me.'

'I once took a life in Burma for the wrong reason.'

'*All* lives taken are for the wrong reasons, but that's the way of man, first or third-hand.'

'I want to feel that I've redeemed myself by helping Rajiv.'

Father Colquhoun swirled the liquor around his glass. 'Who are you trying to convince?'

'Myself, I suppose.'

'I think my god would be happy with you.'

'So I can take it that everything's even?'

'Let's drink on that too.'

***

The train pulled into Amta. Scores of Indians were clinging to it. Those unable to get a seat inside or who could not afford one hung from open windows with their feet on the narrow boards at the side of the carriages. They clung to the ends of the carriages above the spring-loaded buffer pads that would crush them to paste if they were careless enough to slip between them and they gripped the tops of the carriages like limpets. The lucky passengers sat inside on wooden bench seats. The heat within the walls was stifling but there was no danger of death.

Mitchell and Father Colquhoun stood on the platform as

the sweating and dusty travellers streamed past them. The *chapati* sellers gripped their small stoves. A pi-dog skulked around the ticket office and its nose twitched at the pungent smell of food cooking inside. Mitchell looked around anxiously. The platform thinned. And then he saw Rajiv climbing down from the rearmost carriage.

'Rajiv.'

Rajiv ran to his father and dropped his suitcase on the platform. The two hugged and looked at each other and hugged again as the outgoing passengers streamed past them. The stationmaster, who was standing next to Father Colquhoun, watched the white man embrace the brown boy. He looked puzzled. They stood back after a while. Mitchell rubbed the tears from his eyes.

'Damned dust,' he said. 'How are you? How was the flight?'

'I'm very well, Father. The flight was most enjoyable and the second pilot let me sit in his seat while he slept.'

'Did he, now! Let me look at you again.'

The boy took his hands from his father's shoulders and stepped back a little further. He'd grown another six inches and was almost as tall as Mitchell but it was as if he'd been stretched like an elastic band.

'You've not been eating enough fish and chips; you're still like a bamboo stick.'

Rajiv looked him up and down. 'Perhaps I should have brought some back for you, Father, you seem to have lost a lot of weight since we parted.'

'I'm missing your cooking, young man, that's why. Come, look who else is here to see you.' Mitchell turned to Colquhoun but he was standing next to the ticket office, talking to a nun.

'Let's wait for him in the car.'

They walked across the railway line and to the priest's Packard. Many years of exposure to the Indian sun had faded the paintwork; the roof and bonnet showed the red lead underneath. Rajiv talked passionately of England and explained the British way of life as if his father had never been there. Mitchell smiled and listened and said nothing except to prompt him. Father Colquhoun arrived as he was describing the London Underground system.

He grinned. 'Who is *this*? Where is Rajiv?'

Rajiv grinned back and extended his hand. 'Father Colquhoun, it's a great pleasure to see you again. I hope you're keeping well.'

'As well as you look, Rajiv. Is England agreeing with you?'

'It's somewhat cooler than India, but by and large, everything is splendid.'

'And how are your studies going?'

'I'm enjoying them greatly and look forward to every lesson. Did you know that William Pitt the Younger was Prime Minister of Britain at the age of twenty-four? Why, only last week I learned that Queen Victoria spoke Hindustani and there are only thirteen letters in the Hawaiian alphabet.'

The two men beamed and winked at each other. Rajiv was still chattering as they drove away.

***

'It'll take both of us to move him. He looks comfortable enough, let's have another drink.' Mitchell undraped his son's leg from the arm of the chair and straightened it. Rajiv snorted, mumbled something and went back to sleep.

'It's been quite a journey for him, no wonder he's tired. He won't know where he is when he wakes up.'

'Nor will you when we've finished the bottle. You might at least take that dog collar off when you're getting drunk, someone might mistake you for a priest.'

'Expecting visitors?'

'Depends on how much we drink. It was tigers in tuxedos last time.'

'Are you going to tell Rajiv?'

'About what?'

'You know very well what I'm talking about. Your health.'

'No, I'm not.'

'Why? He's your son, for heaven's sake.'

'You know, for a priest, you can be bloody dim sometimes. If I tell him, he won't go back to England. He'll stay here and insist on looking after me. He'll watch me fall apart and die. No child deserves that. No, I won't tell him, and *you* won't, either.'

'And they call the Irish pig-headed.'

'Look, I've made arrangements for him if I should die before he's finished his schooling. A lawyer in Calcutta drew up the papers and I'd like you to have a copy. Some of it concerns you as well.'

The boy stirred but did not wake.

'Let's talk about it later, Gerald.'

***

Rajiv was awake before sunrise. He made breakfast for his father. Colquhoun had driven to the Catholic convent thirty miles away. He would return before five o'clock.

Mitchell took a warm corn cake. 'How does it feel to be back, son?'

'Very strange, Father. It's as if I have never left, but some of me is still in England.'

'Most of you, I suspect. What are you going to do today?'

'I thought I might visit Jaspal. I've brought her a gift.'

'You're very fond of her, aren't you?'

Rajiv smiled shyly. 'She was my first friend when I came

from Vandasi.'

'What did you buy for her?'

'I didn't buy anything. I made a bracelet in the woodwork class. Would you like to see it?'

'Of course.'

Rajiv brought the bracelet from his bedroom and passed it to his father. It was machined from hardwood and stained dark red. The outer face had been cross-milled and the word 'Jaspal' neatly carved into it.

'Well done, young man! How long did it take to make?'

'Three lessons. I broke the first one because I was clumsy with the lathe.'

'That's all part of learning. She'll like it very much, I'm sure.'

'May I go to the village, Father? I'll return at mid-day.'

Mitchell ruffled his son's hair. 'It's your holiday, you can do as you wish for as long as you wish. Would you like me to drive you there?'

'That's not necessary, thank you, Father, I'll enjoy the walk.'

'Don't come back married, eh?'

Mitchell watched as his son ran down the track to the village.

Part 2

'*Sahib* – a great catastrophe has occurred.'

'What is it, Vish?'

He wrung his hands and his feet danced on the wooden floor. 'Oh, sir, oh, sir – it is *Karan*. He is returned.'

Karan! A shadow passed over Mitchell. 'He's back to his tricks?'

'Yes, *sahib*. It grieves me to tell you that he has taken Rajiv.'

It was as if he had been struck by a charging elephant. He clutched at the fly-screened door for support, a singing filled his head and was gone in a surging vacuum, the roof and the walls whirled in a crazy kaleidoscope and then the floor came up to meet him. Vish rushed to Mitchell's side and lifted him to a chair. He was not very heavy, but he was limp with shock. Mitchell heard the *mali's* words as he told him that Karan had taken his son as he walked with Jaspal beside the river, but surely he must have been talking about someone else. So he sat there and watched a team of ants as they dragged a dead cricket across the wooden floor. A leg fell between the boards; they scurried agitatedly around their prize, unable to free it.

Vish stood there awkwardly and chewed his knuckles. It distressed him to see the *sahib* like this.

The truth slowly pushed past Mitchell's crumbling defences. He took a deep breath and looked up. 'Thank you, Vish. Go back to the village, please. I'll come as soon as I can.'

***

They had to help Mitchell from his jeep. His face was white with shock and he was trembling. The villagers gathered around him and stared at the ground. Din was there, the man who'd also lost his son to Karan many months before. He moved closer to Mitchell but didn't say anything.

The headman didn't understand Mitchell's choked words at first. He didn't know if they were English or Hindi. They were very thick as if the man's mouth was full of sand.

'Where … did it … happen?'

'Where the river bends, *sahib*. He was walking with Jaspal. Karan jumped from nowhere.'

'The girl?'

'Rajiv pushed her aside. She ran away. She is with her

family. Oh, it is a terrible thing, a terrible thing.'

'Bring Jaspal to me. I must hear this from her.'

One of the villagers went to find her. She edged up to the jeep a few minutes later. Her eyes were red.

'Mitchell *sahib*, it was a very brave and honourable thing that Rajiv did. He stood before the beast so it could not devour me.'

'I would have expected nothing else from him, Jaspal. He was a boy but he died as a man. Are you hurt?' His voice was little more than a whisper.

'Yes, Mitchell *sahib*. I am sorely hurt in my heart.'

'Did he give you his gift?'

She held out her arm. The red-stained wooden bracelet was on her wrist. 'I shall never take it off,' she said. 'I am very sorry for you.'

'And I am very sorry for you, too, Jaspal. Can you tell me of the tiger?'

'Oh, Mitchell *sahib,* it was so sudden. It leapt from the undergrowth and was upon us in the blinking of an eye.'

'Did it limp, Jaspal? Did it limp?'

'I cannot say, *sahib*, but it stumbled as it stopped before us.'

'And was it big?'

'Very big.'

'As long as my jeep?'

'Yes.'

'Thank you for coming to see me, Jaspal.'

She cried as she walked away.

Mitchell called for the headman. 'Take me to the place.'

The headman and Din and Sanjay were at his side as they went to the river. They supported him as he staggered in the sand. He almost fell as they got there but they caught his arms. There was blood, but not much. A man who is dead does not bleed a great deal. He could see the marks where Karan had dragged his son away. The flies were already settling and a vulture wheeled overhead. Mitchell fell to his knees. The headman and Din and Sanjay stood around him and watched as he ground the reddened sand in his hands.

Sanjay drove him back to the bungalow with Vish in the rear seat. He'd learned to drive in the army but still crashed the jeep's gears. Vish sat Mitchell in the chair on the verandah, put a glass of whisky in his hand and Rajiv's photograph in front of him. They waited with him until Father Colquhoun returned. He did not speak and they did not speak, either.

Mitchell lifted his head at the sound of the Packard's horn. Father Colquhoun was waving from his seat. Vish went to the car and spoke to him.

'It is a calamity. It is all too terrible for words,' they said as they walked back to the village, leaving Mitchell *sahib* and the man of God on the verandah.

***

He sat next to the doorway of the darkened bungalow with an empty whisky glass in his hand and the framed photograph of a smiling boy on his knee. Father Colquhoun had taken the picture with a box camera. The Vandasi Catholic Orphanage sign stood beside him and he had a cotton bag in his hands. It contained no more than a toothbrush, a pair of shorts and a vest. He was waiting to be collected.

'Speak to me as a friend. Don't speak to me as a priest. Please.'

'Gerald.' Father Colquhoun moved his chair closer and held Mitchell's shoulder. 'Gerald, there's little I can say as either that will help. I can't even say that I know what you're going through because I don't. All I can do is wait with you and listen if you want to talk and be quiet if you don't. There'll be no pious platitudes. Can I get you anything?'

‘The tablets. In the locker, next to my bed. And more whisky.’ Mitchell’s words were fractured with misery. He picked up Rajiv’s photograph. The sun was balanced on the far hills and its mauve-pink light caught the glass. He saw his face reflected in it. It merged with Rajiv as he tilted the frame and for a moment, they were one. He put the picture of his son on a table where the last of the sun could keep him warm.

Father Colquhoun pressed the medicine bottle into his friend’s hand and filled his glass. Mitchell took two tablets and washed them down with the whisky. Colquhoun could see the label on the side of the bottle. *Not To Be Taken With Alcohol*. He said nothing.

After a while Mitchell began to speak. Father Colquhoun listened as he told him of his son. He was going to be someone of importance one day … he was a bright boy Stonebridge College was just the place for him …

The moon rose and the whisky went down. Eventually Mitchell was quiet. Father Colquhoun took the empty glass from his hand, went into the bungalow and brought out two blankets. He covered Mitchell and moved his chair a little closer so he could see his friend would come to no harm. It was a long time before sleep came.

***

Father Colquhoun prepared regular meals but it was three days before Mitchell, in his grief, could take anything other than occasional spoonfuls of soup. The whisky bottle was always by his side and although his glass was rarely empty he was never drunk. He sat in silence and stared at the distant hills. Colquhoun stayed close and let him be. He was dozing on the verandah when a flash of lightning lit up the evening sky. Mitchell suddenly stood up and looked at him.

‘I can’t find it in myself to hate him, Michael. I could

hate the Japs for their beliefs and their cruelty and their ambitions, you know as well as I do what they were like. But Karan knew nothing about wars and politics and supremacy – he was crippled and simply doing what he could to survive. I'll respect him for that. You and I would have gone for an easy target in his situation, it's in all our natures. Now I'm going to bed.'

***

Mitchell unlocked the gun cabinet and took out the rifles. He laid them on his bed and began to clean them: first the Springfield, then the Lee Enfield, then the Mannlicher and finally the Gibbs. When he'd finished, he did the same with his Webley and Maximo pistols. His long-unworn army uniform now fitted him. The cancer made sure of that. He chose the jungle greens.

'What are you doing, Gerald?' said Father Colquhoun softly. He was standing in the bedroom doorway. His white hair was tangled and the stubble on his face sparkled in the strong sunlight that shone through the opened blinds.

Mitchell's words were flat in the already-thickening air. 'I'm going to kill him.'

'Gerald. Oh, Gerald.'

'Don't worry your mind, Michael, I'm not going to do it by myself. I *can't* do it by myself. I need your help. And the village.'

Father Colquhoun looked at the guns and back to Mitchell. His face was set and his eyes burned in the circles that surrounded them like dark haloes.

'Are you sure you're up to this? I'm sorry, but you don't look it.'

'I've never been more up to anything in my life. Don't try to stop me. I'll do it by my bloody self, if need be. Do you hear?'

‘All right, Gerald, all right. How do you intend to do it?’

‘With live bait. Then we’ll shoot him. Simple.’

‘I’m worried for you, Gerald.’

‘Then don’t be. Take your choice, the Webley’s for me.’

Father Colquhoun looked at Mitchell doubtfully. ‘I haven’t used a gun in years. I’d better take the Lee Enfield, I’m more used to army weapons. Why the uniform?’

‘I’ve got my reasons. If you’re coming, help me with the rifles.’

Mitchell didn’t talk as they bounced down the sand track to the village in his jeep. Father Colquhoun watched him as he muttered and occasionally bared his teeth. His eyes were fired with intent.

The village was quiet and the rich smell of curry hung in the air. Mitchell sounded the horn several times and stood in the back of the jeep. People abandoned their meals and trickled from their small yards and mud dwellings.

‘We’re going to kill Karan,’ he said to the small group.

‘Mitchell *sahib*,’ said the headman. ‘How are we to do this?’

‘Get everyone together and I’ll tell you.’

‘Are you brave?’ he said when all the men were assembled. ‘Are we to kill Karan tonight? Who among you are the best shots?’

Sanjay stepped forward. So did Din.

‘Who else? Who has been in the army?’

No one moved. Their fear of Karan was plain. Glory would not be enough now.

‘All right, then … the man who kills the tiger may keep the weapon.’

Five men joined Din and Sanjay, who had his own Lee Enfield. Rifles were very valuable; Mitchell knew a man and his family could live for a month on the proceeds of even a worn shotgun.

‘Very well, gather closer. I’ll explain what you are to do

and instruct you in the ways of each gun.'

When he was finished he called the headman over. 'Bring a goat. Don't worry, you'll get it back.'

He sat in the jeep and waited for dusk to settle. Father Colquhoun sat beside him and silently prayed for his friend.

***

There were eight of them as well as the goat. Mitchell pointed to a small clearing between the trees on the opposite bank of the river. It was no bigger than a tennis court.

'That'll do, tie it there.'

The men watched as the goat was chained to a stake. It was little more than a kid and would soon be distraught.

'We'll lie up on the other side,' said Mitchell. 'When Karan comes we'll spotlight the bastard and kill him.'

Colquhoun rubbed his chin. 'And if he doesn't come?'

'He'll come all right, whether it's tonight or tomorrow or the day after. He'll not have gone far with his crippled leg when he knows there are easy targets nearby.'

They waded back through the river and made themselves comfortable where they could on the bank. The jungle slowly came alive with the sound of ratcheting insects and chattering monkeys as the night closed in.

Mitchell nudged Father Colquhoun. 'I'm going to wait in the jeep now. When it takes the bait, I'll turn the headlights on. There'll be no excuse to miss.' He patted the priest's shoulder and crept away.

The slow-moving river burbled over its bed and lapped against the bank. The goat began to bleat after a while. Its cries were unsettling in the darkness, but the men were silent as they lay in the undergrowth with their rifles and pistols. The hours passed slowly and the bleats became irregular.

***

They shot Karan just before dawn. Their tired eyes snapped open at the sound of something crashing through the undergrowth.

'*The lights, Gerald, the lights.*' There was no response. Father Colquhoun ran to the jeep. It was empty. There was no sign of Mitchell other than the glint of an empty whisky bottle in the driver's footwell. He turned the headlights on. The beam carried across the water and into the clearing. The man-eater was staggering through the undergrowth at the edge of the forest as if it were drunk. Din and Sanjay fired first and then the echoes of two dozen shots ran through the jungle. It fell to its side and kicked its legs. Then it was dead.

They ran through the river, sending sheets of water before them in excitement, Father Colquhoun, too. The men jabbered and cheered and prodded the bloodied tiger with their weapons. Its mouth was open in a silent roar and they could see that several teeth were broken and missing. Sanjay lifted a foreleg with the barrel of his rifle. The paw was badly mutilated as if it had once been caught in a trap.

Colquhoun looked around for Mitchell. 'Gerald. *Gerald, we've got it.*'

There was no answer. He looked around and called his friend's name again. Then he saw a shape in the sand. He crossed the clearing in sick anticipation. What was left of Mitchell lay beside the stake that had tethered the goat. The chain had been unclipped. A brown, ribbed bottle lay close to him. It was empty.

The excited chatter died away as the men saw Colquhoun on his knees. They left Karan, gathered round and silently watched as the priest commended his friend to whoever might receive him.

Father Colquhoun found the letter on the rear seat of the jeep as they took Mitchell to the village. It was weighted down by the Webley pistol.

Michael,

You may understand. It wasn't possible for me to kill the beast because Rajiv was part of it. I'm with him now and the morphine will have made my passing painless. Perhaps it made Karan's painless too but I'll never know. You always were a bad shot.

The whisky and jeep are yours. Sell whatever's left and put the proceeds into the orphanage. Perhaps we'll see you again someplace.

Mitch and Rajiv.